Putty in Her Hands

by

Lynn Shurr

This is a work of fiction. Names, characters, places, and incidents are either the product of the author's imagination or are used fictitiously, and any resemblance to actual persons living or dead, business establishments, events, or locales, is entirely coincidental.

Putty in Her Hands

Cover Art by *Diana Carlile*

The Wild Rose Press, Inc.
PO Box 708
Adams Basin, NY 14410-0708
Visit us at www.thewildrosepress.com

Publishing History
First Champagne Rose Edition, 2018
Print ISBN 978-1-5092-1919-3
Digital ISBN 978-1-5092-1920-9

Published in the United States of America

Keeping the shotgun muzzle low,
he paused to observe the miscreant for a moment. Light build, small shoulders, slim hips, snug jeans that didn't sag under the weight of a low-slung tool belt, tanned arms, strong but not muscular, and best of all a thick fall of dark hair showing glints of red beneath the hot sun—not a dude at all. Remy Broussard was about to scare the shit out of a girl who appeared to be boarding up, not tearing down.

She finished driving in the last nail of the highest board, slung her hammer back into its loop, turned, and froze as Remy raised his shotgun to hip level and twanged in old-timey western cowboy style, "You're trespassin' on my property, little lady."

He expected her rather grubby hands to shoot into the air in surrender. Instead, they came to rest on either hip, one on the head of the hammer, the other on the crook of a crowbar. For a woman that he topped by at least six inches, she had a rather commanding voice. "I didn't see any signs, so not trespassing. As you can see, I've been boarding up the place after a short visit to satisfy my curiosity. Nothing stolen. No harm, no foul. You can go inside and see for yourself. I'll be leaving now if you lower your weapon and clear the pathway." She took a few steps forward and unholstered the hammer. Looked like they had an old-fashioned standoff.

Praise for Lynn Shurr

"Shurr is a wonderful storyteller."

~The Romance Studio

~*~

"Very easy read, well written, combined with conflict, believable plots and secondary characters that make the story come alive."

~Jane Lange, Romances, Reads and Reviews

~*~

"Lynn Shurr breathes life into the characters and allows each turn of the page to lead up to a pleasurable ending."

~Cherokee, Coffee Time Romance and More

~*~

"I love the picture the author paints of the town and the way of life, and the characters are strong and interesting. Great read of this summer and for the beach."

~Joan Conning Afman, author

~*~

"Lynn Shurr stories have that distinctive Louisiana flavor…and make you eager for another taste."

~J. L. Salter, author

Dedication

For Sona Domburian,
builder of wonderful libraries,
who gave me the kernel of a plot for this book.
Look how it grew!

Chapter One

They called her the Bayou Queen. Once she stood, stately and beautiful, facing the bank of the river, welcoming all who came her way. Renowned for her elegant teas and grand balls, she played hostess to the best of people. But, the steamboats stopped coming to her landing. The railroad passed her by. Yet, she survived in style until the Great Depression reduced her to penury. Then, she grew shabby and took in whoever would pay her now modest price. The food she served was hearty but cheap. Traveling salesmen and bachelors frequently stayed in her domain as well as soldiers from two world wars on their way to the front. When that second war ended, the surge of automobiles all but ran her over. The interstate highway swung wide around her precincts, and motels gathered at their exits. Some people said she still had good bones like all fine ladies, but her charm dimmed considerably and finally shut down altogether.

****

Dressed in jeans tucked into high-laced work boots, Julia Rossi approached the Bayou Queen with caution. She carried a hammer and a small sack of nails on her tool belt, though neither would do much good if she stumbled across a water moccasin hiding in the heavy brush surrounding the old hotel. The blackberry brambles and green briars impeding her progress made

Julia regret wearing her royal blue company T-shirt instead of a long-sleeved shirt, hot as it might have been on this early May day in Louisiana. The thorns scratched her arms, drew blood, and attracted mosquitoes from the dense shade of nearby live oaks. Really, she should have cut her hair short years ago, but it was a vanity, thick, black and glossy as the tail of a show horse and endowed with natural red highlights sometimes revealed by the sun. Instead, she drew her locks up into a ponytail and shoved them through the loop in her work cap to keep the hair off her neck and out of the way. Despite that, sweat trickled down her back.

Finally, the faint path Julia followed ended at the plain, unassuming rear door of a shed-like addition to the once magnificent building. Her last owners had shown some respect to the aged beauty by hammering stout boards over the door before decamping to Florida and running out on their property taxes several years in arrears. All the ground floor windows she could see through the overgrowth were similarly barred to keep out the vandals, the vagrants, the drug users prone to taking advantage of abandoned buildings. Julia would never have known the Bayou Queen existed, set back from the road and screened by the live oaks and all the trash trees that had sprung up among them over the years if she hadn't been lured by two of most talkative doyennes of Chapelle, Louisiana to share a pastry tray at Pommier's Bakery one rainy afternoon while she and her uncles waited for their plasterwork to dry at Alleman Plantation.

She'd stopped in for a black coffee and ended up with au lait and a pecan pie tart on her plate after the being summoned to sit at the table occupied by the two overweight matrons, each with her white hair dyed an identical champagne blonde and tight, permed curls hair-sprayed into submission. Sisters obviously, they introduced themselves as Patricia Broussard and Pamela Vice, "Please call us Patty and Pammy." Julia knew her Southern etiquette well enough to put a Miss in front of both names when she addressed them despite their overt friendliness. Within a few minutes, they'd managed to work in their status as the wife of a former three-time mayor before term limits were voted in, and the widow of a prominent bank president.

"We hear your company is doing such marvelous work out at Alleman. How wonderful Gaylord Getty can afford to restore the place to its former glory on his proceeds as an artist—though I don't make much sense of his work which always seems so distorted to me, maybe even perverted, but I can't really tell. I hear the gay in Gaylord describes him perfectly. Is that true?" Miss Pammy inquired with a raise of her plucked and penciled eyebrows.

"I really couldn't say. Mr. Getty is staying in his New York loft while the renovation is ongoing. He relays his instructions through Marvin Holcomb, the caretaker."

Miss Patty put her pudgy hands in the air and let the wrists go limp. "Well, we already know about Marv. He should not have been allowed to teach in the public schools."

Julia pretended to miss the implication and did not take the barb baited with old gossip. "Mr. Holcomb has been very helpful. He has a good eye for design."

"Don't *they* all?" Pammy sank her dentures into a

3

pillowy beignet adrift in powdered sugar. "How long will you be staying in Chapelle?"

Julia considered it part of her job to keep an ear out for new business possibilities. Well-connected women like these were a good source no matter how annoying. "Until the work is done, unless we get another contract in the area. You seem like ladies who would know people who might need restoration work done on their homes."

"Oh, we know *people*," both women agreed. "The only building that comes to mind right off the top of my head is the old Bayou Queen Hotel, but once my grandson, Remy, gets hold of it, that place is a gone pecan. He's all about modern," Miss Patty said. "His daddy let him go to architecture school in Chicago and now he has Yankee notions. However, he did come home to start his business. Remy is an eligible bachelor. About time he settled down with a good wife. I think you two would have a lot in common."

Julia wondered if she'd qualify for bride-to-be if she'd worn her work clothes instead of a light blue summer dress, her hair loose around her shoulders, and the sandals on her feet showing off pearl polished toenails while she explored the town. Maybe, Remy was as gay as Marv, and his deluded grandmother refused to admit it.

"Our great-grandmama held her wedding reception at the Bayou Queen in the 1920's. We have photographs. What a grand place it was: four stories tall, the highest building in town, and the first to have air-conditioning, a crystal chandelier in the lobby to beat all. The second story ballroom…just magnificent. Then, the Crash and the Depression," Pammy said with a sigh as if she'd personally endured both. "The Queen hit the skids after that."

Interest piqued, Julia asked where the hotel stood and received excellent if somewhat localized directions. On the way out of town by the bayou road—just past where the old fruit stand used to be on the right, but before the historical marker where a Confederate camp once existed, they told her. She insisted on paying for their pastry tray and met little resistance. On her way back to Alleman, she made note of a patch of gravel and the faint pathway on the bayou side just past the rundown fruit stand buried beneath wisteria vines.

Yesterday's rain had ceased, leaving behind oppressive humidity. They set up drum fans in the plantation home to move the air, but plaster could not be rushed. The brown coat simply had to cure before adding the finishing layer. She'd left her uncles Sal and Sam in the motorhome running its A/C off the generator while they watched a ballgame and knocked back some cold brews. Now Julia, dressed appropriately for exploring, stood before the treasure trove called the Bayou Queen and pried off the boards that prevented her entry with a crowbar drawn from her tool belt. That job done, she pulled a high-powered flashlight from another loop and aimed it at the interior.

Nothing much to see but a very old-fashioned kitchen with rusty appliances dating back to the thirties. She moved quickly into the next room, traversing a large open space until she stood before a grand staircase. Overhead, an ornate plaster medallion of fruit and flowers still possessed a stout iron hook in its center that once supported the legendary chandelier. Julia rubbed some of the dust from the handrail to the second floor and shone her light upon it. Mahogany, certainly, in need of repair and polish, but the real deal. She turned her eyes to the bleak floor covered by green linoleum with a thick layer of dead insects, and used her bar to lift a loose corner. Marble lay beneath, the luxury flooring of the nineteenth century. Did she dare ascend the staircase? The steps seemed stout enough, but you never knew in old buildings. She weighed in at one-twenty-five and had a reputation for being light on her feet, compared to her uncles for sure. Gingerly, she tested a few of the treads, then raced to the second floor without mishap.

Three sets of large double doors marked the ballroom. One stood halfway open beckoning her to enter. She scuffed her boot across the layer of dust and fallen debris—parquet floors—and above them, the source of the chunks of plaster laying everywhere: a coffered ceiling, the equivalent of today's dropped ceilings but much more attractive, consisting of squares and rosette medallions matching the pattern of the inlaid wood beneath her feet. A few of the medallions still held traces of gilding. She spotted four with hooks for chandeliers. Three large arched windows would have illuminated the space if they hadn't been heavily shuttered and provided some cross ventilation on hot summer nights before modern cooling came into existence.

Closing her eyes, Julia imagined what the place must have resembled in its heyday. Her uncles said she had imagination, and she did. Dancing women swirled by, first in hoop skirts, then in bustled gowns, and finally in the loose styles of the 1920's. Maybe injured soldiers billeted here for a while, sleeping in row upon row of cots. Perhaps, doughboys played poker and rolled dice across the parquet floors while waiting for transport to the distant railway station. She'd have to hit the library and do more research on the history of the Bayou Queen. Maybe it wasn't too late to save her from destruction, if she could appeal to the city council to save what should be an historical landmark for Chapelle. Enough speculation. She had real work to do. Before leaving, Julia checked out two narrow staircases at either end of the hall leading to the third-floor guestrooms, but decided not to chance further exploration alone. She descended the main stairs and followed her tracks in the dust through the ancient kitchen and out the rear door.

Selecting the lowest board, she hammered it back into place. On to the next and the next. Julia Rossi would not leave the Queen vulnerable to those who preyed on old buildings, not even that modern-minded Remy Broussard.

Chapter Two

Remington Broussard parked behind the gray pickup truck with the toolbox in its bed. Dusty and dented, it revealed itself as a working truck—probably the kind used to haul away marble mantels or whatever else the old Queen had left to offer. Some people liked antique appliances, not him. He'd owned the crumbling hotel for all of two hours and already she was causing him problems in the form of looters. The building might not have much left to salvage, but what it did belonged to him.

Remy took the shotgun from the rack behind the seat. He always had a varmint gun with him when he checked out overgrown sites to deal with the occasional snake, rabid raccoon, coy dog, nesting alligator, or trespasser. As of last week, the latest crop of new high school grads was on the loose, looking for ways to pass the time until college started, if they weren't desperately applying for jobs. Why not deface the Queen with spray paint or attempt to break a few windows on the upper levels? He needed to post the property with the No Trespassing signs he'd picked up in town sooner rather than later.

Shrugging out of the sports coat he'd worn to the tax auction in the lobby of the parish courthouse, Remy got down and studied the boot prints in the mud leading into the thicket. Yes, small in size, probably some teen who'd borrowed his daddy's truck. No others, so the kid came alone. Remy figured he'd scare the bejesus out the boy and send him on his way. At least, the culprit had pushed through the brambles and cleared the path for him. Usually, Remy approached from the bayou side, tying up his motorboat to a rotting pylon from the old pier, but seeing the truck parked here on his way from the courthouse made him pull over to assert his new rights over the building.

Hammering, sharp as gunshots, sounded in the moisture-laden air. Bang, bang, bang. For sure, some guy trying to break in or destroy Broussard property. Remy gripped his shotgun barrels-down, and moved between the two live oaks forming an arch with their intertwined branches. Once out of their shade, the brambles began. He should have been thankful to the kid for breaking the way, but the vandal wasn't as tall as himself. A wild blackberry cane nearly whipped across his face before he deflected it with his free hand, earning a scratch and a spray of fine thorns across his knuckles. Lower vegetation tore at his dress shirt, but below that he wore sensible jeans and sturdy shoes up to the hike.

The hammering continued in even, steady strokes more like a project in progress than haphazard breaking and entering. He followed the noise to the source. The banging covered the sound of his arrival. Keeping the shotgun muzzle low, he paused to observe the miscreant for a moment. Light build, small shoulders, slim hips, snug jeans that didn't sag under the weight of a low-slung tool belt, tanned arms, strong but not muscular, and best of all a thick fall of dark hair showing glints of red beneath the hot sun—not a dude at all. Remy Broussard was about to scare the shit out of a girl who appeared to be boarding up, not tearing down.

She finished driving in the last nail of the highest board, slung her hammer back into its loop, turned, and froze as Remy raised his shotgun to hip level and twanged in old-timey western cowboy style, "You're trespassin' on my property, little lady."

He expected her rather grubby hands to shoot into the air in surrender. Instead, they came to rest on either hip, one on the head of the hammer, the other on the crook of a crowbar. For a woman that he topped by at least six inches, she had a rather commanding voice. "I didn't see any signs, so not trespassing. As you can see, I've been boarding up the place after a short visit to satisfy my curiosity. Nothing stolen. No harm, no foul. You can go inside and see for yourself. I'll be leaving now if you lower your weapon and clear the pathway." She took a few steps forward and unholstered the hammer. Looked like they had an old-fashioned standoff.

"I just purchased this property. The No Trespassing signs are in my truck."

"I had no way of knowing that when I arrived, Mr. Broussard."

She had bright blue eyes shaded by dark brows and lashes set off by an olive complexion, one of his favorite combinations in women, though he always seemed to date blondes. He appraised her from the heavy soles of her work boots to the crest of her ponytail with a short pause at a high set of breasts. Unfortunately, those blue eyes looked pissed. Maybe it was the little lady remark—or his appraisal. Son of a lawyer and well-educated, he had none of the Cajun accent some of his older relatives possessed, but his mother had been a true Mississippi magnolia blossom and at times, he liked to mimic her soft drawl. "You seem to have the advantage, my dear. And you are?"

"Julia Rossi of Regal Restorations." She took a step closer, moving into hammer throwing range.

He detected an undercurrent of anger in her tone. A preservationist, then, who'd somehow sussed out his intentions. He moved the stock of shotgun crosswise in front of his groin. He'd been hit in the balls by an irate woman when he called off their romance before offering a ring. A hammer to the gonads equaled unthinkable pain. He stepped aside and made a courtly gesture toward the overgrown path. "Your pickup truck awaits you, milady. Feel free to go unmolested."

He gave her plenty of space as she strode past him in her small, somehow endearing, work boots, but she stopped at the entry and pivoted to face him. Did she think he'd shoot her in the back? Remy laid the shotgun carefully in the weeds to make her feel safer. Julia moved toward him, hammer still in hand, so maybe not a good idea to disarm, but he thought he could wrest it from her hand if necessary.

"I know what you plan to do!" she accused.

"No, really, I won't pepper your backside with buckshot or press charges." He'd almost said cute, little backside, but she hadn't holstered the hammer and didn't seem in a playful mood.

"You plan to destroy this wonderful old building and put up some modern garbage that won't last forty years. Have you really taken a good look at her and imagined what she might become with some care and investment?"

He hadn't been inside the Bayou Queen in years, not since he tried to seduce the local girls during his summer visits to his grandparents by daring them to spend the night with him in the supposedly haunted precincts. Only one had gone along with it until she balked at laying down a sleeping bag over the crunchy carcasses of wood roaches and flushing a few live ones as well. Still, they'd had a good enough time in the back of granddad's pickup while sharing a couple of six-packs of beer.

All his defensive hackles went up. "I have investors and good plans for the property. Only the acreage is worth anything, and the hotel will be a bitch to tear down. This town needs some upscale condos, not another rundown relic."

"There we disagree. An historic hotel can bring in a continuous cash flow generated from many visitors, not simply from the immediate sale of condos."

She'd reached poking distance and lightly tapped the head of her hammer against the space over his heart to make her point. Julia Rossi smelled of dust and the light lady sweat that plastered her royal blue T-shirt against those two high, firm breasts almost rubbing against his chest. The lush, dark hair—the kind a man might like to run his fingers through—gave off the lemony scent of creamy, white magnolias. "We could discuss this further over lunch," Remy found himself saying.

Julia Rossi backed up. "I'm hardly in any condition to go out for lunch."

"Not at the Opera House restaurant, but Down by the Riverside is pretty rustic. Believe me, they've seen worse. As long as you have on a shirt and shoes, you're good. Maybe you can change my mind, or I can change yours. Great crab cakes. Tempted?"

"I do love a great crab cake. Okay, the sun is overhead, and we both need to eat." She holstered the hammer.

"Like a true gentleman, I will lead the way, hold back the brambles, and fend off the snakes."

Julia nodded and followed him into the wilderness surrounding the Bayou Queen. He deflected the thorny plants, holding them away from her with the sleeve of his dress shirt. After she refused an invitation to ride with him, he offered a hand up into the cab of her truck, which she also declined. Clearly, his southern charm hadn't won her over, as it did most women, but Remy would figure her out eventually. He always did.

Chapter Three

Julia waited for the charming Mr. Broussard's vehicle to disappear from sight. He drove a truck, far newer than hers, and a vibrant red color more suitable to a sports car. To give him some credit, the sides were splashed with mud as if he did take it out on the back roads to check on construction sites. Her uncles would show disdain for the color but respect the dirt. They often judged men by their trucks, and so did she after working with them for so long.

She doubted if they carried the same equipment. Julia peeled off her soaked T-shirt and replaced it from a pile of Regal Restoration tees on the front seat. When working in the heat, she often changed several times a day. She shucked the tool belt and tucked in the shirt. From the glove compartment, she took a packet of Wet Wipes, cleaned her hands, and rubbed her face with another, as she wore no makeup today. Slightly grateful that she kept her dark brows shaped and her lashes were naturally long and full, Julia swiped on a slash of hot pink lipstick using the rearview mirror. She took down her ponytail and finger-combed away the hat hair. A few little ringlets formed around her face as they often did in humid weather. Nothing she could do about the work boots. A quick spritz from a small bottle of perfume, and she was ready to go. No, she wasn't primping. The man might be a future client if she could be convincing enough.

Of course, Remy Broussard beat her to the bustling restaurant—judging by the crowded parking lot—serving a substantial lunch crowd. She spotted his truck at once, but had to wait for another to move before she could get a space. Like the gentleman he claimed to be, the man waited for her in the reception area. His long, lean form lounged against the distressed cypress wall covered with old advertising signs. He wore a white dress shirt open at the neck, complete with cufflinks, belted into jeans with just enough wear to seem authentic. Eyes dark as a moonless night, midnight hair side-parted, but combed back, definitely styled in a place without a barber pole outside like Ike's of Chapelle. She studied him exactly as he'd leered at her not too long ago, from those compelling eyes to his rugged shoes with a brief stop at his crotch.

His face, also lean and clean-shaven, delivered a wicked, white, deep-dimpled smile in Julia's direction. Damned if he hadn't enjoyed her inspection. "I thought you might have gotten lost."

Oh, a woman could get lost in those dark eyes, be seduced by that devilish smile. She felt a pulse of lust not experienced lately, a year or more actually, if she were honest with herself. Too bad they were already on opposite sides, but not too deeply in conflict yet. Still, nations rose and fell, battles were won and lost in the bedclothes at times. She tried to shake the idea out of her head, but it wouldn't leave voluntarily. He took that as part of her response to his question.

"No, just wanted to clean up a little. I'm more convincing without a soaked T-shirt."

"I wouldn't bet on that." Before she could come

back with a snappy retort, he said, "They're holding a table for us," and pointed the way to a cozy spot for two with a view of the bayou and a gaily painted Victorian house across the water.

Julia led the way and almost reached their destination before she heard, "Hey, Jules, over here! We got plenty of room for you."

Oh great, the uncles had decided to dine out instead of making hero sandwiches in the motorhome. They sat behind massive seafood platters half devoured, the delicate leg bones of frogs stripped of their meat, the crab shells empty of stuffing, and a central cup of seafood gumbo drained. Plenty remained: fried oysters and shrimp, a fish fillet, and a patty of some kind. A crab claw appetizer plate still held a few pinchers ready to dip into sauce. The waitress stopped to ask if they want a second beer. Glancing at Julia, they shook their heads and stuck to ice water. "Say, our niece and her friend are going to join us. Okay?"

Since that meant a bigger tip, the server hurried to grab napkin-wrapped cutlery from a vacant table and ask for their drink orders. With no choice left, Julia slipped into the chair Remy held out for her next to Uncle Sal. He offered a hand to Uncle Sammy, who wiped his greasy fingers with a napkin before accepting, and leaned across the table to shake with Sal, smooth as if no plans had been upset.

"Remington Broussard," he said in introduction since Julia hadn't taken care of that.

She dove in. "My uncles, Sal and Sam Rossi, the most important members of the Regal Restorations team. Mr. Broussard is, um, a potential client." She noticed his dark brows rose, but he didn't deny it. She had to establish a business relationship before her relatives started to interrogate him as a potential husband instead of the sexual playmate she had in mind.

"Polish off those crab claws while you wait, why don't ya," Sammy offered, his broad face made even wider by his grin. "So, what's the nature of your project?"

Since Remy casually selected a claw by the tip, dunked it into spicy cocktail sauce, and sucked the bit of exposed meat from the cartilage, Julia rushed to answer for him. "Mr. Broussard owns the old hotel I checked out this morning. You should see the coffered ceiling in the ballroom. It's not nearly as bad as it seems. We could do molds from the best of the squares to replace the worst, and repair the others. Some new gilding and it would be magnificent. The walls have cracks of course, but those can be patched."

When Remy failed to match her enthusiasm, Uncle Sal chipped in. "Nothing like lime plaster. Withstands damp, doesn't mold or mildew, not like gypsum or Jesus God, that wallboard they use today. Jules knows her plaster, and if she says it can be salvaged, she'll be right."

Remington Broussard mustered a polite smile. "An unusual profession for a woman, plasterer."

"We taught her all she knows. This kid could do perfect flat work on walls and ceilings by the time she turned seventeen. Her daddy wanted better for her, though. Sent her off to college to study history, then historic preservation, and picked up some business courses too, but she worked with us summers saving the money for her education. Some of the old guys around gave her training in ornamental plaster, but we all thought she'd fly the coop once she had those fancy degrees." Sammy made a pair of fluttering wings out of his thick fingers since Sal was busy attacking his baked potato side dish. "But, turned out our girl liked getting her hands dirty more than working up stuff on a computer. Now, she does both. No one puts on a finish coat as well as Jules."

The waitress arrived with the unsweet tea for Julia and a glass of red wine for Remy. He ordered the large bowl of chicken-sausage gumbo, which came with French bread and potato salad. She selected a lady-like seafood salad. The server carried away empty salad bowls and beer bottles to make room and allowed the conversation to continue.

"Very interesting," Remy said.

Sal took over. "Yep, Jules made contacts, turned us into Regal Restorations when we were once only plasterers working on old buildings in New Orleans. Now we can do the whole shebang. Her daddy would be so proud of his baby girl if he'd lived to see this day. And you, what's your game?"

"Architect, mostly high-rises and condos. I generally supervise my own projects." He sipped his wine.

Throat suddenly dry, Julia gulped her tea.

"Remington Broussard, Remington Broussard." Sal pondered. He pointed a finger across the table. "You're the guy who lives in the house they call the Black Box across the bayou and a little upstream from the Alleman Plantation. Marv Holcomb is planting non-invasive bamboo to blot out the sight from Getty's backyard."

"Yes, that's right. I designed the building. I'm

aware the locals don't appreciate its style and call it that, but I believe the world has enough room for all types of architecture. No need to be mired in the past." Apparently, Mr. Broussard took no offense.

Uncle Sammy, always the more jovial of the pair, said, "I bet that place is a chick magnet. Can't see much inside because of the tinted glass, but at night that staircase to the stars shows up when the lights are on. I do believe I've seen some female forms moving up and down too."

"Possibly my mother or sister visiting, but maybe we both need bamboo hedges," Remy remarked mildly. "The first floor is my office with an outside deck and dock. The second is my living room and kitchen, the third my bedroom and bath. Both have balconies overlooking the bayou. I'd be glad to give you a tour anytime—day or night."

He said those last words with his eyes on Julia's face, closing out the uncles for a moment that appeared almost intimate. Sammy missed the suggestion, but not Sal sitting next to Jules. In his youth, he'd possessed the red hair that sometimes popped up among the appropriately named Rossi family. Now with it mostly gone, what remained was shaved close to the scalp. However, his temper remained fiery. Sal's wide face, full of faded freckles, colored. "You hitting on my niece? Because we stand in for her father now."

"Aw, come on, Sal. He don't mean nothing, do you?" Sammy elbowed Remy with a brawny arm covered in dark hair, maybe a little harder than necessary for a friendly gesture.

The man straightened in his chair and offered Sal a cordial smile. "The invitation extends to all of you of course."

The arrival of the gumbo and seafood salad saved the day. Their waitress deposited a refilled bread basket on the table. "Anything else I could get for you, boys?"

"Maybe some more of the honey butter. Bet it's as sweet you are, babe," Sam answered. Despite toting a sold middle-aged gut, he still had all of his hair, a crown of salt-and-pepper curls, and his tendency to flirt intact.

The waitress, also middle-aged, plump, busty, and experienced, smiled. "Not half as sweet as our white-chocolate bread pudding, a house specialty, Junior Polk's own recipe. Can I interest you in dessert, *cher*?"

"Love when women talk to me in French. Yeah, I'll take some," Sammy said.

Sol, scowling, added. "Yeah, make that two."

Clearly, he had no intention of leaving Julia alone at the table with the Broussard guy. Both uncles would stay protectively by her side until they finished eating, not allowing her to get down to the nitty-gritty concerning the Queen. Sometimes working with family was so frustrating. Whenever they left New Orleans, Aunt Franny exhorted her niece to keep Sam away from other women, and Aunt Rosa begged Julia to make Sal stay out of bars where he'd likely get into a scrape. Usually, doing heavy work in the heat took care of both problems as the men turned in early to get a sunrise start before the temperature rose, but sometimes Julia got tired of babysitting them both. At times, she'd posted bail and warned off Sam's latest conquest. They in turn guarded her virtue like two giant foo dogs whether she wanted them to or not.

"We got the time to see your place today. We're

waiting for the brown coat to dry. Shoulda been finished by the end of February, but all the goddamned rain this year set us way back. Good thing our slate man finished up the roof early or there could have been more damage. Most of that was in the attic." Sal helped himself to more bread as the waitress carried away the remains of the stuffed potatoes still encased in foil.

"Do you stay on the job regardless of the weather? That seems inefficient," Remy said, and immediately drew a defensive remark from Sol.

"Hell, no. We go back to the city and do some small jobs. Most of the older homes in New Orleans have plaster walls, even the little places. With all the oyster shells around, they made their own lime in pits way back to do the job. We found horsehair in Alleman's walls used to bind the plaster. You could still tell it came from a brown horse or maybe a mule. Now, it mostly comes with wood fibers."

"Enlightening." Remy Brossard spooned his gumbo and offered the accompanying potato salad to anyone who wanted it. Julia felt a trifle embarrassed when Sam took him up on the offer after his gargantuan meal.

The bread pudding arrived swimming in a sweet sauce. Sal pressed half of his dessert on Julia. "You can't do heavy work on a salad."

She pointed out they weren't working today, but she ate it anyway. So good!

The final check came, a hundred dollar plus whopper. Three credit cards belonging to Sal, Julia, and Remy hit the table. Sam shrugged. "We each have a company card. Doesn't matter which of us pays."

"I insist," said Remy Broussard. "I invited Julia,

Ms. Rossi, to dine here and am happy to include her co-workers."

The uncles did not fight his offer, nor did Julia. This was a business luncheon, or should have been, not a date. Mr. Broussard could write if off on his taxes just as Regal Restorations did. Too bad Sal and Sammy didn't forget about the offer to tour the Black Box.

"You lead the way. We'll follow." Sal jingled the keys to the second Regal Restorations truck they had at their work site, same gray color but closer to silver than the one Julia drove, and newer. Its Regal Restorations logo still stood out with the royal blue lettering topped by a crown while her vehicle's sign had long since peeled away.

They followed the red truck out of the shell parking lot, made a left at the bridge, a right by the vast cemetery, then drove along the bayou until they came to a lengthy paved drive guarded by two massive live oaks of distinguished age and a metal electric gate. They had arrived at the Black Box.

Chapter Four

It pleased Julia to see that Remy Broussard wasn't entirely nontraditional. He'd planted the way with young live oaks that would eventually form an impressive alley, but not in his lifetime. She noted he'd placed a parking pad with a two-car garage and storage shed off to one side in order not to conflict with the sleek, dramatic presentation of his home. He'd also boxed in his narrow lot running from the road to the bayou with metal pipe fencing matching the stark modernity of the house. A couple of chestnut horses grazed on one side of the fence and a decrepit trailer occupied the lot on the other.

They parked on the pad and paused to gaze up at the black monolith. "Cool," said Uncle Sammy.

"I don't trust this guy," Uncle Sal whispered in Julia's ear.

Entering through a door only distinguishable from the glass exterior by a silvery handle, Remy showed off his efficient office space sporting a wall of diamond-shaped cubbies filled with rolls of architectural plans, the latest in computers and specialized copiers, plus a traditional drawing board, and modern glass-topped desk scattered with small sculptures. A few sketches of a project filled a corkboard. The Regal Restorations team took a long look at that.

"Sort of similar to this place but laid out in a

connecting row of diamonds," Julia observed.

"Exactly. Ultramodern condos the like of which Chapelle has never seen before," Remy said, enthusiasm warming his voice.

Julia shook her head. "I can't see much market for them in this small town, and retirees won't want a three-story home; too many stairs."

"What she said," Uncle Sal agreed.

"The end units are three-stories, but the rest run crosswise, three layers of apartments with elevators, of course. Bayou views, close enough to town for shopping and taking advantage of the many local festivals, restaurants, and the little theater. Not far distant from Lafayette if you want more action." Remy Broussard had his sales pitch memorized.

Uncle Sammy nodded. "I could dig it. Yeah, I could live there." Through his own lack of restraint and his wife's strict Catholicism, he and Aunt Franny had seven kids, some grown and out, four still creating chaos at home. He liked being away on a job a little too much. Julia glared at him for betraying their bread-and-butter business. Renovate and restore; don't build new.

"Let me show you the rest of the place." Their guide led the way to a metal staircase almost industrial in style. "The plumbing core runs up alongside the stairs, half-baths on the first and second floors, and a full on the third."

They clanged to the second floor in their work boots and emerged next to a kitchen and dining area, all open floor plan. A free-standing fireplace vented to the outside, stood across the way surrounded by black leather sling chairs and a sofa of the same material accented by a few red pillows. Remy flicked on recessed lighting that made table lamps and electrical cords running across the floor unnecessary. A pewter-toned contemporary chandelier hung over the dining table. The white subway tiles of the kitchen backsplash reflected its light. All the appliances were stainless steel and the counters black granite flecked with white. A small bar stood ready to fill the round metal cocktail tables scattered around with a variety of drinks or wine from the rack.

"No laundry area?" Julia asked, criticism in her voice.

He heard it. "There's a washer and dryer stacked in that cabinet. I send most of my stuff out to be laundered. The cleaning lady does the rest."

"A true bachelor pad." She'd noted even his worn jeans had been pressed.

"Step out on the balcony. You'll love the view."

Julia opened the sliding door and moved to the curved smoked Plexiglas topped with a metal railing enclosing the space, which held deck chairs and more of the little tables for drinks. "You *can* see Alleman from here, almost eye to eye with its second-floor gallery."

From the site where they'd been working, the metal railings of the Black Box made two shining slashes across the modern building which threw a dark shadow over the bayou below. Yes, that bamboo should give Mr. Getty his privacy. Uncle Sal tested the railing for stability and found it solid. He grunted but conceded nothing.

"The third story balcony provides shade for this one, but you can catch the best breezes up there or take a tan." Remy took them back to the staircase, the one that lit up at night, and showed the way to the next level, his bedroom. "Feel free to explore the bathroom. Esther cleaned this morning. It should be presentable."

Julia, always a sucker for a nice soak which she rarely got on the job, opened the double doors exposing a large, well-lit mirror placed above twin sinks set in the same granite as the kitchen. In its own room on the right, a free-standing tub big enough for two sat on a pedestal. Small baskets containing fragrant soaps, fizzy bath bombs, and soft washcloths sat around the base. A heated towel rack held, what else, thick black towels, and a private commode hid behind a half wall. Off to the other side of the sinks, a clear glass box of a shower had its own space, and beyond that lay a closet hiding a toilet. Her gaze returned to the tub, and she emitted a soft sigh she hoped no one heard.

Making room for the uncles, Julia returned to the bedroom, attempting to avoid staring at the king-sized bed covered in a black satin quilted duvet cross-crossed by a zebra hide, and a stainless-steel headboard which mimicked brass beds of old. She stared anyhow. As Sal flushed the toilet to check the water pressure, Remington Broussard came up behind her. His closeness made the hairs on the back of her neck prickle and her nipples harden.

"Like it?" he asked.

"You kill that zebra yourself?" She hoped a little snark might chase away the sensations he provoked.

"No. The decorator said this room needed some striped relief from all the black. She swore it wasn't an endangered species like the Grevy's zebras they have at the little Acadiana zoo."

Julia had to agree with the decorator. Even the two

nightstands were black lacquer standing out against the prevailing neutral pale gray walls. She moved away to escape his body heat.

Out on the second balcony where a nice, cooling breeze blew as promised, sat a double lounger, a hammock on a stand, and more of the small metal tables he must have bought in a wholesale batch. Again, Remy approached from the rear, this time caging her against the railing with his arms as she took in the view, though he didn't touch her. Julia refused to flinch or retreat, but if he kept this up, she'd give him an elbow to the gut. She'd dealt with plenty of aggressive construction workers in her line of business.

Instead, she said, "You can see the Bayou Queen from here, her upper stories, and make out where the path from the dock ran."

"I cleared that. Usually I take my boat up the bayou when I want to survey property rather than fight the undergrowth."

"Wise idea. I should have brought a machete instead of a crowbar."

The balcony door slid open. His arms dropped. He stepped back. Julia exhaled as Sam entered the space and stared down as well as out. "Hey, that's a nice dock right off your office and a boat. She looks pretty speedy."

"She is. I could use her to water ski if I wanted to chance the bayou water. Mostly, I just tool around. You get a whole different view from the water."

"You ever grill out on the dock?"

"Occasionally."

"Yeah, I could see myself in that hammock, a nice big burger on the table, a brew in my hand."

"This is my favorite space too."

"But not a family home with only one bedroom," Julia said, breaking up the love fest between Sam and Remy.

"It wasn't intended to be. The bedroom is large enough to be split into two if necessary, but I'd really hate to do that."

"I'll bet you would."

Sal joined them. "Hey, you can see that old hotel Jules explored today."

She wanted to thank her uncle for opening the subject again. "Imagine if that place were beautifully renovated, and the gardens planted again. What a picture the Bayou Queen would make lit at night with her reflection glittering in the water. Put in a new dock, and boaters could stop for a drink or lunch. If a reception or ball were held there again, she'd be ablaze with light. That's something to be proud of, something you'd save for posterity, yours and others, like planting those young live oaks along your driveway."

Remy met her challenge. "What if I want to make the buildings of the future instead of preserving the past?"

"Surely you could find undeveloped property to do that. Lots of cane fields around here with plenty of room. Buy one of those."

Remy snorted. "You really are a city girl. People around here hold onto their land whether it's in use or not. The daddy or granddaddy or great-granddaddy left them that land. All the heirs must agree to sell, and believe me, those families are large. Right here, this is my tiny piece of family land carved out of a cow pasture my paternal great-grandfather, a man they called Tubbs, left his children, all seven of them. My grandmother nagged granddad to let me purchase his sliver to entice me into moving back to Chapelle because land is so expensive around New Orleans."

"You got that right," Sam agreed.

Remy expanded his arms, pointing from one fence to the other. "A second cousin lives in that trailer. Another one grazes a few horses on his share. Finding a plot large enough for a big project is nigh well impossible, and if you do, it might take years to get all the heirs to agree to a sale and the price. I got the Bayou Queen property for a pittance at the tax auction. Another deal like this won't come along any time soon—if ever."

Julia played her ace. "I had coffee with your grandmother and great-aunt at the bakery. They are both in favor of seeing the Queen restored. Wouldn't you like to make them proud?"

Remy threw back his head and barked out a hard-edged laugh. "So that's where you found out about the Queen—and me. Those two are already proud. You think I haven't had to listen to their tales of past grandeur over and over. My grandmother married down, taking on Guidry Broussard, a country lawyer whose main clients were his own disreputable kin. She polished him to a shine and got his family to back him in a run for mayor. He won three terms. His pride and joy is bringing Hartz Technology to town, though most people think Jonathan Hartz moved here because he fell in love with and married a Cajun girl. Believe me, Patty Broussard still likes to manipulate people. If one way doesn't work, she'll try to destroy her opponent with vicious gossip. When my mother wouldn't bow down to her, she started rumors of an affair going on behind my father's back. He moved us and his law practice to Mandeville to get away from her."

Considering the outburst, Remy felt little affection for the woman who had gotten him this land. Julia backed up a little, but didn't concede. "Whatever Miss Patty has done in the past doesn't make her wrong about the Bayou Queen."

He ignored her statement. "You know what I see when I stand here? My row of Black Diamonds condos reflected in the water. Accept that's the way it is going to be."

"Maybe not. We'll have to see about that." She'd gone into stubborn mode, her hands on her hips. Her uncles said she could be harder than plaster, more like concrete, once she set on a course.

Uncle Sammy checked a rugged watch nestled in his black arm hair. "Time to go, Jules." He'd extricated Sal from more than one tight spot with timely exits, and Julia suspected he did the same for her now.

She decided to exit gracefully before she lost her temper. Sal grumbled about not having time to fully appreciate the view from the third floor. "The same as the second only higher," she snapped. He raised his russet eyebrows at her as they charged down the staircase and retreated to their trucks. Remy Broussard followed, getting ahead of Julia on his long legs. He opened the door for her and offered her a hand up again, one she didn't need.

"Maybe you'd like to stop by this evening and see the stars from the third-floor balcony. I could crank up the grill, make a couple of steaks, uncork a bottle of wine."

"No, thank you, Mr. Broussard."

He was quick to say, "Remy."

"I have other plans."

"Maybe another time."

"Perhaps." Julia shut the truck door and turned the engine over. She did have plans to make and people to call—to save the Bayou Queen.

Chapter Five

After the Rossis left, Remy went to his office, awakened his computer, and tried to work on the specifications for a project, but his mind kept straying to Julia. Contrary to popular opinion, he didn't care for easy women and preferred a challenge. He'd earned his reputation during his teen years while being forced to spend summers in Chapelle, a pretty dull place for a guy who grew up across the lake from New Orleans. His parents had made some kind of agreement with his grandparents long ago when they fled this town and its nasty gossip. So, he'd endured having his grandmother pressure him to commit to a career in law in order to mold another successful politician.

Sitting in the mayor's chair while his granddad worked was fun as a child, not so much as a teen. When he acted out, Mayor Broussard took him fishing on Indian Lake and told him he understood. The Broussard in Remy was coming out, but he must understand he had a grander future than settling down early with some gal he'd gotten pregnant. Even if he went on to college, the whole town would remember what he'd done and to whom, killing any chance of public office. That lecture didn't prevent Remy from running amok among the loose girls of Chapelle, but he took care to carry condoms.

With a great deal of teen sulk, he'd replied, "I

don't want to hold public office. I plan to be an artist."
He'd held up his sketchbook, showing Guidry
Broussard a remarkable likeness of himself done with
the charcoal that blackened Remy's fingers. Like Julia,
he didn't mind getting his hands dirty.

"Excellent work, but not very practical unless you
plan to spend your life sketching tourists on Jackson
Square," his grandfather said.

By the time he graduated high school and got into
Tulane, Remy realized this to be true. The Broussards
were nothing if not practical realists and opportunists.
Asserting himself, he selected a major in architecture
and went on to pursue post-grad work in Chicago, far
from family pressures. But as his father warned, the
Broussards always found a way to suck you in. He
glanced at the deed to the Bayou Queen still sitting on
his desk and looked around at the house he'd built on
family land.

At least his taste in women had improved. At
Tulane, he dated girls from good families, Mardi Gras
ball debs with great breeding. The last of those
expected an engagement ring upon graduation and
received only his decision to leave the area presented at
fancy restaurant where he believed she wouldn't make a
scene. Instead, she stood when he did and delivered a
girly hit to his balls. It hurt, but not as much as it would
have if he hadn't seen it coming and arched his back.
He didn't return to the city until she'd safely married
someone else.

In Chicago, he slept with serious women intent on
their careers, not marriage, and sought the same type
after coming back to New Orleans. They wanted a
handsome escort to society events where they made

contacts, furthered their agendas, and enjoyed purely recreational sex. One whom he hadn't dated exclusively did turn up in the family way. He called her bluff. A DNA test proved him right. She married a man lower down on the social ladder. He had no idea if that guy was the father or not, but he sent both a wedding and baby gift. No sense in making extra enemies.

Remy suspected Julia Rossi fit his type, a strong, career-centered woman—who could probably hit harder than any of his other lovers. He recalled the way she'd held the hammer and crowbar, ready to fend him off even if it meant breaking his skull. That made her a little bit dangerous, and he liked the idea. Let's face it, her kind was thin on the ground in Chapelle where every young woman appeared to want marriage and children as soon as possible, and even divorcees were on the prowl for their next husband. Any with other ambitions left town right after college.

Six o'clock. He didn't feel like firing the grill or delving into the contents of his refrigerator. The idea of eating alone at the Riverside or Opera House did not appeal. Not in the mood for Chinese buffet. Maybe he'd get a large sub at the sandwich shop on Main Street, bring it home, and pair it with a red wine. Since Julia had turned him down, he'd watch the sun set alone from his balcony. Sounded like a plan. He put it into execution.

The last person he expected to see sitting at an outdoor table in front of the new Starbuck's was Julia Rossi looking very professional dressed in a crisp white blouse and slim dark skirt. Her dark hair, freshly washed, waved over her shoulders. She sat with two other women, acquaintances of his, not sexual but purely business and social. They had their heads together over coffee and high-priced desserts. The locals would say the same of the coffee, claiming they made better and just as strong at home, or in the case of the senior citizens, that Mickey D's was good enough and you got a free refill. Maybe they could get better pastries at Pommier's, but the bakery closed at four each day.

Remy recognized a female cabal when he saw one. He parked on the street not far from where they plotted and walked casually into the buzzing hornet's nest. "Mind if I join you ladies? Just let me put in my order."

In other words, he wasn't taking no for an answer. The way the volume of their whispers increased when he turned his back told him he'd been the topic of their conversation. He ordered a double espresso and a panini sandwich. Whatever the older generations thought, the interior tables were completely occupied by younger residents immersed in their laptops or engaged in lively conversations. He paid, returned, and took the fourth seat at the ladies' table.

"Beautiful evening, lovely company," he said with his best smile. "We don't get too many opportunities to sit outside once summer starts. Mrs. Hartz, Mrs. Tauzin, how are your families?"

Both agreed that their husbands were fine and their children thriving. Mrs. Hartz was still often referred to as the Billionaire's Cajun Bride as if she'd been the heroine of a romance novel. Starting out a kindergarten teacher, Celine Hartz grew in sophistication being the wife of Jonathan Hartz. She now ran his charitable trust, doling out scholarship money to deserving students and funding worthy projects. Though she must have been heading toward forty, had two half-grown children and one at the Naval Academy, she still possessed a clear olive complexion, luminous brown eyes, and thick, dark hair that might have been touched up, but by the best salon in Lafayette. He'd sat at her table several times during the endless fundraisers the rich were expected to attend and always found her gracious.

On the other hand, Jane Tauzin was a scrapper when it came to causes she embraced. She fought for the environment and had brought back recycling to the parish, Louisiana's equivalent of a county. Since her parish councilman husband worked offshore every other week, she took care of business in his absence and ran her own environmental testing company. Remy had hired her a few times to check sites for polluted soil or hidden gas tanks, all of which could drive up the cost of a project so high as to make it unfeasible. Originally a Montana girl, she owned dark green eyes, a perky brown bob, a pretty face, and a nice rack. He would never mention that last fact to anyone. People still called her husband Crazy Merlin Tauzin though he'd stabilized considerably with a wife and two sons in his life. No sane man would want to take him on in a fight. Jane appeared to be around the same age as Julia, early thirties, a few years younger than him.

Powerful women, all three of them. Was he ready to take them on? No time like the present to start. "I hope I didn't interrupt anything important, though I understand why Julia turned down my invitation to dinner if she had better company waiting."

Celine raised her eyebrows, and Jane tossed a coy smile in Julia's direction. Both women finished the final bites of their strawberry-topped cheesecake and last drops of coffee. They left a reply to Julia who seemed caught off guard by his remark. He watched her high breasts rise as she took a breath.

"As a matter of fact, we met to discuss the fate of the Bayou Queen. We've come up with some alternate ideas to tearing her down."

"Since I own the hotel, maybe I should have been included."

"This was only a brainstorming session. We might try to get the Queen landmark status. The hotel has a long and colorful local history. After I left your place, I stopped by the library. They have a huge file on the hotel, all the balls held there, its role in housing troops on the way to World War I, its use as a hospital during the Civil War—just as I imagined when standing inside its walls."

"How about its decline into a boarding house and then a flophouse?" Remy asked.

Before Julia could stab him with her fork, his coffee and panini arrived at the table. When one sat with the town's richest maven, the food came to you, no shouting out your name and sitting it on the counter for pickup.

Julia quelled the look of attack he'd seen in her eyes. She applied the fork to her cheesecake instead, swallowed, and answered, "All that is part of the hotel's story, if not very glamorous. Jane agreed to begin the process to have the Queen declared a landmark. She's good with bureaucracy."

"Might have been nice to ask me first."

"We were getting around to that."

Sure, once she'd stirred the bayou waters into a

fine froth. Celine Hartz spoke in her soft voice. "Would you consider selling the property to my husband for five times what you paid? The profit to you would be considerable. Then, we'd hire you to oversee the restoration. You certainly did a fine job on this building."

Remy could tell that came as news to Julia. Jonathan Hartz had bankrolled the business when a local couple wanted to buy a franchise. People joked that he missed his Seattle coffee so badly he had to bring it to Chapelle. Remy took the empty derelict storefront on Main, repointed the bricks and left some exposed, others covered with plaster for a French Quarter sort of style.

Evidently, Mrs. Hartz intended to blow his horn for him. "Remy went before the town council to get permission to put up the iron posts that now support what used to be a second-floor screened porch. They'd intended to have the part of the building that jutted over the pavement condemned before it fell on someone. Instead, he reinforced it with metal beams and glassed the area in. The new posts blend in with the character of the town, as do the exposed bricks on the inside. The second floor, all up to code, has become a gathering place for many groups. It has a wonderful view of the green and the church. Jonathan owns the building of course, but rents it to the entrepreneurs at a very reasonable price. The young people find work here, and the property tax has gone way up to the advantage of the town. We know we could trust Remy with an even bigger project."

Celine Hartz certainly knew how to add cane syrup to her words. Remy switched to a diplomatic half-smile.

"I'm flattered, but I have plans for my own development. The investors approved the project and expect to see it completed within the next year."

"Might they not consider a buyout by Jonathan Hartz a better deal?'

Jane Tauzin fought her way into the conversation. "Move your project elsewhere. Restore and recycle this landmark building. Once it's gone, we'll never have another like it. Take the money." Her Montana roots showed an unseemly Yankee haste.

Celine consulted a delicate wristwatch, the dial surrounded in tiny diamonds that winked in the late afternoon sun. "My family expects me for dinner shortly. I had my dessert in advance. Please consider our idea with an open mind, Remy." She offered her hand.

He rose and shook it, but made no promises. Since Jane also got up, he remained standing and did her the same courtesy.

"Merlin took the boys for pizza since he's onshore this week. I'm sure they'll save a slice or two for me." She didn't try to hold Remy to any promises, but said to Julia, "We'll talk some more." Still plotting, Remy thought, as both women sauntered off deep in conversation to the small parking lot at the end of the block. He took his place at the table again.

"And that leaves us," he said to Julia. He sipped his coffee and noticed her empty cup. "Can I get you another?"

"No, thank you. My uncles will wonder where I am."

He wanted to keep her right where she was, or better yet, at his place viewing the sunset. "The others hadn't had their dinner yet. How about you? Want half this panini? I'll share my chips." He ripped open the packet.

"A tempting offer, but I should go."

"Your uncles keep you on a pretty short leash, I guess." He knew that would rile her independent spirit.

"It's a family business, but I can do as I please. I simply don't like to worry them."

"Then come back to my place and look at the interior floor plans of my condos. I think you'll be impressed. They have every amenity. You had no time to study them earlier." He thought he detected indecision. She didn't stand to leave. In fact, she pinched a couple of chips from his bag and stalled for time by eating them one by one. He'd bet her lips would taste like salt if he kissed her right now.

"How did you get to know Celine and Jane?" Julia wasn't from Chapelle, but she'd sure honed in on its most powerful women.

"They've stopped by Alleman several times to see how the work progressed. Mrs. Hartz owns a couple of Gaylord Getty's paintings, which your grandmother seems to think are obscene. Both women are very interested in historic preservation."

"His paintings are abstracts and can be whatever you want them to be," Remy said.

"Like a good prostitute?"

Her unexpected answer made him laugh and slightly spill the espresso he had raised to his lips. He blotted his mouth with a napkin before the dribble stained the white dress shirt he still wore, sleeves rolled up now to his elbows, strong forearms lightly furred revealed. "I don't believe Mr. Getty would appreciate the comparison, but yes.

She stole a few more chips from the bag. No, she hadn't had dinner. Remy put half his sandwich on a napkin and handed the other to her. She didn't shove it back. In fact, she bit into the ham and melted cheese. First, feed her, then seduce her. He summoned the deep, double dimpled smile. "You know I'd be putty in your hands if you'd just let us happen."

Julia set the sandwich down and replaced it with a glare. "Is that the best you can do for a pickup line? I've heard it a hundred times. I'd expect an architect to know that putty and plaster are two very different things."

He had prepared for this reaction. "Isn't lime plaster made with a base of lime putty mixed with sand, water, and fiber?" Remy bit a chunk out of his sandwich while he waited for her reply.

"I'll bet you looked that up this afternoon while I was at the library researching the Bayou Queen." She pointed at him with the crust that remained in her hands.

He didn't cop to that plea, even though he had done the deed. Remy merely continued to eat his sandwich and waited for her to let off steam—as lime did when mixed with water.

"Do you know I learned about making plaster from scratch in one of my restoration classes. We made a lime pit, filled it with crushed oyster shells, heated it, then slaked the lime with water. It gives off tremendous heat before it cools enough to produce putty. It is both dangerous and volatile. Sacks of quick lime have been known to burst into flame and burn down the ships transporting it. It's not something to play games with."

Julia's blue eyes narrowed at him.

Remy understood the warning and ignored it. He gazed at her across the table. "You have gorgeous blue eyes."

How those blue eyes rolled in disgust. "Next you'll tell me I'm beautiful when I'm angry."

"You are. Where did you get such blue, blue eyes? They aren't common among Italian girls." He was surprised when she answered.

"My mother is Irish, but I suspect you know all about Italian girls," she countered.

"I did study abroad my junior year. Nothing like Italy for architecture—and girls."

"Yes, I spent some time there myself. Italians believe in preservation. All the men think they are Romeo."

"Italians believe in tourism, yet so many of their monuments are decaying from lack of care."

"Would you tear them down and put up condos?"

"Of course not, but people don't flock to Chapelle to view rundown hotels."

"They visit the church and plantation homes. Why not add an historic site nearby where they can stay? All the motels are out on the highway."

Remy felt as if he'd just played a fast round of tennis with an able opponent and perhaps hadn't won the set. He crumpled the empty chip bag, stuffed it into the paper coffee cup, and balanced both on his plate. Heading for the waste can, he said, "I'll be back in a minute."

He didn't expect her to be there on his return, but there she was, balling the used napkin in her fist. What to try next? "I don't know about you, but I could use some wine and savory snacks. That wasn't much of a dinner."

"I had enough with the cheesecake, but a glass of wine does sound good." Her blue eyes glittered. "Where did you have in mind?"

"My place, top deck to watch the sun set." He checked both his watch and the position of the sun. "We still have time to look over my plans before it goes down."

"Goes down," she repeated.

He wasn't sure if this was a challenge or a sexual suggestion, and didn't care. "Your truck or mine?"

"We'll take both."

Ah, she didn't trust him and wanted to keep her escape options open. Admiring the hip action beneath that slim, booty-hugging skirt assisted by the high heels she wore, Remy watched Julia move toward the parking lot. After she got into her truck and pulled up behind him, he climbed into his and led the way. At the Black Box, he left the electronic gate open once they'd passed. He wanted Julia Rossi to be comfortable with him, very comfortable indeed, with no fear of being trapped.

Chapter Six

Julia had driven the newer of the two trucks—the one with the nice logo—to her power meeting. Naturally, Jane arrived in a gas-saving hybrid and Celine Hartz in a discreet silver Lexus also bearing her bodyguard, and she'd wanted to put her best foot forward. Speaking of which, the high heels were killing her. She made note that Remy left the gate open after they passed. She wouldn't have to ask his permission to leave, and she appreciated that.

Though she'd boldly asserted that the uncles did not rule her life, sometimes getting out the door with them around proved difficult. Like good parents they asked the pertinent questions: where are you going, with whom, when will you return? And like a naughty teen, she'd told them about the meeting and fudged on how long it would take. Remy Broussard hadn't figured into the white lie, but now Julia knew exactly where they were headed, conflict or not, and she'd agreed to come along to see his equivalent of etchings. She wanted some Julia-time, which she didn't get when sharing a motorhome. Thanks to Marv Holcomb, she had a room in the house and a bath with a tub down the hall. Hopefully, the uncles wouldn't notice when she returned.

Remy held open the nearly invisible door to his dark tower and got right down to business as if he wanted to keep to a schedule. He rolled out his floor plans on the large table meant for exactly that, and weighted down the ends with small statues: a Degas ballerina, a Roman goddess—both naked—an Egyptian cat with a ring in one ear, and a sleek golden bee resting on a block of black marble. Julia found the assortment of museum replicas both tasteful and quirky, but said nothing. She gave her full attention to his floor plans that resembled shotgun houses of old in a very modern design. The living room/dining area flowed into a kitchen open enough to allow for conversation with guests but sheltered enough to hide dirty dishes. Across the aisle, he'd hidden the utility area. Passing down the hall, two small and one large bedroom and master bath sprouted off the main trunk. The master bath resembled his own on the third floor. The other bedrooms shared bathing space. The hall ended in a large linen closet. He'd included a free-standing fireplace, not that anyone in the deep south needed one, but people liked them. Blank wall space came wired for a television and any other technology the owners might want. Cleverly concealed doors like his own opened off each bedroom to a narrow terrace. The vertical versions mimicked his tower with the living room and kitchen on the first floor and bedrooms on the second and third.

Julia applied a critical eye to the layouts. "No parking, no porches?"

"You do realize with the advent of air conditioning, no one sits outside anymore except on rare occasions, but we'll have benches along the walkways, a picnic and grill area, and other outdoor meeting space as well as indoors at a club house with a pool. As for parking, each condo gets a spacious carport with a small storage building that will blend in attractively with the buildings."

"If you didn't intend to knock down an historic building to do this, I'd say bravo. You might even attract jaded city dwellers tired of traffic and crime."

"Not might, will. I'm ready for that snack now. How about you?"

"Definitely ready for wine."

Remy led her up the stairs to his kitchen. While Julia watched, he rummaged in his refrigerator for plump red grapes, a block of cheddar, a wedge of brie, along with the obligatory cracker assortment taken from a box in his pantry, what she thought of as typical male seduction food. When he sliced rings of crawfish boudin sausage and laid them out on the plate, she gave him extra credit for originality and local color. He uncorked a bottle of red from his wine rack, then gently shoved the cork back in and handed her the bottle plus two long stemmed glasses. "Carry those up to the third floor for me. I'll be right behind."

Julia let her skepticism show. "The bedroom, really? Why not this balcony?"

"Like I told your uncles, better view up there, nice breeze."

She shook her head at his transparency, but went along with it for now. They did go directly to the balcony. Remy set down the platter on one his little metal tables and positioned another to take the wine and glasses. He snapped open a folding chair with a black canvas back, and seated himself. "Please, take the lounger and be comfortable."

"How comfortable do you expect me to be?"

"Take your shoes off. I'll feed you some grapes,

but you must try the crawfish boudin. It's really great." He poured two glasses of wine, half full.

Julia took part of his suggestion. She removed her pain-in-the-arch heels and put her feet up. Remy dangled a stem of red grapes over her mouth. She bit one off and tried hard not to laugh at her Cleopatra imitation. All they needed was a discreet servant fanning both of them with ostrich feathers. After she swallowed, he offered a circle of boudin impaled on the end of a toothpick. Really good, she acknowledged with a nod, but now she'd have crawfish breath.

"Why don't you have some too. You're the one who's hungry."

"I will, but ladies first. Cheddar or brie?"

"Brie."

Remy smeared the soft cheese on a cracker and offered it to her mouth with his fingertips. They grazed her lips when she took it in, sending tingles right where he intended. Oh, he was good at this, very good. Next, he handed her the glass of wine to sip and helped himself to the spread. Leaning back in his chair, he said, "The sun is going down right behind the Bayou Queen."

The live oaks stood out in black relief as the red orb drew tendrils of orange, gold, and pink from the sky and pulled them into night. The bayou reflected it all in a hazy brown mirror. Treetop breezes kept the mosquitoes off when darkness and their feeding time descended. Peeper frogs and crickets tuned up for their mating serenades.

Julia finished her wine. Remy refilled it immediately—attentive or trying to get her drunk, she couldn't tell. She allowed herself to relax on the comfortable cushions covering a lounger big enough for two. It had been a while since she'd been with a man. The demands of the company kept her on the road, and she wasn't one to pick up a guy in a bar, or cavort with a construction worker she'd hired. Usually too tired anyhow. Right now, here sat a fellow, handsome, clean, and well-spoken, who obviously knew his way around women. Why not enjoy despite their differences? She sensed she should make the first move, give the green light, whatever.

"That chair seems uncomfortable. There's room enough for two over here." She moved to one side. He hadn't turned on a bug-attracting outdoor light. Hard to read his expression in the dusk. Julia got her answer when Remy set aside both wineglasses and took up her offer. As he settled beside her, one arm went around her shoulders and drew her close. The other cupped one side of her face as he moved in for the kiss. She'd been told she had voluptuous lips, and his weren't so bad either. Remy Broussard knew what to do with them. They nibbled and tongued before going deep. He completed the job of seducing her mouth before moving his free hand to open the buttons of her blouse.

She did the same, working his shirt open and enjoying the lack of a T-shirt beneath as well as a patch of dark hair on his tanned chest that her fingers combed through lightly. Remy shivered beneath her hand despite the warm evening. She circled his nipple with a fingernail and delighted in its pucker. He'd removed her blouse and made headway with her nude-toned bra, nothing fancy, but uplifting, and applied those talented lips again to the peaks of her breasts. Her turn to shiver.

They took their time with each other. Despite the

strength of his erection, Remy didn't grope beneath her skirt. He unzipped it, laid it aside, and slowly removed those nude bikini panties down the length of her legs. He came up kissing her thighs, working his way to her center. No danger he'd miss those nether lips or the firm clit throbbing for more. His fingers thrust inside of her, bringing on the slick of passion. She felt the gathering of her orgasm, the tightness, the release like a bowstring being plucked.

Time to reciprocate once she'd savored her moment by removing his trousers and a black pair of boxer briefs. Somewhere along the way, he'd toed off his shoes and shed his socks. Somewhere handy, he'd retrieved a condom.

"Let me do that for you." Julia smoothed the rubber over the swollen tip of his penis and rolled it down the hardened shaft. "Not like putty, strong as plaster."

He rewarded her comment with a slight laugh. "I certainly hope so."

Spreading her legs, he went onto his knees and took the first plunge deep inside of her, touching her womb. She jerked, still close to the edge from her first orgasm. He wouldn't have to do much to guarantee a second, but Remy was not a man who rushed. He teased her with short thrusts, then longer, holding on beyond her expectations until she wished she had longer nails to score his back, urging him on. As her body started to seize, Remy allowed his release. He stayed only a moment collapsed against her breasts before rolling to the side and disposing of the condom into its open wrapper. They lay side by side allowing the night air to dry their bodies of love sweat. The stars twinkled in the humid air. The gentle lap of the bayou water against his dock far below lulled.

Julia bolted upright. "What time is it?"

Remy checked the glowing dial of the watch he'd left on a side table. "Only nine-thirty. We have plenty of time for more wine and another round."

"You do. I don't. May I use your bathroom?"

"Absolutely."

Julia gathered her clothes and the small purse she'd slung aside earlier. He gave a soft sigh of regret when she moved away, certain her backside glowed in the moonlight. She'd intended merely to clean up a little, but that big bathtub and all its amenities beckoned. She closed the door and turned on the taps. As the water rose, she selected a bath bomb and tossed it to foam and fizz and release its fragrance. Another little basket contained packets of hair clips and scrunchies. Remy Broussard did think of everything.

She selected a clip and twisted her hair to the top of her head. Stepping into the warm bath, Julia laid her head back against the cold of the porcelain and washed her still sensitive nether regions with a black washcloth and a tiny, scented guest soap. She selected another cloth from the baskets and patted her face hoping to keep her makeup in place for the return to Alleman and the uncles who might still be up waiting. Her swollen lips stung a trifle. She'd definitely need a new application of lipstick.

Sorry she couldn't linger in more ways than one, Julia emerged from the bathtub to dry with one of the thick, black towels so nicely heated. She dressed again and shoved the hated shoes onto her feet. The nice thing about having the sinks and mirrors in a separate space, they hadn't steamed over. She bent close to apply lipstick. A masculine hand released the hair clip and sent her hair tumbling again.

Remy lifted the strands and kissed her neck. "If I'd known you were taking a bath I would have joined you. That tub is big enough for two."

"So I noticed. You certainly thought of everything a woman could want in there, right down to a way to put up her hair." She picked the clip off the counter and snapped it at him playfully.

"The last person to use that bath was my sister, probably the woman your uncles saw on the staircase. She makes the obligatory trip to see our grandparents once a month, but can't be bribed to live here like I was. Amelia has more integrity. Anyhow, I keep the clips and scrunchies for her because she forgets to bring them or loses hers."

"And she's the only one who does?" Julia raised her dark, defined brows.

"Obviously not, since you did—but I'm not seeing anyone at the moment. You?"

Julia shook her head. "I don't have much time for relationships."

"A thing we have in common. Tonight was good though, very good for me." He waited for her to say the same.

She hated to inflate his already large ego, but she also believed in giving credit where it was due. "Very good, excellent in fact. I'd hire you for a gigolo any day, if you ever give up architecture."

"Good to know I have an alternate career waiting in case the Black Diamonds deal falls through. You must understand I have a lot riding on it."

"Move your development elsewhere. Sell out to Jonathan Hartz and accept the position as project manager. He pays well for expertise."

"I can't do that. I owe the investors."

"You could if you wanted." They'd moved so well together on that double lounger, but apparently were no closer on the fate of the Bayou Queen. Wondering if her uncles watched the lighted staircase tonight, Julia headed rapidly down the steps and out Remy's front door. Flicking on the garage lamps, he followed her all the way to the truck. Julia mounted the cab before he arrived to lay those tempting hands on her. She did lean out for a goodnight kiss that went on way too long.

"Despite our differences, I hope we can do this again sometime," he said in parting.

"Maybe," Julia answered. She turned over the engine and backed away. Maybe—if they didn't end up becoming enemies about the Bayou Queen.

Chapter Seven

Remy rolled the plans for the Black Diamonds development he'd left out overnight and secured them with a stout rubber band. He replaced the small sculptures that had held down the edges on his desk. Often, he could tell much about clients if they remarked on one of them: cat lover, nature lover, lover of women, free spirit. But Julia had given nothing away. He suspected she rarely did.

After she took her leave, he'd gone back to the top deck, polished off what remained of the wine and boudin, and went to bed. He slept well, very well, only sorry Julia hadn't agreed to join him under the black satin spread. In the morning, he didn't bother to shave. A little dark scruff would help him fit in better at the noon luncheon investors' meeting as would a black fitted tee that showed his lean strength, and the jeans he donned after his morning run and a brisk shower. He placed the plans next to a slim briefcase that contained the prospectus headed *Black Diamonds Development— Find your perfect setting*. Julia had it right. His target buyers were city people seeking an escape from crime, noise, and traffic—who still didn't want to mow lawns in order to live in the country.

Breakfast consisted of two cups of black Community Coffee and a couple of slices of toasted whole wheat bread smeared with strawberry preserves from a hand-painted jam pot, both made by the local *traiteur*, the faith healer Rosemary Leleux. Supposedly, her pots brought luck. He'd need it today. Considering he'd run five miles, it wasn't much of a meal, but the provided lunch would tilt toward fried and greasy.

He fiddled away the rest of the morning making calls, the most important to the man who would bush-hog the Bayou Queen property and make it accessible from the road again. He phoned another to install heavy-duty culverts in the drainage ditch that could handle the weight of heavy equipment. When his watch showed eleven, Remy set out for the shady home of his ancestors and their contribution to Cajun culture, Broussard's Barn, an old-timey dance hall, some distance out in the country among the cane fields.

The Barn had started out as a country general store way back before the turn of the twentieth century. Barely providing enough income for a very large family, the Old Broussard of the day cleaned out his barn, knocked down the stalls, and turned the place into a dance hall with enough lively chank-a-chank music to whet the thirst of the dancers for his wife's lemonade and cherry bounce. Should they get hungry, the store stayed open to provide soda crackers, tins of sardines, and other salty snacks, or canned peaches in heavy syrup for those who had a sweet tooth, all innocent enough.

Eventually, an enclosed ramp connected the store to the barn to keep the customers out of the weather and above the mud. Everyone entered through the store, nowadays to pay a modest cover charge, but the hall, expanded and updated over the years, had many exits that satisfied the fire marshal but owed their origins to its days as a speakeasy. Even a trapper could get a jar of white mule, known for its kick, in exchange for a muskrat pelt during the days of Prohibition. Hot jazz bands out of New Orleans replaced the accordions, fiddles, and triangles. The high and low classes mingled and got drunk at Broussard's Barn. The family kept the peace with a shotgun, a baseball bat, and a pearl-handled pistol still kept beneath the counter. Cops were not called then or now. The Broussards made a fortune that even the Depression didn't whittle away. No stocks for them. They bought up land from defaulted farmers and sold or rented it later for solid profits when the good times rolled again. "Because da land, it never goes away, no," became a family adage.

Remy parked in the shell-paved lot near the store. Across a half-grown cane field stood the ancient cypress and bousillage house where many a Broussard had been born and died. Two-hundred-year-old oaks shaded its newer tin roof. As the barrier of the cane field implied, business was never conducted there.

The strings of clear bulbs that illuminated the lot were turned off for now, as were the lights by each door of the rundown motel to the rear of the dance hall. The girls who rented them by the hour at night probably still slept. Starting out as cribs for prostitutes, the ladies of the evening now had slightly better accommodations and the protection of the Broussard's bouncers for a cut of their profits. Everyone knew. No one talked about it.

Remy also turned his eyes away. He had nothing to do with this end of the family business. Entering through the darkened store, not open as this hour, where the shelves of old canned goods had only fairly recently been replaced with convenience store foods and a large beer cooler—cigarettes, snuff, and condoms still kept behind the counter—he descended the creaking ramp into the Barn. The stage and the dance floor, now more likely to host country/western bands and their fans, stood empty. Overhead, the house lights burned illuminating a section of four tops pushed together and set for a meal with cutlery wrapped in paper napkins. Sweating bottles of beer sat at each place.

The smell of meat splattering fat on a griddle filled the air. All the aroma and noise emanated from the kitchen behind the substantial and well-stocked bar. Well, he'd arrived a little early. Remy pushed two more tables together and unrolled the Black Diamonds plans. No handy sculptures around, he used a bottle of hot sauce, the salt and pepper shakers, and a metal napkin caddy to hold down the edges. As he fanned the brochures out to one side, thunder sounded in the tunnel, and he knew his great-uncle had arrived along with—he counted the place settings—six of his minions, all relatives.

Hard to believe the currently reigning Old Broussard was his grandfather's brother. A morbidly obese belly strained at his bib overalls, a white T-shirt with stained yellow armpits worn beneath. Sure, the former mayor possessed a prosperous gut well-hidden beneath his tailored suits, but nothing like this rotundity. Both still sported full heads of thick, steely gray hair, his grandfather's beautifully styled and his grand-uncle's cut saying he'd paid all of twenty dollars to have it clipped.

"*Nonc*," Remy said, using the regional term for uncle, technically *noncle*. He braced for an all-encompassing handshake from the huge, puffy hand, but got instead a crushing hug to the fat man's belly, once a hard pile of lard, now as soft and drooping as a woman who had birthed a dozen children and nursed them all judging by his sagging breasts.

Remy stepped back and gestured to the table with his brochures. "If you'd like to take a look before we dine..." he said and heard the snickers from his relatives at his formal use of the word dine.

"Where you from, boy? First, we eat, den we take a look at dem plans." From deep in his treble-chinned neck, Old Broussard summoned an impressive holler. "Dose burgers 'bout ready, NuNu?"

"Comin' in a few minutes. Gumbo is up." Remy's second or third cousin, anyhow the one who lived next door to him, appeared toting a tray of thick-walled soup cups. He gave Remy a grin missing two top teeth. Unlike most of the family, NuNu had long dirty blond hair coiled under a hairnet, and light blue eyes most folks described as crazy. Acne scars studded his pale face like seeds on an unripe strawberry. Some thought he'd been born of one of the prostitutes from the motel, but if so had definitely been folded into the family and raised accordingly.

NuNu plonked down a cup at each place, spilling some of Remy's on the checkered oilcloth and barely missing his lap. The gumbo came with an island of white rice in the center and a spoon tucked in the side. "Soup's on. Turkey/sausage. Broussard Burgers next on the menu." Shaking his skinny behind practically in Remy's face, NuNu boogied back to the grill.

Old Broussard sank into his custom-made armchair at the head of the table, the one usually behind the cash register out front. He patted the place on his right with a heavy hand. "Sit by me, Remy. Talk wit' me. Slick, take dat udder end chair."

Slick Broussard, head bouncer, conceded his usual seat. Maybe five years older than Remy, he slid toward forty with bulging biceps from pumping iron and a hard gut on him like a Romanian weightlifter. He still wore his hair in a greasy pompadour ending in a ducktail as if he'd never gotten over the death of Elvis. Now, it bore a few threads of gray. No one messed with Slick or ridiculed his retro style. Most predicted he'd become the next Old Broussard when this one died of the expected heart attack.

Remy started to pick up his spoon, but let it drop when the old man bowed his head and muttered the usual Catholic blessing. Then, the slurping began, and conversation ended. The burgers with a side of fries arrived just as Remy finished, leaving much of the rice in the bottom of the cup. A Broussard Burger consisted of a half-pound of ground beef topped with two slices of cheese, double bacon strips, and a mound of grilled onions, all on a toasted bun slathered with a special sauce Remy suspected to be spicy mayonnaise. Devouring one tested a guy's manhood. Not to finish every bite earned taunts of "wimp". Remy knew that. His appeared to be topped with extra onions and more goop than the others. He ignored the fries and applied himself to getting the enormous wad of meat and toppings down with sips of beer in between. "Great burger," he muttered.

"Damn right, it is. Best in da parish. Dat NuNu, he turned out to be some cook, him. Learned in prison. Got his GED dere too. Made good use of his time dere."

"Considering the condition of his teeth, I hope

that's all he's cooking." Remy should have let that observation slide.

Old Broussard puffed up like an offended bullfrog. "He don't do none of dat drug shit. Anybody does, dey off my payroll." Broussard eyed the men around the table. Each one dropped his gaze and focused on downing the burger. "NuNu, he lost his teet' in a bar fight da way a man is supposed to do."

One of the minions, all of them dressed in boots, jeans, and bicep-revealing black T-shirts with Broussard's Barn in white lettering across their chests, looked up and bared a grin showing off a gold incisor. "That's how I lost mine, throwing a guy already hopped up on dope outta here."

No surprise that the Broussard posse also served as the old man's bodyguards. Remy forced down another bite of burger, almost done with it. But, some special sauce leaked from the side of the bun and down his shirt. Remy wiped off the glob of pink with a napkin, and figured he'd have to do the presentation with a grease stain on his front. Since a couple of the men around the table had wiped their fingers on theirs, he should feel right at home.

However, the old man issued an order. "Slick, you get da boy a clean T-shirt from da store."

Slick delegated the errand to the scrawniest of the bodyguards who most likely only weighed two-hundred pounds, all muscle. Eyeballing Remy, he said, "I'm guessing a medium."

Remy couldn't deny it. When the T-shirt arrived, Slick said, "Go ahead, put it on." It didn't bear the plain white block letters of the security force, but instead had a couple doing a two-step beneath the words, "Pass a

Good Time at Broussard's Barn." Another challenge issued. Remy stripped off his shirt for their amusement. The dozen eyes studied his chest and armpits for hair, which he had, along with a lean set of defined abs that declared him a welterweight if he cared to enter a boxing ring. He gave them a minute to satisfy themselves that he wasn't a sissy, then donned the shirt.

"There, you one of us now," Old Broussard declared.

NuNu slinked out of the kitchen with another tray loaded with bread pudding anointed copiously with rum sauce, and made the rounds of the table. "Coffee?" He received a unanimous round of nods.

"Why don't I do my presentation while you enjoy dessert?" Remy suggested. "Pack mine to go, NuNu, because it really looks great." Truthfully, he couldn't hold another bite and looked forward to the coffee to wash down all he had eaten. Before anyone could insist he stay at the table, he scooped up the brochures and handed them around, then went into his pitch, pretty much the same one he'd given Julia and her uncles. He invited them to study the floor plans and outlined the kind of clientele he hoped to attract to Chapelle.

"We're not good enough for you?" Slick flexed his verbal muscles again.

"Give me your down payment now. I'll let you have a discount." Remy kept his salesman's smile on his face and dearly hoped Slick wouldn't take him up on the offer.

"Nah, I got my own place on five wooded acres. I like my space. Don't want to be stacked on top of nobody."

"To each his own." Internal sigh of relief.

Still, Old Broussard heaved from his chair and pawed through the plans. Since he took an interest, so did his men. Grease stains marred the edges. Remy put running a fresh set on his list of things to do. The old man looked up with his piggy, yet very shrewd black eyes, like an aging boar that still knew the exact time the slop arrived in the trough and was the first to eat. "What else you got to show me for my big investment?"

Always make eye contact. To glance away showed weakness. Remy met his stare. "I bought the Bayou Queen site yesterday for an incredibly low price. No one bid against me."

"*Mais*, yeah. Maybe word got around I was interest in dat deal." Old Broussard chuckled deep in his chins. "Anyt'ing else?"

"I've got a man to bush-hog the lot and arranged for some culverts that will support the heavy equipment for the demolition."

"You hire Stelly?"

"Yes. He's reliable and careful."

"Married to one of my granddaughters. You done good." Having made the effort to stand long enough, Old Brossard returned to his chair. NuNu circled the table filling the coffee mugs from a large granitewear pot. He jumped a little when a phone rang from somewhere deep in the old man's anatomy, but no harm done. His grandfather fished out a cell from his bib overalls. "Broussard," he answered gruffly, though dozens of Broussards populated the parish. Someone had him on speed dial and kept the conversation short. "Dat so. T'anks. Anytime you come around, I stand you for a free drink." No goodbye. He simply disconnected and gave Remy a hard look.

"Dat I-talian gal from New Orleans you foolin' around wit', she axed to be put on the agendas for bot' da parish and city council meetings next week."

"I not fooling around with…"

"Yes, you is, Cuz," NuNu cut in. "She got nice tits. I saw 'em last night."

"You spied on my house with binoculars?" Remy rose up from his seat. He had some height and more muscle than the scrawny second cousin. The urge to smash the Styrofoam box of bread pudding into that gap-toothed mouth was difficult to restrain.

"Hell, no. I picked up some night vision goggles at the surplus store. When you're on parole, legal entertainment is hard to come by." NuNu's comment drew a laugh from the audience.

"I believe being a Peeping Tom is still against the law."

"Way out in the country? I was lookin' for owls just about the time she stood up naked as a jaybird. A birdwatcher, that's me."

Remy gathered the man's soiled apron in his fist. "Don't do it again."

Old Broussard's hand slammed the table and splashed the coffee from the cups. "Enough. You see dat girl don't interfere wit' our plans, Remy. Never was a Broussard welcome at da Queen when she lorded over da bayou in her best days. Now da sabot is on da udder foot, heh. Tear her down, you. NuNu, you watch for birds somewhere else. *Bon,* no?"

Remy released his grip on the apron and wiped his hand on a napkin. NuNu scuttled back to the safety of the kitchen like the cockroach he was. "I'll speak to Ms.

Rossi." He rolled the plans, collected the spare brochures, slipping them back into his slim briefcase, and started for the exit.

"Hey, you forget your bread puddin'." Because the old man recalled him, Remy accepted the box and the hearty slap on the back that signaled dismissal.

Chapter Eight

In his sweltering truck, Remy cranked up the air-conditioning and aimed for Alleman Plantation. As he bucketed along crumbling country roads, he rationalized that his father's family wasn't really the Cajun mafia as some people called them. Those same people certainly hadn't voted for Guidry Broussard as mayor or welcomed him into their social circles either.

No one "made their bones" slaying enemies or dealt in drug trafficking. Every one of them had the fortune or misfortune of being born into an actual huge, tight-knit family that accounted for a lot of small town corruption, most of it victimless crimes like backroom gambling, prostitution, and paying off politicians for favors. Hell, since the parish voted gambling back in to garner more taxes, the Broussards had gone legit and owned a couple of mini-casinos out on the highway, and another situated in a truck stop on the parish line, all very lucrative. The Black Diamonds development was another step in the direction of becoming completely legal. That's what Remy told himself.

Remy figured after last night, he owed Julia a face-to-face conversation, not simply an email or text saying cease and desist or stay out of my business. He hoped they could remain friends, maybe with benefits, since she was from out of town and really didn't understand the dynamics of Chapelle. He got to New Orleans fairly often and could look her up—if he'd remembered to ask for her email address or her phone number. Making a mental note to get that information, Remy steered between the two whitewashed brick pillars that denoted the entrance to Alleman.

He knew immediately that Julia Rossi and her uncles had gone. No motorhome sat parked under the shade of the oaks. However, Marv Holcomb heard the crunch of oyster shells beneath tires and appeared at the front door before Remy had a chance to turn around. He approached with arms wide, a welcoming smile expanding beneath a neatly trimmed silver mustache set in a thin face. Marv wore his hair in trendy short spikes of gray. When Remy looked down on the shorter man's head, he could view the pink of his scalp between the peaks.

"Remy, have you come to see the progress on Alleman? It's going to be stunning, absolutely stunning. Let me show you around."

He had no choice but to get down. This man had encouraged him to draw, paint, and study art during those long summer stays with his grandfather. If Marv was disappointed that he'd given his support to a kid who later became an architect whose style he did not admire, Remy never would have known it by the greeting, a heartfelt light hug so different from being enveloped by Old Broussard's flab.

"Actually, I was trying to track down Julia Rossi, but sure, I'd love to see the place."

Marv's hollow-cheeked face fell a little. "Julia and her uncles went back to New Orleans to do a small job and pick up an apprentice. She'll return in time for the council meetings next week. That woman is on a crusade, I tell you." He fanned the air with an artistic, long-fingered hand.

"Yes, I know."

"Must you really tear down the Queen?"

"As I told Julia, I have investors for a new project."

Marv shrugged his slight shoulders. "See what Regal Restorations has done for the house. Mind, the first floor is empty until they can do the finish coat, which should happen shortly. I've jammed all the furnishings into the second-floor rooms and the attic. What a boon the roof no longer leaks, and we can make use of that space again. Mr. Getty has vast collections of, well, this and that, he likes to rotate on display."

Remy followed his old friend into the hallway of the mansion and peered into the parlor and sitting rooms on opposite sides. Farther on, a dining room sat across from a large master bedroom. All had huge fireplaces, paper covering the heart pine floors, and magnificent Corinthian molding topping the walls. Julia's team had repaired that trim. Not a single acanthus leaf remained broken or chipped. They passed a rather decadent bathroom hewed from the kitchen space at the rear, which had once been a brick-floored pantry area and now housed modern appliances. That brought them to the rear verandah sporting the same four gracious Corinthian columns as the front of the house. Marv sank into a cushioned rattan chair and gestured Remy to take another.

"So very hot for May." Marv picked up an old-fashioned paper fan distributed by funeral homes back in the day and stirred the air. "One of Mr. Getty's collectables. I really shouldn't be using it, but the ceiling fans are temporarily disconnected. I'd take you upstairs. However, it is simply chaos there. I culled out space for myself and Julia. The bathroom isn't nearly as grand as the one downstairs with the tub inset in marble. She says she is simply grateful to have a bathtub instead of a shower. Such a nice young woman. Might I offer you coffee, iced tea, lemonade?"

Remy's thoughts had drifted from Marv's chatter to a vision of Julia in his bath. He imaged his hands slicking across those firm breasts so admired by NuNu, sliding down her back and under her buttocks as he lifted her on top of his erection hidden in a froth of foam. He felt himself going hard. That wouldn't do in front of Marv who waited patiently for an answer to his question. He'd never put the moves on Remy despite what his grandmother believed, but didn't want to give him any ideas either. "Uh, iced tea, no sugar."

"Coming right up." Marv bustled to the kitchen.

Without his host blocking the view, Remy could see his black tower of a house very clearly a half-mile away on the other side of the bayou. The glass glinted in the sunlight, but it still cast a long, dark shadow over the water. At least, his home hid the view from Alleman's porch of NuNu's rundown trailer.

Marv returned with a tray holding two tall, icy glasses decorated with a slice of lemon and a spring of fresh mint. He liked to make things nice. Even his khakis and short-sleeved cotton shirt were pressed. Remy accepted the glass. The chill against his skin made his hands less sweaty and burst the thought bubble of Julia in the bath.

"I hear you're planning to plant bamboo to block the view of my house from Mr. Getty."

Marv's olive complexion showed a spot of color on

the cheekbones. "Mr. Getty's idea, not mine. I live to serve him. Alleman has become my haven since the school board let me go when they cancelled the arts program—due to lack of funds, they said. I should be glad I made the twenty years for my retirement before that happened."

"I hope my grandmother had nothing to do with it. She tried to out you more than once."

"No, no. I think the downturn of the oil industry meant less taxes collected. Time for a change for me regardless. Gay men of my generation never played in town. We took ourselves to clubs in Lafayette or New Orleans. Some of my friends married, had children to please society and the Catholic church, but I always thought that unfair to the woman. If you kept up the façade, people here looked the other way. When AIDS came along, the wives caught it too. Just another tragedy to add to the rest. Remy, I'm HIV positive myself, but I take my meds and stay fairly well. I'd appreciate if you kept that to yourself. Others guess, but they don't really know."

Remy clasped his old instructor's hand which now appeared frail. "I can keep a secret. Thank you for entrusting me with yours. You were a great art teacher."

"You're better than most of the Broussards in this parish, dear boy."

"I don't know about that. I'll come to visit again, but for now, I need to get back to work, make some calls."

"Of course."

Marv walked him to his truck and waved as Remy made the turn to take him away from Alleman. He should have looked in on his old mentor before now, not that he hadn't greeted him cordially if they passed on the street. But, he'd been living in Chapelle for three years and never once sat down for a good visit. Exactly how good was he even if he'd never engaged in gay bashing like some of the Broussards. That had stopped with the fear of getting splattered with HIV blood.

Remy crossed the nearest bridge, one of four across the bayou, to return to his house. When he sat behind his desk again, he checked his computer for the number to Regal Restorations and called. No answer. He left a cordial message, "Please give me a call." Tried later. Left another message. "It is important that I speak with you." A third try late in the afternoon went to leave a message again. He didn't bother. She could be up to her elbows in plaster, but he doubted it. Julia Rossi was avoiding him.

Chapter Nine

Dressed in a navy-blue suit with a red power blouse and sensible heels to give her more height, Julia entered the city council chambers late. Familiar with the folderol that went on in political meetings, the pledge, the reading of the minutes, the old business before the new, she'd used some time to put last-minute details into her presentation.

Remy, with a thick roll of plans propped up next to him, sat in the first row.

Even with his back turned he looked good, dark hair as well-cut as his suit, his neck tanned, a tan she knew went down to his waist. Wondering if he still bore the scratches she'd given him in their sexual encounter, she stripped her gaze from the breadth of his shoulders and forced her eyes to settle on one of the less attractive councilmen as an antidote. Imaging doing it with a tubby older man possessing an excess of nose and ear hair drove her mind far away from sex and back to business.

Julia had a feeling Remy knew she'd arrived. Yes, she'd been avoiding him and his messages. He'd probably figured that out. What sort of businesswoman would she be if she didn't answer her inquiries? Whether he was the kind of guy who really did call the next day to say he'd like to see her again or merely an architect who wanted to argue for his plans again, she couldn't be involved right now. Remy's name wasn't on the agenda. Hers was. She had to keep her head in the game, not in the bedroom.

When they finally reached her issue on the agenda, Julia beckoned to her new intern standing in the rear of the room holding an easel and a low-tech poster board. She had no idea what kind of technology this small-town government owned and went old school with interesting pictures and printed reports entitled *The Bayou Queen—an Historic Gem* with a nice cover sheet showing the hotel in its 1920's heyday. Women in drop-waisted dresses and cloche hats strolled on the arms of natty men wearing straw boaters and striped trousers before the Queen's impressive façade. She'd gotten it from the library's file. Her intern/apprentice, Todd Whitcomb, fumbled setting up the easel, lank blond hair falling in his eyes as if he'd never worked with anything so primitive before, and at last hoisted the large poster board into place. Julia entered the U-shaped arena surrounded by councilmen seated behind their nameplates and mics like a toreador about to face multiple bulls. She averted her eyes from Remy and began with a smile. The man with the hairy ears smiled back. Julia cleared her throat.

"Thank you for giving me the opportunity to speak to you about a vital issue. You might already be aware that the Bayou Queen, a landmark hotel, is in danger of being torn down for development. I am here to ask your support in saving her." She didn't get any farther before one of the councilmen interrupted. His nameplate read Theriot "Terry" Broussard. Figured that Remy's relatives were everywhere. Other than dark hair and deep brown eyes, she didn't see much of a resemblance to the thick, squat man without the manners to hear her out.

"That falling down hotel is none of our business. It sits a mile out of the city limits. With the oil industry as it is and tax collections down, we're hard put to keep the potholes filled and the parks mowed. If you are asking for financial support, we have none to give."

"No, I'm not asking that." Though she had hoped there might be some. "I simply want an acknowledgement that saving the hotel would be an asset to the town, supplying jobs to the construction trades and bringing tourists to spend money in the area. We can use any written support given to obtain grants for the renovation."

"Mark my words, the place will turn into a money pit and never give a good return to the community. We need to move forward, not back into the past."

Mayor Folse, surprisingly a woman of well-preserved middle-age, thin, with blonde hair pulled into a chignon, said, "I'd like to hear her out. Go ahead, Ms. Rossi."

Julia did, presenting the arguments she'd given Remy and referring to pages in her handout picturing the Queen of the past and pointing out its future potential with photos she'd taken only yesterday with a good low light camera that revealed a swept portion of the parquet floor, the stunning plasterwork, the mahogany staircase, and long bar of the same wood she'd discovered in her further explorations of the first floor. The last lay beneath a rotting tarp heavy with dust. Someone had cared enough to cover it right down to its tarnished brass rail. Of course, she'd ignored Remy's No Trespassing signs and entered through a more easily jimmied window to get the shots. Julia concentrated on the mayor, whom she sensed might be an ally, with occasional glances at other members of the council, but never at Remy. She could almost feel the heat of his stare right between her shoulder blades.

The moment Julia finished, he jumped to his feet asking to be allowed to address the gathering, to show his vision of the future. Remy cut in front of her to distribute his shiny, professional pamphlets with their architectural drawings. "This is what Chapelle needs. Luxury condos that will draw more taxpayers to our community, the kind of people who will shop in our stores for groceries and tires, jewelry and clothes, not just transients who come and go after buying a few souvenirs."

"Employment," Julia countered. "Running a grand hotel takes a large staff from managers to groundskeepers, all paid from the hotel income. Condos won't do that except for some maintenance staff." She knew she'd struck a chord with the two black members of the council, one man, one woman, by the nodding of their heads as if she played a favorite song.

Remy turned on her. "Excuse me, Ms. Rossi, but I own the property—make that private property—and can build what I want there. I don't know why we are bothering the council with this matter."

Did he know she'd been snooping around the Queen again? Not hard to figure out considering the pictures she'd taken. Before she could open her mouth, Councilman Broussard spoke. "I move we table this request and get on with our agenda." Julia swore he gave Remy a subtle "thumbs up" partly hidden by the glossy brochure of Black Diamonds.

Though the mayor offered her a sympathetic smile, she asked for a second, given by the man next to Terry Broussard after he took an elbow to the side. Mayor Folse called for discussion, and none came from the council, but a woman's voice shouted from the rear of room. Julia noted a few of the male council members cringed and the tall, light-skinned black woman with the long red hair grinned, showing the white of her teeth.

"Do not endorse this outrageous and destructive land grab through inaction. Restore and repurpose!" Jane Tauzin strode toward the front of the room as she spoke, drawing Mrs. Hartz along in her wake. "We have already applied to get historical designation for the Queen. If granted, we can stop this project. Ask yourselves whether you'd rather have a marker put up where the hotel once stood or the real thing revived to its former glory."

"A good point," said the mayor.

Remy, clearly irked, raised his voice. "This is not a land grab. I paid for the Queen at a tax auction where anyone could have placed bid and didn't bother because they didn't care."

Jane had reached the arena. "You didn't find it strange that no one else showed any interest? Could it be someone scared them off?"

"I don't know anything about that." Remy suddenly hooded his eyes.

Celine Hartz arrived to put a gentle hand on Jane's arm. She might have been out of order, but no one removed the billionaire's wife from a room. "Regardless of how the land was obtained, my husband has taken an interest in restoring the Queen."

"Then, why didn't he bid on it?" Terry Broussard insisted.

"Not being from here, I believe he was unaware of this treasure hidden in the weeds until Julia Rossi brought it to his attention. He is willing to put a substantial amount of money into the project."

Julia watched opinions change before her eyes.

"Well, that does put another spin on things," said the male black council member.

"I'd like to call the question," Terry Broussard barked.

"And I'd like to propose a secondary amendment saying this issue will be sent to the proper committee to consider and a statement phrased after proper study of the matter," Topaz Senegal offered with a shake of her red locks.

Her counterpart from the district next to hers seconded her motion. No one cared for more debate. The first motion failed by one vote, the second passed by two. Julia made a point of shaking Ms. Senegal's hand before leaving the floor with Jane and Celine. They moved directly to the creaking old elevator that hoisted people to the council meetings and took them down again at the pace of thick cane syrup being poured on pancakes.

"We didn't win, but we didn't lose," Jane declared. "Could Jon exert a tad of pressure to facilitate getting that historic designation?"

"He hates pressuring people, but feel free to use his name as a backer if that would help."

In the privacy of the small space, Julia gave both women a hug. "Tomorrow night counts for more since the Queen sits in the parish rather than the city. Can I count on both of you to be there?"

"You got it." Jane stepped off first.

"Of course," said Celine Hartz. "You might also contact the Historic District Committee and the Live Oak Preservation Society. The first only has clout in town, but should support you. The live oak ladies are fierce when they feel trees are endangered. Most of them are elderly and might not have computer access, so keep that in mind."

"We'll start a phone tree tomorrow," Jane vowed.

The women moved to the parking lot and parted for their cars. Julia continued to her vehicle now sitting in a dark area of the lot beneath a burned-out streetlight since night had fallen. Before she could open her truck door, a man stepped from the shadows and grasped her arm. She twisted to shake him off and opened her mouth to scream.

"Julia, it's me, Remy. I took the stairs, faster than that ancient elevator." Trying to put her at ease, he said, "My grandfather once got trapped in it trying to get to his office and had a panic attack. He wet his pants. That machine isn't to be trusted."

"Are you?" Julia countered.

"Absolutely, but you don't know what you are getting into. It's more than local politics. Let me see you home."

"Yours or mine?"

"Alleman if you are staying there again, but if you want to come to my place…"

"Don't worry. I have an escort. Oh, my God, I forgot Todd. I have to go back."

"That pathetic dweeb? Some protection."

"He's simply wiry, but totally devoted to

restoration. I can't say the same for you."

Something scraped along the paving, putting both of them on alert. A large, headless white form appeared. Remy pushed Julia behind him and assumed what she supposed was a martial arts stance. It looked good on him, but she'd taken a similar self-defense class.

"Ms. Rossi, Ms. Rossi, it's only me, Todd. I missed the elevator because I couldn't get the easel to fold, but I knew you wouldn't leave without me."

She almost had. "Certainly not. Put that stuff inside and climb aboard."

"Some protection," Remy muttered again.

"Give him a break. He's a grad student in historic preservation and a well-intentioned millennial. We need more like him," she whispered as Todd struggled to shove the chart and easel behind the seats. "The New Orleans Master Crafts Guild gave him a one-year apprenticeship. We'll make a manly plasterer out of him by the end of summer."

"I think you could make a man out of any guy."

"I'll take that as a compliment and be on my way—alone, alone with Todd, I mean."

"If that's what you want."

But Remy waited for her to exit the lot and tailed her all the way to Alleman, tooting his horn as he veered off to his tower.

Chapter Ten

To Julia's delight, the parish council chambers bulged with her supporters, thanks to many phone calls made by her, Jane, and Celine. Patty Broussard and Pammy Vice sat amid the members of the Historic District Committee. In one of life's delicious ironies, Remy's grandmother chaired that group. Two very elderly women, one with shoeshine black hair, and the other with thin locks dyed flaming red, going by the names of Miss Lolly and Miss Maxie, represented the Live Oak Preservation Society. Peppered among her ladies were forbidding, unshaven men wearing jeans, boots, and tight black tees. One thin guy in a dirty white T-shirt and missing his front teeth appeared to belong to no group.

Remy had taken a place directly behind Julia and sat beside a sinister fellow with a greasy ducktail and bulky biceps. She regretted wearing her hair up for this occasion as the guy's hot, beery breath bore down on her naked neck like a stalking predator about to grip her nape with his fangs. Not a man she'd like to meet in a dark parking lot.

With the help of Todd and Office Depot, she'd run more reports for this larger body and had her intern practice with the smooth setting up of the easel. She noticed the parish courthouse had electronic voting, and several members fiddled with smart phones and computer tablets. Behind them, the stern portraits of former parish presidents lined the walls, and a videographer recorded the event. This was the big league who made the county-wide decisions. Julia remained quietly poised as the minutia of parish business passed and stood when called upon. Todd set up the easel and mounted the board flawlessly this time. She went into the same pitch she'd performed the previous night.

The youngest councilman who had spent the entire time enraptured with his iPhone, watching baseball or playing a game Julia thought, raised eyes delineated by heavy black frames. "I'm against new taxes, raising existing taxes, or dumping money into foolish public projects like the proposed campground."

Sounded like his campaign platform. Julia scanned his nameplate, Darin Duke. "Councilman Duke, as I am sure you heard, we are not asking for money, simply the written support of the parish government to help us obtain historic designation and grants to save the Bayou Queen which is a hotel, not a campground. The hotel will generate taxes, not raise them. It's all laid out for you in the handout."

He shrugged. "Words are cheap. Send your proposal as an attachment to my parish email account." And went back to studying his phone

As she finished, Remy stood and asked to speak to the question. He distributed his professional brochures again and did his spiel. The chairman of the council asked if anyone else wished to comment—and his grandmother, wearing a frilly, floral dress she thought still fit even though she'd had to pin the top over her bulging breasts shut with a large antique broach, barged to the front of room. To Julia's delight, Remy winced.

"As the wife of the former mayor of Chapelle and current head of the Historic District Committee, our group lends its support to saving the Bayou Queen, part of our noble heritage."

"It's an eyesore and needs to be torn down," a councilman said, another Broussard, this one with the forename of Hulin. Was there no end to them, Julia wondered?

Miss Patty's soaring blood pressure turned her face an alarming red at the disrespect. Julia dove in to save her. "An eyesore that could become a sight for sore eyes. We thank you for the committee's support."

"Her committee has no power here. Barely does in the town except to hassle incoming businesses to death about their facades. They can't prosecute anyone or levy fines," Hulin gloated.

"Thanks to our work, the Subway and the Starbucks have not defaced Main Street with modern exteriors. I am proud to say my son, standing right there, did the work on the coffee shop. He could do the same for the Queen. And Huey, I'm telling my husband about the way you treated me."

Hulin Broussard didn't seem overly concerned by the threat. Remy took his mother's arm. "Thank you for the vote of confidence. I'll be sure to make Black Diamonds a beautiful development you can be proud of. Let me escort you back to your seat."

"But, Remy!" Despite the protest, he steered his grandmother away from the action.

"Does anyone else have something to say before we entertain a motion?" the stone-faced chairman asked.

The elderly women rose just as Remy deposited his grandmother into her seat. They held out arms as thin as chicken bones but latched onto his with the talons of raptors. "If you could lend us a hand, Remy."

Unable to do anything else, he helped them totter forward to address the council. "Our concern is for the two-hundred-year-old oaks adorning the property where the Queen sits," the red-haired Miss Maxie quavered. "Those trees were on the property when the hotel was built. Heavy equipment will destroy their fragile root systems, and who knows how many trees will be hewn down in the name of progress."

"I don't plan to destroy any of the oaks. Well, maybe a couple will have to go to make space for the project, but—"

"There you have it!" Black-haired Miss Lolly came alive. "When that big box store came to the parish, they chopped down the oaks surrounding the property and put up their gas station and parking lot. Yes, they landscaped, but if you kill fifty-year-old oak trees what will you have left in a hundred years? I recall when those trees were planted and how beautifully they grew."

The youngest councilman raised his eyes again. "I am sure you remember when the oaks at the Queen were planted too, witch."

Miss Lolly cupped her hand to her ear. "What did you call me? Bitch or witch?" Her frail body shook more with outrage than age.

Duke smirked. "I didn't finish. Which means we've heard enough about oak trees. Why don't you sit down before you fall down? We wouldn't want that, now would we?"

The chamber grew quiet as all held their breath after this appalling breech of respect for the elderly. Miss Lolly leveled a knobby finger ending in a red-painted nail at Darin Duke. "Your first term will be your last, young man."

Her target appeared to pale beneath his olive skin, but he held his hard line. "Sit down—please."

"Remy!" The old women summoned him again, and using his support, returned to the rear.

"Anyone else?" the chairman inquired with a weary sigh as if hoping there wouldn't be more clamor.

"I'd like a few words," a heavy voice said.

Julia hadn't met the man, but from local sources she gleaned this was Jane Tauzin's husband, Crazy Merlin, though it didn't say that on his nameplate. A big man with a long, unshaven jaw, he did have electric blue eyes that flashed, *Don't mess with me*. Jane adored him. "Y'all know the Bayou Queen is one of my wife's causes. Hi, there, honey babe." He nodded toward Jane in the audience and drew a smatter of laughter. "Because of this, I must recuse myself from any vote on the matter—as should Huey since he's related to Remy Broussard. You might get away with that at the city council, not here." Merlin Tauzin drilled the councilman sitting opposite him with his hard lapis gaze.

The pause was brief before Hulin Broussard answered, "Yeah, I guess I recuse myself too."

"Other than that," Tauzin continued in his deliberate, deep voice, "I was taught to respect my heritage and listen to my elders, not make fun of them." His scary gaze shifted to Darin Duke who slouched and kept his own myopic eyes on his phone as if working some difficult equation. "The Bayou Queen deserves our support. I hope all y'all will give it." His eyes scanned each council member one by one and stopped at the black woman, Norma Bell, short, dark, plump, and wearing her hair in a knot on top of her head. Merlin gave her an almost friendly showing of his teeth. "I'm done."

"Thanks, Blue Eyes," Jane shouted to the amazement of Julia. She shrugged. "It's our thing."

Norma Bell immediately moved, "That the Ste. Jeanne d'Arc Parish Council supports having the Bayou Queen designated as an historic landmark building and being renovated to serve as a hotel again." She got a rapid second to her motion.

Having sat through most of the meeting, Julia suspected Norma Bell enjoyed putting Duke on the spot as he'd earlier proposed another delay to the building of a new library in her poor district by saying no one used libraries anymore since everyone had the internet, and a study should be done before proceeding. Because her motion cost nothing and made for good PR, it passed with the support of most of the council minus the votes of Duke and his cronies. But until that historic designation came through, Remy could proceed as he wanted. The fight wasn't nearly over.

Again, Julia took time to thank Bell and Tauzin and shake hands. Hers practically disappeared in Merlin's big grip. She herded her ladies out in a large group and stuffed the most feeble into a larger, better elevator to the ground floor. Jane, who had given her husband a little finger wave on the way out, and gotten one of those almost smiles in return, took the stairs along with Julia and Celine while Todd followed toting the easel and board. By the time they got to the parking lot, Miss Lolly and Miss Maxie had sailed off in their big boat of an ancient Lincoln Continental and Patty in her Mercedes.

"What did you think of my husband?" Jane asked, clearly proud as could be.

"He's, um, very impressive."

"He's scary, but he wouldn't swat a mosquito—most times, unless the mosquito was a really annoying bloodsucker."

"Good to know."

The women put their heads together to plan for tomorrow now that they had an endorsement from the parish to add to their plea for an historic designation. Remy in the company of the duck-tailed bruiser passed nearby. The preservationists strained to hear their conversation.

"You better set that bitch straight, Cuz. That pissant idiot, Duke, was worthless tonight, and we paid for his campaign. He got the ladies all wound up. The old man don't like that kind of thing. Miss Lolly taught him in third grade, and he has a soft spot for her. I think the old dame is right. He won't get another term unless he finds other backing." Remy and his cousin kept right on walking.

"He called you a bitch," said the outraged Jane.

"It's a name I've been called before when I've taken a stand to save a building. I don't care about that—most of the time."

Celine wore a troubled expression. "I'm more worried about the implied threat that Remy should do something about you. I think we were meant to overhear that and consider it a warning. I can lend you one of our family's bodyguards. He's sitting in the car right over there waiting to see me home as usual."

"I'll protect Ms. Rossi!" Todd said. The offer would have been more effective if his long legs hadn't tangled in those of the easel in that moment and sent him tumbling into the side of the truck.

Julia offered a hand and set him upright again. "Remy won't hurt me, Todd. Never fear."

"Glad you understand that," said the man himself who had approached during the minor chaos. "Julia, we do need to talk. Don't evade me this time. Come sit with me, and let's hash things out. I'll see you get back to Alleman."

"Why not?" She turned her keys over to Todd. "Don't wreck it."

"Ms. Rossi, should I call the police if you don't come back by a certain time?"

"No! And don't tell my uncles where I am. I'm sure I won't be long as there isn't much to discuss."

She walked away with Remy and left the others goggling at the sight. He helped her into the cab of his truck, took his seat, and turned on the engine. "We need the air-conditioning." Except he locked the doors and pulled out of the lot too.

"Where are you taking me? I thought we'd talk here."

"Back to Alleman eventually, the long way around. I can speak and drive at the same time."

Julia had made a big mistake and knew it. Outside of beating her fists against the window and making a scene, she would go along for the ride and simply must trust Remy. Still, the manner in which he drove swiftly out of town and onto the back roads gave her the feeling of being abducted—kind of thrilling in its way since she believed herself absolutely safe with him.

Chapter Eleven

What worried Julia more was the huge, black SUV tailgating them so close its headlights blinded anyone looking in the side mirrors. Celine's bodyguard? Julia didn't think so. Remy flipped his rearview to night driving and continued on steadily at sixty, slightly above the limit.

"Julia, we're bush-hogging the lot on Friday, and we'll be putting in the new culverts to handle the bulldozers and the wrecking crane early next week. I know how slowly the government works. You won't get your historic designation on time. Please back off."

"What will happen if I don't?"

"Trouble. My backers are the Broussards, my daddy's people though he has nothing to do with them. They might not look like much, but believe me they have money, connections, and power. The old man who heads the family bears a class grudge against the Queen and wants her torn down."

"You mean that obese geezer who takes the cover fees out at the Barn and tells everyone to pass a good time?"

"You've been to the Barn?" Remy gave her a quick glance, his face easy to see in the glare of those SUV headlights.

"Sure, we've been working at Alleman since January. My uncles wanted to try the burgers, and I wanted to listen to the music. Both were awesome in their own way. The old man doesn't seem like much of a threat."

"Believe me, you won't be doing any more work in this parish if you cross him."

"Not a big worry since most of our jobs are around New Orleans or out of state. I figured some kind of fix was in when you got the property for next to nothing and no one bid against you." She got in her little dig.

"Knocking down the Queen will cost more than the value of the land she sits on, so not much of a fix, I'd say."

"Anything else I should worry about?"

"Accidents could happen, nothing fatal, but discouraging." Though Remy kept his eyes on the road, she read concern in the tense set of his shoulders and grip on the wheel.

"Would they do anything to Alleman?"

"I doubt it since they have nothing against the man who bought it, just you."

The cab of the Remy's red truck went dark as the SUV decided to pass on a curve and pulled into the other lane. The driver, hiding behind heavily tinted windows, didn't speed up as he should have, just crowded Remy, their side view mirrors only inches apart. Julia's heart accelerated as adrenaline rushed through her system. Out of her passenger window she saw only a narrow belt of clay, and deep, weedy ditches still holding water from the last rain.

Remy spoke no longer. He held the wheel steady, dropped his speed, and fell back as they came out of the turn. With a blast of his horn, the other driver screamed into the night.

"My God, was he drunk?" Julia hated how her voice quavered.

"No, just my distant cousin, Slick, playing chicken. You saw him sitting next to me at the meeting. You'd think a man pushing forty would be over childish games. When I was a teen driving a cherry red Mustang my granddad gave me, he scared me into a ditch one night. Totaled the car, but I survived with seatbelt bruises."

"You could have been killed. We could have been killed." Julia willed her hands to stop shaking.

"No, he picks his spots where there aren't any oak trees or culverts to smash into—just in case *he* loses control. Slick isn't a man who believes in seatbelts. Tonight, I let him win. I have precious cargo with me."

She saw the gleam of his smile in the moonlight—and realized they'd arrived at the Black Box, the gate opening and closing as they passed. "Did you plan this?"

"Nope. You're shaken, and we were closer to my place than yours."

"I'm f-fine."

He reached over and touched her arm. "You're shivering. Let's get you inside and settled down before I take you back to Alleman. Do you drink whiskey?"

"Not often." Not since college when she'd had a couple of shots on a dare, but she didn't want to sound like a wuss. Since she continued to sit in the cab, Remy came to her door and lifted her down. Her legs felt rubbery. He kept an arm around her as they walked to the door.

"Are you sure Slick wasn't sending us a warning?"

Remy's shoulders lifted and fell against her side.

"Could be. You never know with him, whether he's playing around or dead serious."

She hunched at the word "dead". Remy got her inside and up the stairs to the second level. He lowered her into one of his ultramodern chairs, went to the small built-in bar in the kitchen, took out a couple of glasses, and poured two shots of amber liquid. He handed her one, watched her sip, and wince. "Toss it back if you aren't used to it. Get it down quick—though that is good sippin' whiskey, as my grandfather would say."

Julia followed his instructions. From her last experience, she recalled it went down hot and burned in the belly, but this seemed smoother than the cheap brand at the frat house. The warmth of the liquor spread through her rapidly.

Remy took her fingers his hand. "You're still cold on a warm night like this. Have another."

He handed her his glass. She tossed back the contents and slammed it down on one of his tiny tables next to the other. Julia attempted to stand up, but fell into the deep pocket of leather. Why fight it? At the moment, she had no good answer. Relaxing into the sling chair, she closed her eyes. The sound of Remy climbing his metal stairs with her in his arms woke her again. Headed to the bedroom. He provided a ready excuse.

"I thought you'd be more comfortable on the bed, Julie."

"Sure you did...do, whatever." She waggled a finger at his very nearby face. "Never call me Julie. That's a little girl's name. It's Julia or Jules. The men like to call me Jules."

"Because you are a jewel."

"Oh, another cheesy comment I've heard a million times. No, no. no." She shook her head against the arm that cradled her. "I think it makes them more comfortable with having a female boss. That's my theory."

"I'll stick with mine. You are a rare gem." Remy nudged open the door to his bedroom with his hip and crossed to his bed. The black satin felt so cool and smooth against her cheek, and the zebra skin a little prickly against her bare legs.

"Let's make you more comfortable." He unbuttoned the jacket of her suit and removed her heels. Propping Jules against a pillow, he raked his fingers through her upswept hair. Pins and clips went flying. It fell, thick and tangled into his hands. "All through that meeting I imagined doing this." His lips moved along the side of her throat, and she no longer felt chilled.

Her finger wagged again. "Ah-ah-ah, we are enemies. We can't be doing this."

Remy raised his head and nearly poked his eye on that finger. He curled it down. "We're frenemies, or maybe enemies with benefits, I don't know which. Either way, I've thought about being with you again every day since the last time. This, between us, has nothing to do with deals or projects. It's chemistry."

"Like turning putty into plaster." Her hand drifted down the length of his body. "I see the formula has worked again."

"Are you willing?"

"As long as it has nothing to do with the Queen or Black Diamonds. We must keep this separate. I'm not nearly drunk enough to forget that."

"Deal. Shake on it." She offered her hand, and he

91

kissed it.

Her cell rang in the pocket of her jacket folded neatly over a chair. "Don't answer," he whispered as if someone might hear.

"Have to. I'm sure Todd wants to call the police by now." She walked to the chair and extracted the phone. "Hi, Uncle Sal. No, no, all is well. You don't have to come anywhere for me. Our debate lasted longer than I thought it would and got very heated. I'll be home shortly. Thanks for checking on me." She rolled her eyes at the last statement as she disconnected. "You'd think I'm his daughter, the one he wouldn't let date until she turned eighteen."

"At least your relatives are caring, not downright scary." Remy helped her into her jacket. She finger-combed her hair. No use trying to find those scattered clips and pins. "Will I pass inspection?"

Remy reluctantly gave her fully clothed body a once over, clearly wishing she wore less. "If they don't remember how you wore your hair tonight."

"Men rarely do."

"I guess we're ready to go. Your uncles have a deflating effect on me. Unless you want to stay the night."

"Want to and must not are two very different things. I have to work tomorrow. Remember, we're still at war."

"The truce didn't last nearly long enough."

She tried to make it up to him with a prolonged kiss that required a lipstick check and the command, "Down, Boy," to the action in his slacks.

The distance to Alleman wasn't far. Julia asked to be dropped by the white entrance pillars. "Less trouble for both of us."

He nodded. "Sorry it has to be this way."

"For now." She trudged up the drive toward the motorhome where Sal and Sam sat waiting in camp chairs, cold beers in hand, and Todd by their side. Their intern slept in the loft space over the cab so no sense in going to bed until the other men did. They'd put a bottle in his hand, too. Julia stayed far enough away to keep any of the men from smelling the whiskey on her breath.

"The guy didn't have the manners to walk you to the door?" Uncle Sammy took a suck on his beer. "You make any progress on the hotel?"

"I asked him to let me out at the entry. No progress on the hotel, but I did learn his immediate schedule to tear her down. Todd, tomorrow we activate the phone tree again and organize a protest for Friday, early."

"Couldn't we just message everyone? It would take a lot less time."

"Considering the average age of the members of both the Live Oak Preservation Society and the Historic District Committee, no. I doubt if they read their messages even if they have a smart phone."

"Oh, I didn't think of that." Todd studied his beer bottle with ashamed gray eyes.

"You're here to learn." Thinking of a hot bath, Julia turned toward the plantation home.

"But, when am I going to get my hands dirty, make some lime putty, and spread plaster?" His earnest eyes were on hers again.

"Learning how to fight for preservation is just as important as mixing plaster, Todd, but maybe next week sometime."

"Great! Oh, you look really nice with your hair down, Ms. Rossi."

Her uncles did the double take with their thick necks. "Thanks. All those pins were giving me a headache. I took them out."

At the moment, she really didn't care if Sal and Sammy believed her or not. A hot bath awaited, and tomorrow she went into battle again.

Chapter Twelve

Remy's phone rang far earlier than he'd planned to get up on Friday morning. The light slanted on his deck like a sundial reading seven or eight a.m. He planned to meet Stelly at the Queen around nine. Maybe the bush-hogger couldn't make it since that was his number showing on the phone.

"Hello?"

"Remy, we got us a situation here at the hotel. Old ladies everywhere chained to the oak trees. You want I should call the police or go back home and get some bolt cutters?"

"No, no. That's exactly what they want—to make a scene and get publicity. I'll be there in a half hour or less."

Dammit. He shoved himself into jeans and a T-shirt, put on boots, and did a quick brush of his teeth in case he ran into Julia close up. The hell with the shower and shave. Taking the stairs two at a time, he went to his truck and took a minute to find his bolt cutters in the storage shed just in case it came down to dragging senior citizens to squad cars. Not what he wanted. Maybe he could reason with them. Ha! The people of Chapelle went rabid over oak trees. The closer in age they grew to those trees, the worst they were.

Remy barreled to the Queen and braked into the turnoff to the hotel. The tractor, hooked to the parallel blades of the bush-hog, sat in the road with orange safety cones fore and aft while Stelly waved traffic around it. He gave Remy the nod. "Good to see you, boss. Look close. They almost blend with the trees."

Miss Maxie's red hair gave her away, though. She sat on the roots of one of the sentinel oaks at the entry, a cushion beneath her behind and a thermos of coffee by her side. The dark green sweater and matching afghan swathing her body against the early morning damp made her appear like a mossy growth on the wide trunk. A lightweight chain and padlock dangled where her waist might have been at one time. She unscrewed her thermos and poured a cup. "Would you care for some before I drink, Remy. Looks like you could use it."

"No, thanks. You go ahead. Won't be an hour before you need a bathroom break."

"Oh, we're all wearing our Depends this morning, even the youngsters, aren't we girls?" Echoes of *yes!* sounded all over the grove.

He turned to Miss Lolly attached to the other entrance tree. "You don't seem too comfortable there."

Miss Lolly glanced up from the large print library volume splayed on her lap and illuminated by a book light. A small cooler sat by her side amid the gnarled roots that greatly resembled her fingers. "A good book and a light snack is all I need, thank you."

"I'm telling you, we aren't going to harm the trees. They're an asset to the property." Remy spoke loud enough to be heard deep into the lot.

"We have to be sure," said Miss Lolly with her turkey neck jutted forward in defiance.

"All right, then." Remy returned to his truck and

took a retractable measuring tape from his glove compartment. The boles of the ancient oaks had swollen over the drive in the years since anyone used that path. He took a careful measure between the twisted roots of the two trees, then walked to the bush-hog and compared the widths.

"We have a couple of inches on both sides, Stelly. Can you do it without barking the trees or taking a limb off an old woman?"

Stelly rubbed his short, dark beard, took off his LSU cap, and put it on again as he considered. "Yep, but I'll have to back over the road and get it real centered before I move. You'll take care of traffic?"

"Sure." They laid out more safety cones in a bright orange lines. Several drivers waited unhappily on either side of the barriers as Stelly backed up, pulled front, backed up again as Remy waved the bush-hog closer and closer to the opposing ditch. He signaled to stop before the hog went over the edge. A pull forward and another back up to get everything straight. The tractor inched forward. The impatient sounded their horns.

A young man with a camera bobbing on his chest raced along the roadside. "Wait, wait! The *Chapelle Clarion* wants a picture of this." He clambered into the ditch and out the far side, scrambled past the oak roots, and positioned himself directly before the tractor but a few paces back to get it and the trees in the shot.

Remy hoped his groan couldn't be heard over the panting of the tractor. Stelly craned his head looking for directions. "Go ahead."

The tractor eased forward and cleared the trees with little space to spare. The driver started to turn into the brush, but the reporter ran to his side. "Just a sec. I want to get one from the rear that shows the protesters. Your name?"

"Jim Stelly of Stelly's Land Clearance Services. Make sure you get that right."

"Absolutely will, Mr. Stelly. Let me just ease around you."

With mud caked on his khakis from his foray into the ditch, the guy moved with the agility of a student who once ran track and field. Remy suspected that was exactly what he was, out for the summer, and picking up some cash from the notoriously tight local newspaper. Remy let him take the shot, then asked him to leave the posted property.

The cub reporter followed him around spouting, "Freedom of the Press!" as Remy picked up the cones and waved the accumulated traffic forward. For the first time in his life, he played the family card. "I'm Remington Broussard, yeah, one of *those* Broussards, and I want you off my land. We have work to do here, and I wouldn't want you to get hurt." He scraped his black scruff with his fingernails and tried to look as mean as Slick on his worst days.

"The men who run the Barn—and other things?" The allure of Freedom of the Press dimmed in the boy's eyes.

"Yep." Remy took out his measuring tape and slapped it into his palm a few times as if it were a sap about to be used on the kid's face.

"I think I have enough, thanks. I can call for interviews later." The reporter hightailed it back to subcompact car he'd parked at the old fruit stand. Miss Lolly and Miss Maxie made "call me" signs with their arthritic fingers as he fled.

Shaking his head, Remy walked to the tractor. "Go as wide as you can around the live oaks. The brush isn't heavy there with all the shade and fallen oak leaves killing the growth. Whatever you do, don't get near any of the women."

Then, he heard her, Julia's voice calling, "Put on your safety glasses, ladies," but couldn't see her. Putting on the sunglasses in his pocket, he followed in the wake of the bush-hog as it mowed its first path, chewing up the brambles and snapping off the small prolific chicken trees that took over vacant land. Narrow paths that could have been made by wild game but weren't shot off on either side, each one pushed through to a live oak that harbored a chained lady like some kind of weird fairy tale. He suspected his grandmother might be among them, but not Julia who stood by the old kitchen door with cases of bottled water, a pile of safety glasses, a large cooler, and a first aid kit. He approached her as the tractor swung out to make its first circle around the building.

"You haul all that stuff in here by yourself?"

"No. Todd and my uncles helped. Our company donated the safety glasses. We use them a lot. Subway gave us sandwiches and several of the convenience stores offered a case of water. We even have cookies from Pommier's. The town supports our cause."

"The Broussards don't."

"That can't be helped. Here, put on a pair of safety glasses. Those shades aren't enough protection if you're going to follow the tractor around."

"Hadn't planned on it until I saw this mess. Now, I'll have to stay on-site." Remy leaned back against the barred door to the kitchen and folded his arms. He didn't accept the safety glasses Julia held out.

"As you should. You're very grumpy this morning. I'll bet you didn't stop for breakfast. Here, have some water. Want a sandwich?"

"I want coffee." But he accepted the water, cracked it open, and took a deep swallow.

"Maybe Miss Maxie would share hers."

"Stupidly, I already turned that down." His eyes followed the bush-hog going round and round, not penetrating the sanctity of the live oaks, most of which had limbs hanging too low to accommodate the machinery anyhow. "You made me threaten a reporter who couldn't be more than eighteen."

"Oh, good, the *Clarion* sent someone out. Eat something. You sound absolutely petulant." Julia opened the cooler and selected a turkey and veggie on whole wheat as if concerned for his cholesterol.

Not about to turn down another good offer, he unwrapped the sandwich and chewed thoughtfully. "Besides me and Stelly, you are the only one who knew when the bush-hogging was scheduled. Can I expect more interference when we put in the culverts on Monday?"

"Maybe. It depends on whether or not you'd consider meeting with Jonathan Hartz about selling the property to him at a profit."

Those blue eyes he'd found so attractive the last time he'd caught her trespassing glittered like the shards of broken glass lying in the weeds. They went soft and dark when she came. Frenemies.

"I don't want to sell my land. I intend to build Black Diamonds here."

"Your choice, then."

"Julia, you've run big projects before. Culverts have to go in whether we tear the Queen down or not, just like the bush-hogging needs to be done. Be reasonable."

She wasn't listening. Those blue eyes had a smile in them now as the undergrowth fell to reveal the old carriage drive as it parted to make a circle around the hotel. Broken oyster shells flew into the air every time Stelly crossed a patch of the path. The oak tree warriors closest to the drive settled their safety glasses more firmly on their noses.

"Tell me you won't destroy the carriageway when you bring in the bulldozers to level the land. We'll find some old garden paths too, that should be preserved in their original spots."

"I guess I could work them into my plans. I want pathways, oaks, and shade. Easier to work with what's here than do it all new."

She took that as a concession and gave him a rewarding smile. "Now you're thinking like a preservationist." Julia picked up a case of water bottles. He admired her muscle. No asking for help. She started off along the areas his man had already cleared.

"I have to keep my women hydrated. It's already getting hot."

He admired her hips in the snug jeans and her confident stride. "You want to come over tonight and have another discussion?" he called.

"No good reason to since you won't meet with Hartz," she shouted over her shoulder.

"You don't need one. Any time you want."

"I'll keep that in mind." Julia bent to slip under the canopy of an oak and deliver water, a modern Molly

Pitcher fighting for her cause. If only they could be on the same side.

Chapter Thirteen

Julia didn't darken his black door all weekend. Remy took solace at Broussard's Barn, the one place in the parish where no one would hassle him about the demise of the Queen. The *Clarion* made the most of the oak tree protest with full color pictures on the front page. The kid got a photo credit and a by-line for his interviews with Miss Lolly and Miss Maxie, who vowed to keep such a close eye on the project not one leaf would be bruised in its execution. Julia stayed in the background, not commenting, letting the society have all the credit. No matter that once the bush hogging was done, they'd all gone home one by one, unlocked by a master key she'd kept in her bra as if he might try to seize it from her.

Remy danced with women he didn't care about, had a few drinks, and if he didn't cry in his beer, he did brood over it. Old Broussard summoned him to the front and asked how the project was going. "Culverts go in Monday," he said, telling the truth, but not telling it all.

"*Bon*," the old man replied and sent him back to his table where a free drink he hadn't ordered appeared within minutes. Definitely time to go home after that.

Bright and early on Monday, he had a good breakfast and lots of coffee before donning his hardhat and heading for the Queen. His contractor was there with a flatbed loaded with concrete culverts, backhoes to ream out the clogged ditches, and a small crane to lift out the crumbling pipe under the drive and insert the new ones. The police he'd requested to handle traffic during the process stood by their squad car awaiting his arrival—as were the protestors who lined the road for a quarter of a mile, staying on the public access strip between the ditch and the roadway, careful not to step over the white line and get in the way of the cars or equipment. Each one held a placard reading, "God save the Queen" with a little crown over the Q remarkably like the one on Julia's truck. Now, she'd brought God into the fight.

Not just eccentric women this time either. Some had dragged their retired husbands into the fray. Waving their signs, Patty and Pammy stood side-by-side overdressed in lime green and orange pantsuits. Julia's reedy intern had locked arms with two very elderly men who were telling the cub reporter they'd stayed a short time at the Queen before shipping out for WWII. "The food was hot and good, and the sheets clean even if she wasn't in her prime," one said very loudly, probably hard of hearing. Todd winced at the volume, but continued to hold the ancient veterans upright.

Remy didn't see Julia. However, Jane Tauzin was there with a bullhorn rallying the troops. "Stand firm. Don't break the line."

He approached the officers. "What can we do about this?"

Officer Chauvin shrugged. "Not much. Miz Tauzin has a permit to demonstrate. The protesters ain't in the street or on private property so we can't remove them with or without force."

"No force!"

Officer Ancona raised his eyes skyward. "Maybe it will rain, but not a cloud in sight. God does seem to be on their side today. To think I left New Orleans for days like this!"

The Regal Restorations truck drove up and squeezed into a spot on the other side of the road. Julia got down and sauntered across to Jane. "Sorry I ran late. I've been on the phone with Jonathan Hartz."

"Is he coming?" Jane asked with unbounded enthusiasm.

"No, he and Celine are in Seattle for a few days, but we couldn't wait for them. Nice job getting everyone here and into place."

"Oh, one of the churches loaned us a bus. Really convenient. We parked on the Ste. Jeanne d'Arc lot as a central meeting place, and the Baptists delivered us here. They're standing by for pickup." Jane raised the bullhorn to her lips. "Julia is here!" A hoorah went up from the protesters.

Enough was enough. Remy left the company of the police and the cultch of workmen waiting to get started. He approached Julia and Jane. "Yes, nicely done and remarkably fast."

"Thank you," both women said simultaneously.

"You know this culvert work has to be done, Julia, whether we tear the building down or renovate it. Why don't you let it happen?"

"Maybe we will once we get the historic designation."

"It won't come through before my demolition permit. That is already in the works."

Julia and Jane exchanged glances as if mindreading. Their synchronization gave Remy a slight chill. "What?" he asked.

"Would you hold off on demolition until we can arrange a meeting with Jonathan Hartz? You need to hear what he has to say, but he won't be back in town until next week. I can't speak for him," Julia said.

Remy took a deep breath. "I could wait a week, but only if you stop blocking my culverts." He heard a click-whirr. The Jimmy Olsen of Chapelle was back taking pictures and gathering news. Jeez, the kid had freckles and red hair exactly like the original. Remy pointed a finger at him. "Leave."

"I'm not on your property. That starts on the other side of the ditch." The reporter literally walked the white line edging the road and made for the two veterans who let go of Todd and straightened their VFW caps. They gave the boy their best denture smiles and a smart salute before grabbing Todd's elbows in case they lost balance and pitched into the coulee. An interview ensued. Remy could hear their shouted answers where he stood, though he wasn't sure what their battle stories had to do with a few days stay at the Queen umpteen years ago.

"That sounds like a deal to me." Jane put the bullhorn to her mouth. "Mr. Broussard has agreed to delay demolition for a week. We will be back if no compromise can be reached. Hang onto your signs in case we need them again. The bus will be here in fifteen minutes. Thank you so much for coming." She pumped her fist into the air, and cheers rose loud enough to stir to leaves of the oaks.

Julia reached for Remy's arm. "I appreciate the

concession." Her blue eyes shone with warmth, maybe even heat, and stared directly into his. Her voice lowered to seductive. "I'm going to teach Todd to make lime putty and turn it into plaster early Monday morning, say around eight. Want to come and watch?"

"Sure sounds hot to me."

"It will be. Wear old clothes you don't mind getting dirty."

"Dirty. You got it."

Jane intruded. "If you two are done having a stare-down with heavy sexual overtones, we should herd everyone over to the fruit stand for pickup and get out of the way of the construction workers. How about asking the cops to stop traffic so we can cross the road safely, Jules?"

"Will do." Julia turned to leave.

Remy stopped her with a light touch. "See you Monday—if not sooner."

"Not sooner."

Looked like he had a long and frustrating weekend ahead.

****

Once the volunteers were loaded on the bus and headed home, Julia retired to Jane's cozy office in her renovated Cajun cottage. An abundance of family pictures and thriving houseplants bedecked the spots not covered by the stacks of Jane's projects. Jane cleared a chair of papers topped by a child-sized baseball mitt left behind by a son and beckoned Julia to sit.

"That went well. No violence, and we've set Remy up to meet with Hartz. But we have to push for the historic designation, especially since he spilled that he's applied for his demolition permit. Funny how he let you know when he was going to bush-hog and put in those culverts." Jane leaned back in her office chair and regarded Julia very seriously.

"Those things came up in conversation when we were trying to change each other's minds. I think he'd come around to our way of thinking if he didn't have a commitment to his family to build the condos. They're backing him." Julia kept her eyes on her short, clean nails. Jane's green Mother Nature gaze could be very perceptive.

"Ordinarily, you don't want to mess with the Broussards," Jane agreed.

"Remy said there could be trouble. Are you afraid? I didn't mean to drag you or your family into danger."

Jane shook her brown bob. "Heck, I jumped in with both feet, but I'm not worried. My husband used to run with Slick Broussard, and his mother and sister once worked out at the Barn. They're still on friendly terms. I know Merlin put the word out to let his wife do her thing. She wins some, loses some, he says. He was one of my hopeless causes, so he ought to know. A lot of people are still scared of him, which I guess helps in this case." Jane picked up one of her photos of herself and Merlin surrounded by apple blossoms and gazing into each other's eyes. With a dreamy look, she said, "I mean does he look like a dangerous man? We danced to *Apple Blossom Time* at our wedding."

"Hell, yes, he looks dangerous. I'm glad he's on our side. Maybe having an in with the Broussards will help too."

"Well, I think Remy is leaking information about his plans because he wants to score with you."

Glad her olive complexion didn't give too much away though she felt the heat rise in her cheeks, Julia said, "I doubt that." Because he'd already scored.

"His attraction could be useful, not that I'd want you to prostitute yourself for the Queen."

"Maybe his heart isn't truly in those condos."

"Ha! I've never seen a man more into his own project than Remy. He might think the sexual attraction could work both ways and convince you to cease and desist."

"No, we agreed…" Time to change the subject. "I didn't get a chance to tell you that Celine prodded Jon to make some calls to expedite our historic designation. He hates bludgeoning people with his wealth, but it does help move things along, especially with politicians. The Office of Cultural Development has all the information Todd and I put together. We could get the Queen added to the survey of Louisiana Historic Standing Structures any time now. I only hope we can delay the demolition long enough."

"We'll file an appeal against it as soon as we get on that list. You keep working on Remy."

And that would be a pleasure for Jules.

Chapter Fourteen

Marv put out a nice breakfast of egg and sausage casserole for his workers at seven and left some of the fruit and extra homemade biscuits on the kitchen table for their breaks along with an urn of coffee. Julia would give the man a marvelous host award. She needed to work off his meals. Directly after eating, she set Todd to sifting sand for the finish coat, tedious work, but that's why God made apprentices. The finish coat wouldn't require much, but she wanted to attain a perfectly smooth surface.

Remy arrived promptly at eight wearing old jeans, thin in some interesting places, a long-sleeved red tee, dismally faded, and work boots. He grinned at Julia's clothing and committed his first faux pas of the day. "You look adorable in that getup."

She regarded her coveralls, the long-sleeved jersey with the royal blue Regal Restorations logo on the front, and tipped back a cap roomy enough to stuff her hair beneath—all of the apparel spotlessly white for the moment. "If I wanted to look adorable, I'd be wearing pink polka dots. This is professional attire for a plasterer. Here's the rest of yours." Julia handed over a cap, safety glasses, and a pair of rubber gloves.

"Am I going to be washing dishes?" Remy quipped.

Todd by the sand pile sucked in his breath at the

irreverence. Knowing how irked she'd be at not being taken seriously, her uncles merely stood around amused, and waited.

"No, we don't want the lime to burn your soft, pretty hands. There's a bowl of vinegar water over there if any gets on your skin. Wash it off immediately. We wouldn't want to mar that handsome face of yours."

The uncles guffawed. Remy put on the gloves.

"Okay, Todd, that's enough sand. Let's make the lime putty." She handed Remy and her intern five-gallon buckets. "Fill them two-thirds with water." They took turns at the hose.

"Carefully open the bag of lime. Don't breathe it in. This is hydraulic type S lime. Don't use anything else. Pour it slowly into the water. Never pour water into the lime."

The sack weighed fifty pounds. Todd struggled to hike it up. Remy took it from him and split the sack between the buckets. Julia admired his muscles like a schoolgirl with a crush on a lifeguard, but she didn't let it show on her face. This was serious business, and Remy needed to learn that.

"Good. Todd, why don't you use the drill with the paint mixing attachment? Remy gets the hand whisk." He gritted his teeth at being given the harder task, but he complied. "Scrape the sides fairly often. Add a little more water if you need it to blend all the lime. You must make a smooth, thick paste."

"What do you think, Ms. Rossi?" Todd turned off his mixer to let her examine his job.

"Nice work. Let Mr. Broussard use the electric mixer now. He isn't nearly done." Maybe she enjoyed this a little too much, payback for his long-ago remark about being putty in her hands. Now, he was totally at her command. "All right. We add a little water on top and seal it up."

"Are we going to use it to make the plaster?' Todd asked, all eagerness.

"No, lime putty is better if it ages a while like wine or cheese. We'll use some we have on hand. Meantime, soak the tools in some water, and we'll take time for coffee. Oh, Remy, I'd remove those gloves the way a doctor would, turning them inside out in case they have any lime on them, and wash your lovely face too. See you in the kitchen." Julia walked away while her smirking uncles stowed the newly made putty.

She had coffee in hand and a bite of a biscuit slathered with butter and blackberry jam in her mouth when Remy stomped into the kitchen and poured himself a cup. "Putty making wasn't that hard," he claimed.

"No, it isn't, but it has to be done safely and right like all good jobs. Want to try your hand at plastering next?"

He recognized a challenge when he heard one. "I'm ready whenever you are."

"Great!" She gave him her perkiest smile. "Todd, have a cup of coffee and something to eat."

"Just water and fruit for me. I like to stay hydrated and full of fiber—kind of like plaster." The intern laughed at his own joke. Julia gave him an appreciative smile, ignoring her uncles who rolled their eyes behind the kid's back. Remy shook his head slightly as if to say, "Young and trying too hard," but at least Todd showed enthusiasm.

"If we're all finished, let's make that plaster."

"Boo-rah," Todd shouted, lofting a melon slice into the air. Since no Marine Corps service showed up in his resume, Julia was fairly certainly he played video war games.

Back at work, she asked the men to put on their gloves and glasses again and lay out a ring of aged lime putty. They added gauging plaster in the center, a bit of very fine sand, and a small amount of water. Julia handed Remy and Todd hoes to blend the mixture. When satisfied, she picked up a steel trowel, scooped a bit of their plaster onto it, and turned the trowel sideways.

"Good job. You want it smooth, not too heavy, but it should cling to the trowel and not fall off."

Todd raised a hand as if he were still in the classroom. "Did we forget to add fiber?"

"Not needed in the finish coat. I wish we could have convinced Mr. Getty to use a float finish when we mix in a lot of sand and then rake it with a broom to make swirls, but he wants to paper over our beautiful walls now that they are fully restored." Julia sighed at an opportunity lost. "Apprentices, go dampen the parlor walls. We'll be along with the plaster shortly."

Todd grabbed a brush and trotted off obediently. Remy glanced at the smiling uncles. "Bossy, isn't she?'

"Nope, she *is* the boss," Uncle Sal told him with glee. "Better get hopping."

Remy didn't hop, but he picked up a brush and caught up with Todd. Once they'd prepared the surface, Julia literally rolled up her sleeves in the stuffy room and showed both how to apply the plaster starting at the bottom and working their way up. She loaded her hawk and wielded her steel trowel across the surface like a lethal weapon. When she got to the point where the twelve-foot walls went beyond her reach, she climbed a ladder with no hesitation and worked up to the cornices. "We'll need scaffolding for the ceiling."

Sal and Sammy followed behind, working a two-man float to remove any bumps or other regularities in the plaster when they weren't working on their own wall. For Remy, a lunch break—late because they wanted to finish the parlor before eating—came as a welcome relief. "Hard on the back," he said.

"Maybe you should stretch first or try some yoga like me," Todd advised.

"Next time," Remy said, obviously not meaning a word of it.

The uncles snorted. Both were as sturdy as live oak trunks.

Julia examined their work. "Too thick, Remy. Yours isn't quite as bad, Todd. We'll do over after lunch." The uncles scraped away both of their hard work.

"I have to leave after we eat," Remy replied, but first he got to enjoy the spread in the kitchen after they washed at the sink.

Marv had driven to the Whole Foods in Lafayette to bring back artisanal breads and exotic mustards made by secluded monks, though the cold cuts—ham, and Cajun-spiced chicken, plus three types of cheese, Swiss, cheddar, and muenster—were easily recognizable. A plate filled with pickles—dill, bread-and-butter, sweet, and French cornichons in addition to olives, ripe, green, large, small, and some stuffed with almonds—impressed even Remy. Sam and Sal slapped their sandwiches together without comment, but Julia graciously complimented the hovering Marv. "No one has ever treated us better."

Their host beamed. "I had no time to bake, but I did pick up a lovely rum cake at Poupart's on my way back."

"You are too good to us," Julia assured him.

"Oh, I forgot the sun tea. It's still out on the porch." Marv hurried outside.

"That guy is okay for a…" Sammy started to say.

"A gay American citizen who should have the right to marry?" Todd surprised them all by speaking up as he made a sandwich with three slices of cheese and a daub of mustard.

"Yeah, exactly the way I wanted to put that." Sammy loaded his bread with meat of both kinds and lots and lots of cheese.

"He's a good man. We're old friends. It's always a pleasure to be in his company," Remy commented as he built his sandwich and added a handful of olives and pickles on the side.

Uncle Sal raised a russet eyebrow. "So, we don't have to worry about Jules being alone in your company?"

"Marv was my art teacher, period. I think Julia can handle herself in anyone's company."

"Thank you for that. Neither of you have any business in my business whether Remy is gay or not." Julia cut her modest lunch decisively in half.

Marv returned with the large jar of sun tea afloat with lemon slices and mint leaves and set it on the counter. "Oh, Remy isn't gay. I'd keep an eye on him if Julia were my niece. He can be very *canaille*."

"I'm not tricky!"

115

Marv went on as if he hadn't heard the denial. "Tea, anyone? It's very refreshing. Help yourself to a glass and ice from the fridge." They did. No beer on the menu during work hours and not much talk once every one settled into eating, and then finished it off with big chunks of rum cake, except for Julia's smaller piece.

Remy arose. "Thanks for the lunch, Marv. Great as usual." He leaned over Julia's shoulder, lightly brushing by her cheek. "You'll be exhausted by tonight working in this warm weather. Want to come over and relax? I'll throw a couple of steaks on the grill."

"*Canaille*," murmured Marv.

Uncle Sammy stepped right in. "That sounds great. Can we bring anything? Marv, you coming, too?"

"I'd love that. I haven't really seen Remy's new place except from the backyard."

Julia turned and gazed up at Remy's flummoxed face. He'd had a hard day too. That made her smile. "What time should we be there?"

"Seven is good. I have wine. Bring beer if you want. I need to get going. Seems I'll need a few more steaks."

Todd waved a hand. "Fish for me."

"Sure, fish for you. Anyone else want fish?"

The rest shook their heads. Good-natured laughter followed him out of the room.

Chapter Fifteen

Remy fumed all the way to Duane's Specialty Meats. One thing he could say about Cajuns, they'd still patronize a butcher shop with custom cuts rather than running to the nearest chain store. A massive smoker puffed behind the freestanding building cooking the next batch of brisket and ribs. Duane himself in his stained apron came from out back when Remy's entrance rang the bell over the door. He leaned his fleshy arms on top of the refrigerator case displaying loops of boudin sausage, thick-cut pork chops, and generous rib-eyes rubbed with Duane's special seasoning. Judging from his flushed jowls, sweating forehead, and odor of charred hickory, he'd come from stoking the smoker. "What can I get you, Remy?"

"Five of those rib-eyes." He let his eyes rove around the shop while Duane packaged the meat in old-fashioned butcher paper. Loaves of LeJuene's brick oven, chewy French bread sat sleeved in white wrappers twisted at the ends by the register. He added two to his order. "Give me an order of *gratons* too."

Duane shoved a scoop into a bin of greasy cracklings, bagged, and sealed them. "That it?" At Remy's nod, he totaled the bill, ran the debit card, and shoved the purchases into a large plastic bag.

"You forgot to add in the *gratons*."

"A little *lagniappe* for you. Thanks for your

business."

Often, it paid to shop local. Next stop, the market run by a Vietnamese couple whose family owned a boat. The catch at Nguyen Fresh Fish was better than any place in town, but you had to take whatever the Gulf provided recently. Really, he was going out of his way for Todd. Small, persuasive Mrs. Nguyen tried to convince him to buy a whole fish because the bones made it tastier, but he took a couple of pounds of seasoned, boiled shrimp and two redfish fillets instead. Wouldn't want Todd to choke on any bones—or would he?

The guy clearly adored Julia, following her every order like an orphan afraid to be put out on the street. The intern had garnered many more encouraging words on his novice plastering than Remy, even if she had to go over some spots again. Todd wouldn't know what to do with a strong, vibrant woman like Jules if she offered herself to him. The thought that he might be jealous crossed Remy's mind. Ridiculous!

He went to a small grocery next—not that Chapelle had any big ones—and dumped bags of salad, bell peppers, and red onions into his cart. Throw in some olives, toss with a light bottled dressing, and he'd have what passed for a vegetable dish. He guessed he could grill some thin asparagus spears coated in olive oil and garlic salt too. Enough! Done. What he'd envisioned as an intimate evening with Julia had turned into a cookout for five men and one woman.

With everything but the *gratons* and bread stowed in his refrigerator, Remy showered, and put on pressed khakis and a short-sleeved cotton shirt in a deep green that flattered his dark coloring. He'd pre-heated the gas grill on his deck and set out the cracklings in a basket and the shrimp in a bowl of crushed ice covered by napkins to keep off the flies just before his guests arrived. The uncles shamelessly showed off hairy legs and toes in baggy shorts and heavy sandals topped by company tees. Marv and Todd came attired much like Remy right down to the deck shoes. And Julia—short shorts over tanned and toned legs, a tucked-in tee, wedge sandals on her feet and her red-highlighted hair piled carelessly on top of her head in a way that made Remy want to take it down. Let the party begin!

The uncles sank their beers into the ice chest before cracking open a couple. Julia, Todd, and Marv accepted the red wine sitting on the small table where Marv had placed his offering of the leftover rum cake and dark chocolate brownies he claimed paired well with the Cabernet. Everyone unfolded a chair and made themselves at home, crunching on cracklings and peeling cold shrimp to be dipped in cocktail sauce with an extra dash of hot sauce. Only Todd hung back, avoiding both.

Sammy placed a crackling in Todd's palm. "Go on, they taste like bacon."

"Yes, bacon. I really don't eat…"

"Try it!"

Julia took the offensive crackling and pressed it to her intern's lips. "Just chew and swallow. You'll like it." Of course, he obeyed, and chased the *graton* down with wine. Then, she showed him how to rip the head off a shrimp and peel its tail. All the while, Remy toiled at the grill, not rushing the steaks but getting hotter and hotter himself. The grill cages with the asparagus and Todd's fish mixed with onions and bell pepper, seasoned with Cajun spice, sat to one side waiting their turn. That guy was so much extra trouble.

Todd didn't spit out the crackling, but didn't take another. He complimented the shrimp. "We don't get seafood like this in Chicago."

"That where you from? I studied architecture up there. Hey, how about peeling a shrimp for the chef, Jules." She did him that service, and Remy made sure his lips touched her fingertips. Neither uncle noticed, though maybe Todd did. Just staking his claim.

"Really, I grew up in Oak Park, a great place to learn reverence for preservation with Frank Lloyd Wright once living there." Julia fed the kid another shrimp as if he were her trained seal being rewarded for doing a trick.

"Believe me, I appreciate his work, but times move on. Say, why don't you go inside and take a closer look at my Black Diamonds plans. Explore the house if you want. It's my design. Oh, and bring the salad from the fridge on the second floor when you return. Marv, how about putting the garlic bread in the oven and watching it for me." Both men left the scene to do as suggested.

Sammy stretched out his thick, muscular legs. "This is the life. A house on the water, no noise, no traffic fumes." He popped another *graton* into his mouth.

Remy flipped the steaks and did some probing. "Where do you live when you aren't on a job site?"

"Same place the Rossi family has always lived since they got off the boat from Sicily. We have our own block in the French Quarter, used to call that whole section Little Palermo with so many Italians there. People don't know New Orleans is the most

Italian city in the U.S., or once was."

Sal chipped into the conversation. "Yeah, we come from a long line of masons, bricklayers, and plasterers. Our people built a lot of those fancy tombs in the cemeteries. Works of art, they are." He polished off the last of the shrimp.

"The Quarter has all kinds of rules now. You can't do this, you can't do that when it comes to rehabbing, so our places still look like the originals spiffed up a little, but modern on the inside thanks to Regal Restorations taking off big time."

"Do you have a place there, Jules?" He went to the New Orleans area fairly often.

"An apartment a little farther away from the old neighborhood. I rent out the ground floor for income. NOLA isn't a cheap place to live unless you inherit the property. I renovated the place myself."

"I'd like to see it."

"One day when all the controversy is over."

Once he won and tore down the Queen would that offer still stand? Remy put the fish and vegetable baskets on the grill, piled the steaks oozing red juices on a platter. Todd trotted out the door bearing the salad and set it down on the picnic table. "Cool house, Mr. Broussard." He glanced at Julia. "But you know there is only one Bayou Queen." She'd indoctrinated him well.

Marv arrived with the garlic bread perfectly browned and artfully arranged in a basket. Remy turned the fish and vegetables, almost done. "Bring your drinks, move over to the table, and snag a steak on the way. Todd, your special order will be ready in a minute."

"Sorry to put you to extra trouble, Mr. Broussard. I

try to watch my cholesterol."

Right, that skinny reed of a guy needed to watch his cholesterol. Evidently, Sal felt the same. "Hard work and good Italian cooking will keep your arteries clean. A nice thick steak every once in a while don't hurt." He speared the largest of the rib-eyes and brought his dish to the table. Julia chose the smallest and did the same. Sam followed. They loaded up on salad and bread.

Remy plated the redfish and delivered it to Todd before taking the last steak and doling out the asparagus with a pair of tongs. He sat determined to see what else he could learn since he'd be denied Julia's company later. "So, how is work on Alleman going? When do you think you'll be done with the project?'

"Oh, we have couple more rooms to do on the ground floor, then the plaster will need two or three weeks to cure. We'll fill in the cracks on the second floor, go back to NOLA and wait. Jules will want to return to supervise the paperhangers and painters. After that, we'll be done. Goodbye, Chapelle." Sal attacked his steak with gusto and a sharp, serrated knife.

"You'll be gone in week or so."

Julia appeared to read his mind. "Whether I'm here or not, you promised to meet with Jonathan Hartz."

"It's already set up. His personal assistant got in touch with me, and we're on for a meeting at Pecan Grove in a few days. I swear I'll listen to what he has to say." And reject the offer, not only because Black Diamonds was his dream, but because the Broussards would accept nothing less. Still, he didn't want to begin the demolition until Julia left the area. He already felt like a parent putting down a favorite pet grown too old to live.

When everyone was full as tick on the ear of a Catahoula hound, they stretched out to watch the sun set over the bayou and the silhouette of the Queen. Marv insisted on cleaning up and putting the meager leftovers away. The rest polished off the last of the wine and beer.

"Great feed, Remy," Sammy acknowledged.

"Yes, you are a man of many talents," Julia agreed.

"Not so much. Mostly I grill for company."

"Now you wouldn't think it, but Julia is a great cook. Learned at her Sicilian grandmother's knee since her mother is Irish blood," Sal boasted about his niece.

Todd fingered a soul patch so light as to be unnoticeable in the dent of his chin. "The Rossi clan is Sicilian?"

"You bet, from way back," Sammy said.

"Are you connected?" Todd swallowed hard without taking a sip.

"Connected to what?"

"You know, the Brotherhood, the Mob, the Mafia. I heard they used to be pretty strong in New Orleans." Todd's light eyes widened. Obviously, he's seen all the Godfather movies.

"Everyone in Little Palermo is connected in some way or other," Sammy said, punctuating that statement with a belly laugh. "Better watch out for us, Remy."

"I'm connected to the Broussards," he answered, for better or worse. He thought he'd spied Slick's dark SUV next door at NuNu's trailer, but a lot of those vehicles looked the same.

"I don't think they bat in the same league, son," Sal replied.

"Cut it out! You're scaring Todd. We have a full day of work tomorrow and need to get rest. I'm calling this very nice evening to an end. Thanks for having us, Remy. If you open the gate, we'll find our way out." Julia made shooing motions at the men in her life and got them moving through the office and out the front door.

Remy followed, pushing the button to open the gate along the way. His eyes tracked Julia's truck, his mind regretting what might have been. He heard feet hit the ground as someone jumped his pole fence. Slick materialized out of the dusk dressed all in black like the thickening night. "You fraternizing with the enemy again, Remy? NuNu gave me a call about your party. You didn't invite him."

"Just trying to bring the Rossis around to our way of thinking," he lied. "They plan to finish the plaster work and return to New Orleans until it cures within a week or so. Only Julia will be back to see to the final details. Once she's gone, some of the pressure will be off tearing down the Queen since she's the motivating force. We can wait until then."

"Yeah, well, the old man ain't happy. He saw in the paper you cut a deal to meet with Hartz to get your culverts finished. You caved to a bunch of old ladies tied to trees."

"I won't be tempted by whatever Hartz has to offer."

"Better not be."

Remy groped for some protection no matter how imaginary. "The Rossi family might be connected to the mob."

"The mob won't be your problem if Black

Diamonds doesn't get built. Get moving!"

"As soon as my demolition permit comes through."

"That's what your *nonc* wants to hear. Have a nice evening." Like a Cajun ninja, Slick disappeared into the night and thudded to earth on the other side of the fence.

A nice evening was what he'd had until Slick showed up. Now, it promised a lack of sleep and maybe a few bad dreams about what happened to people who crossed the Broussards—or the Mafia.

Chapter Sixteen

One thing Remy could move on, and not Julia, was a new dock for the Queen, or rather *his* property. The rotted boards and pilings need to be pulled out and replaced by stout new timber. He put the demolition crew he had waiting in the wings on that. The new culverts supported the pile driver and other heavy equipment as the machinery carefully skirted the oaks and rounded the Queen to begin pounding away along the bayou. Remy envisioned his well-heeled condo dwellers fishing off the pier or tying up their boats after a recreational cruise down the bayou.

Unfortunately, the reverberations shook the earth for miles and called attention to the project. They came, the oak tree ladies and the preservationists, and left once they were sure the destruction of the hotel wasn't the reason for the noise and not a leaf had been lost. The thumping brought Julia racing from Alleman in her plastering gear. She clamped her hands over her ears. "How long is this going to continue? You'll open the cracks we just sealed at the plantation."

"Regardless of the fate of the hotel, a new dock is needed. As soon as it gets done, how about cruising up the river with me from my place? We can have a moonlight picnic here—just the two of us this time. Will you still be around this weekend?"

"I think so. Okay, fine."

"Saturday, my place around seven."

After Julia went back to her job, he re-assigned some of the crew lounging around on the piles of timber and waiting for the pile driver to finish. "I want you to go up to the second floor and clean the ballroom of debris."

"Why, boss, if you are just going to tear the place down?"

He started to say none of your business, but thought better of it. "I want to see if any of the parquet is worth salvaging."

They accepted the task with minimal grumbling. It did make sense to take any profit out of the old wreck that he could. Remy's mind moved on to thoughts of Saturday and Julia, a woman unafraid of ghosts. The thud of the pile driver matched the beat of his heart. If only he could convince her of the merit of his plans and make her part of them.

****

Julia arrived precisely on time dressed as she had for the barbecue except for the more practical sneakers. When on a job, she didn't drag a lot of wardrobe with her, and on this visit to the Queen, had no brambles to fight. They had been shorn to the ground. She supposed they'd picnic on the new dock and not enter the premises unless she could persuade Remy take her inside after they ate. She'd put that on her agenda. He simply had to fall in love with the place, and their conflict would be resolved. Then, they could move on to their strong mutual attraction.

Her date wasted no time on chitchat or trying to persuade her into ditching the picnic and spending the time instead in his bed under the zebra skin, though she thought she'd seen that invitation in his dark eyes. Instead, he led her directly through the office to the dock where the speedboat, as sleek and black as his tower, waited stripped of the tarp that had covered it the night of the barbecue. He'd named her the *Cormorant* after the black seabirds that knifed through the water to spear fish with their serrated beaks.

Remy helped her aboard the already stocked vessel. Julia noted the necks of two bottles of white wine poking from the picnic basket and a couple of padded mats rolled tight under a seat. They pulled slowly out into the current, passing his shiftless neighbor who wore a wife beater and sat in a plastic chair leaned against the backside of the sagging trailer. The guy saluted them with the Bic lighter he'd just applied to his cigarette.

Remy didn't drive directly to the Queen's new dock. It wasn't that far, and he seemed determined to give her a thrill ride first and get her adrenaline pumping. Once out into the deepest part of the bayou, Remy opened the engine and sped, bow-up under all of Chapelle's bridges until turning the *Cormorant* back toward their destination. People dining at On the Riverside stared at the performance and little boys ran alongside the bank in excitement until easily outdistanced. The wind loosened the clips holding the hair off Julia's neck. She surrendered to the breeze and removed them, letting them plink into the bottom of the boat. Remy smiled his approval.

He slowed as they approached the new dock smelling of the fresh timbers and tied up the boat. Remy jumped off first and helped her ashore, then went back to retrieve the basket and the mats, which turned out to be sleeping bags he unrolled with a flourish.

"I guess I could have asked Todd to lend me his yoga mat, but these will be more comfortable. I ordered the food from the Riverside. It will be good, but not dainty." He followed that statement with a white smile and a glint in his eyes, maybe reflected off the water, maybe not.

"I'm not a dainty kind of girl. Like my uncles, I work hard. Bring on the eats." She sat cross-legged on one of the bags while Remy unpacked the feast: cold fried chicken, individual containers of potato salad and slaw, the famous white bread pudding for dessert. He uncorked the wine and poured it into glasses rather than paper cups even though they'd be eating with their fingers and plastic utensils.

Remy let her have her choice of the double-breaded chicken pieces while he talked about the new dock. "All cypress so it won't rot. We don't have the guardrails up yet. I wouldn't want any of the occupants of the condos tottering off the edge. I plan on a few built-in benches too and some other nice embellishments, maybe decorative caps for the tops of the piles and of course, a gate from the water in case anyone wants to visit by boat. It will be a gathering place to watch the sunset."

Julia sipped her wine and left greasy marks on the glass from the chicken. "It's in the same place as the original steamboat landing. Imagine how many hundreds of people must have used it to stay at the Bayou Queen." She wiped her prints from the glass with a napkin, but sucked her fingers clean one by one. Though they'd fed well, Remy watched her with hunger.

"More will enjoy this dock in the future. We'll have a pool and a clubhouse for celebrations."

For the moment, Julia declined to argue with him. They spooned up the bread pudding so sweet it made the fragrant Riesling seem sour as the sun began to set. Remy didn't immediately turn on the two battery-operated lanterns he'd brought along. He repacked the basket sitting between them, all but the wine, and returned it to the Cormorant. After he came back, Remy moved his sleeping bag next to hers and put an arm around her waist.

"This is a wonderful spot and will be great again in a new way. Stop trying to prevent progress, Jules."

She didn't shove him away, even if she did briefly consider pushing him into the bayou. Two could play this game. "A clubhouse and a pool will never replace the grandeur of that ballroom. Have you actually taken a close look at her interior? If we put a marble dust finish coat on the walls, they'd gleam in the light of the chandeliers. Replace the gilding on the coffered ceiling, maybe create plaster pilasters along the walls highlighted with gold, and the Queen would be magnificent again, no other like her."

"I've looked at her many times—from my teens on. Used to be my second favorite make-out place, but most of the girls were too afraid to go inside, ghosts, they believed. I've recently gone over the whole place looking for things we could salvage. They built her of brick and cypress and a good slate roof, otherwise, she would have fallen down decades ago. We'll save those bricks and slates, maybe move that mahogany bar to the new clubhouse, give new life to old things." Remy moved in for a kiss as if he were still that randy teenager.

When she pulled away, he dropped his arm, stood, and began rolling up his sleeping bag. "Okay then. I guess we should go. Unless you are brave enough to spend the night here."

"Maybe if we did, you'd feel the spirit of the place and change your mind."

"I'm willing to give it a try."

The way he glanced at her with his head cocked, Julia realized she'd fallen in with his well-laid plans. He rolled up the other bag, tucked both under his arm, and made her custodian of the remaining bottle of wine and the glasses. Each grabbed a lantern. They moved to the portico and the regal front doors, twelve feet tall and so substantial no vandals had been able to enter that way. Intruders like Julia always forced the flimsy door on the shabby annex, he said. "I've blocked the original rear entrance. No more creeping inside through the kitchen."

Funny how he'd brought the massive key to the front doors and how easily it turned in the lock as if recently oiled. As the doors creaked shut blocking out the twilight and leaving them in darkness, they flicked on their lanterns. Julia observed the prints of many feet in the dust, obscuring her own from her earlier trespass. They moved to the staircase, the treads cleaned, the mahogany handrail waxed, and up to the ballroom with its three entries standing open. Stepping inside, the parquet floor gleamed as if it, too, had been polished, all the debris and dry husks of insects gone.

Remy dropped the sleeping bags in the center of the dance floor. "It's stuffy in here. I'll open the windows for some air." He applied some muscle to a lower sash, but it swung upward easily. After he'd opened all three, he spread the bags out to full length and offered her a seat. "They zip together."

"I noticed. It's too hot to crawl inside right now. Wine?"

"Absolutely." They sipped in silence as the dusk thickened, wrapping the Queen in a black velvet cloak of night.

The bottle finished, Julia stretched out full length and contemplated the magnificent ceiling. "Not as much work to restore that as you'd think. I'd give you a rock bottom price simply to be part of it."

"I'll bet you would." Remy lay down beside her, his arms cushioning his head.

"You must be considering the idea since you went to the trouble to damp mop and oil the parquet floor. Even the windows are clean."

"Nope, I had a work crew just sitting around waiting to build the dock. I don't pay for idleness so I put them to work. This floor is definitely worth taking up and saving. You don't see this kind of workmanship or the varieties of wood that went into making up each rectangle anymore."

Speaking of good quality wood, Julia felt it beneath her hand as she lightly ran her fingers up and down the fly of his jeans. She rolled on her side and gave him the kiss she'd denied before on the dock. She filled it with desire and the force of her will. Her hands stripped off his T-shirt and caressed the definition of his muscles lightly dewed by the heat of the night. He let her take the lead, going down on him as she loosened his erection from confinement and placed her lips on its engorged head.

Remy groaned. "Not so much of that. I'm too ready for you. I have been all week." He raised her up to her knees, pushed down her shorts and panties, and seated her firmly atop him. She began the ride slowly as he raised her shirt, discarded her bra, played with her nipples, molded her breasts in his hands. Stimulated, Julia picked up the pace, turned it into a wild ride. The sex became more than recreational to her as her hair flailed about her shoulders. She felt their connection to this place, their union of similar passions, what they could have together if either relented. So much to gain. So much to lose. They went over the top together and parted to lie side by side, too overheated to do any cuddling.

Julia closed her eyes. "Did you feel it, Remy?"

"I think we forgot the condom—but it felt great!"

"On the pill. Forget about that. And not what I meant. I can almost hear the music played in this room, the waltzes and the foxtrots, see the flicker of the candlelight bouncing off the chandelier crystals or the gleam of electric bulbs above the dancers, even the fear of men who might have died here or the dread of those going off to war."

"Ghosts, you mean. No, not a bit."

"Not ghosts, merely the weight of the past and all that has gone before. We're part of it now."

"I doubt we are the first ones to make love here." He shook his head against the sleeping bag. "While this was my teen dream come true, mostly I feel sticky. Ordinarily, I wouldn't advocate swimming in the bayou, but how about a quick skinny dip from the dock to cool off? Not much traffic on the river at night and only a pasture across from us."

133

Despite a twinge of disappointment that what they'd done was still only great sex to him, she took the dare. "I'm game, but I'm wearing my shirt and shoes to get down there."

Remy zipped his jeans and shoved his feet into his shoes. He gave her a hand up and an arm around her shoulders as they descended the staircase and pushed out the front doors again. The heavy, humid air did little to cool them. They raced for the dock, shucked off what little they had on and dived in. Surfacing, each placed a hand on the boat to keep from drifting in the mild current.

"Much better," Remy said.

Julia combed her hair back with her fingers. "Truly, I swore I caught the whiff of ladies' perfume and the hair oil of the men upstairs. Nothing...you experienced nothing?"

"Not a thing but your heat. Smoke! I smell smoke." He stared toward the Queen where a cloud lighter than the night rose from the rear of the building.

Chapter Seventeen

Remy catapulted out of the water and groped the pocket of his discarded jeans. A strip of condoms fell out, but he found the phone. Julia followed him, wet and sleek as a seal. She fumbled trying to get her shirt over her head. Remy ripped it away. "Later. Call 9-1-1 right now."

He drew up his jeans, stumbling along over shell shards and close-cut brambles as he headed for the temporary water line he'd had installed for the work crew and its pitiful single hose. He turned the tap on full and stretched the line toward the old kitchen as far as it could go, wetting first the shingles, then working down to the ground where the flames licked at the old, grease-saturated boards with relish.

Julia came rushing to his elbow. She'd had the sense to put on her sneakers as well as the T-shirt that clung to her as if she'd entered a contest to show off her body. Sensible woman had his shoes and phone in hand. No panic about his Julia.

"The fire department is on its way. Put your shoes on, and I'll hold the hose." She directed the water to the outer corner of the wooden annex, but the fire seemed to run completely around its base. The glow penetrated the deep shadows of the oaks. "Do you see him?" Julia questioned. "A man over there watching the hotel burn!"

Remy peered at where she pointed. A figure, slender and white, light-haired, lurked there. "No ghost," he said. The form took off, swinging two red gas cans like exercise weights.

"I'll follow him!"

Remy held Julia back by grasping the neck of her shirt. "No way. He could jump you anywhere out to the road."

A truck gunned its engine. In the distance, sirens sounded, rushing aid to the Queen.

"I think he's gone. I should steer the firemen."

"I wish you had your crowbar along, but okay. Be careful."

As she scooted off toward the road, Remy asked himself why he bothered trying to put out the fire. Instinct? Trying to impress Julia? The connection Julia spoke of that he'd felt and denied? Letting the Queen burn hewed to his best interests. Nothing more to stand between them with the ancient hotel reduced a heap of ashes. Still, he didn't turn off the hose.

The fire engines took advantage of the new culverts and pulled into place. Part of the crew emptied the well of the pumper truck onto the inferno while another ran a line to the bayou to suck up more water, a far cry from the bucket brigades of the Queen's youth. Remy shut the spigot, recoiled the hose, and let the professionals and well-trained volunteers work.

Chapelle's new fire chief, a younger man with the fitting name of Ashton Blaise, stalked over to him. Julia dogged the heels of his fireman's boots like an eager Dalmatian. Remy wondered if she noticed how handsome the man was, how heroic in his gear.

"Any idea why this started and who might have

done it?" Chief Blaise questioned. "Ms. Rossi said you saw a man carrying gas cans leave the area."

"We did."

"A thin blond man," Julia prompted.

"Only person I can think of fitting that description is Todd, Julia's intern."

Her outrage burned as hot as the fire. "How could you even suggest that? Todd totally supports restoration!"

Because the other man resembling Todd was his cousin, NuNu. Broussards did not rat on each other, even if they defended a rat.

The sheriff walked up and caught the tail end of the conversation. "I can think of another, Nolan "NuNu" Broussard. He has a record, but not for arson. Cousin of yours, Remy, right? We'll check out both of them." A man on the job for years, he knew about everyone in the area. Anyone focusing on his middle-aged gut and gray mustache instead of his shrewd eyes made a big mistake.

"Todd isn't used to hard work in this climate. He was in bed before I left Alleman." Julia staunchly defended her apprentice.

"And you were here because…" Sheriff LeDoux probed.

Julia shrugged, lifting the T-shirt that covered her to the thighs a little too high for Remy's comfort. "We had a picnic on the new dock and went for a dip in the bayou."

"That's what you were doing out here in the middle of the night?"

"It's my property and not the middle of the night, barely past nine o-clock." Remy let his irritation show.

"Even you were still awake."

"Just thinking burning this place down would work in your favor." Sheriff LeDoux contemplated the annex as its roof caved in over the old kitchen.

"I think Julia, who is highly in favor of saving this place, can vouch for me. We were both in the water when I noticed the smoke."

"Yes, that's right." She spoke as if she begrudged Remy the alibi.

"Sorry we couldn't spare this part of the hotel. Can we get in the front to make sure the fire hasn't spread?" Chief Blaise asked.

"It's open. Go ahead. I did block off the old kitchen recently. That might hold back the flames." He truly regretted polishing the bannister and the parquet now, only more fuel for the fire.

"Lex," Blaise called to one of the firemen heading up a group of volunteers. "Take a few men inside and make sure we don't have worse to handle. Check upstairs as well."

Remy winced at what they'd find in the ballroom. The answer wasn't long in coming when Lex reported in to his leader. A broad smile split his black face. "No penetration on the main floor, but maybe some kids fooling around upstairs in the ballroom: sleeping bags, empty wine bottle, and this." He dangled a delicate bra from his gloved finger and glanced at Julia in her damp tee as if assessing her cup size. "Could be they started the fire for more fun and games."

"I'll take that!" Julia snatched her underwear from the fireman's grip. "As I said, we decided to go for a swim after having a little wine. No crime in that."

Having given his report, Lex backed away. "Surely

138

not a crime, ma'am." But he failed to wipe that suggestive grin off his face.

"Glad we could save most of the hotel. My wife would not forgive me if I allowed it to burn. She's solidly with the preservationists," Blaise said.

Great, the fire chief's wife ran the local animal shelter. Even the animal activists were on Julia's side. At least, Julia now knew the guy was married. Although still clearly pissed at him, she eyed Remy avidly. "You could have let her burn. I think in your heart of hearts, you want to restore this building."

He denied it. "Plenty of good salvage to be taken out of the Queen yet. All I did was turn on a hose to protect my own best interests. The firefighters saved her."

They stayed until the last coal drowned in water, and the firemen packed up their gear. The sheriff had gone on his way with a promise to stop by both Alleman and NuNu's trailer. Reports would be ready Monday morning if Remy needed them for insurance purposes. Black streaks of soot marred the rear of the Queen, not that the cracked stucco over her bricks was all that attractive anymore.

Julia mused, "We'd wash that old plaster and put a new top coat on it. The hotel would gleam in the sunshine again like a white temple."

Remy didn't answer. "Can we go inside and check things out?" he asked Blaise, really meaning could they retrieve the sleeping bags and the rest of Julia's clothes. At one point during the wait, she'd slipped into the deepest of the shadows and put on her bra, guessing rightly they were fooling no one.

"Sure. Glad we could put this one out with so little

damage to the main structure." Tipping his fireman's hat, Chief Blaise left in his official red vehicle.

Julia charged ahead of Remy, up the stairs to the ballroom. The firemen had closed the windows, but a smoky haze hung in the air like the ghosts that supposedly haunted the place. She sat on the sleeping bags to draw up her panties and shorts, but let her shirt hang out over her thighs. No tucking in to show her shape.

Worth a try he figured, Remy asked, "Do you still want to spend the night?"

"No, I do not! Trying to foist the blame off on Todd when your own relative is responsible—I cannot believe you did that."

"We don't know NuNu is guilty." He offered a hand to help her up. She slapped it away and sprang up on her own. Nothing more to do than roll up the sleeping bags and pack out the empty bottle and glasses.

"All I can say is you had better be at that meeting with Hartz if you expect me to trust you again. The Queen deserves a fair chance, not death by arson." Her last words of the evening.

The ride to his house was swift and silent. Julia jumped ship at his dock before he had the *Cormorant* properly tied up. She sat in her truck until he opened the gate, then roared off into the night, her vehicle sounding as annoyed as she.

Yeah, he'd be at the meeting on Monday since he'd made a deal to attend. Too bad it wouldn't and couldn't make any difference to the fate of the Queen.

Chapter Eighteen

Remy got through Saturday night easily enough, satisfied after sex with Julia and tired from dealing with the crisis at the Bayou Queen. Sunday night didn't go nearly as well with the worry over the upcoming meeting with Hartz, the possibility that NuNu had been arrested since he hadn't spotted him at the trailer, and total silence from Julia.

How to deal with a powerful billionaire and still keep his obligation to the Broussard family? Remy guessed he could bail NuNu out, but how suspicious would that look to Sheriff LeDoux?

And Julia, whom he'd pegged as being just his type, a career woman who enjoyed recreational sex without a mention of marriage and children. The trouble was, Jules ran hot, not cold. She poured passion into everything from restoration to making love. Maybe that was the problem. He loved what she did and how she did it. Every once in a while, he caught himself wondering how many of their offspring would inherit her blue eyes—strictly from an interest in genetics. What if they merged their businesses as well as their bodies? Not likely to happen since he'd insulted Todd.

Monday morning inevitably came following a sleepless night. Remy shook off his fatigue with a hot shower and counted on Starbuck's for breakfast and a hefty shot of caffeine. He braced himself to enter

Chapelle's modest police department and inquire if Sheriff LeDoux had solved the crime over the weekend. Shown right into the office, LeDoux stood to shake his hand after a quick bush of powdered sugar off his belly. Remy suspected the source as Pommier's beignets.

"Got your report right here. Blaise faxed me his statement. No need to make two stops. Definitely arson using a gasoline accelerant. We went back to the site in the daylight to look for shoe prints or tire tracks, but it's been too dry. Good thing you mowed recently, or the fire department would have had a hell of a brush fire to control. We strung some crime scene tape just for good form. Don't think the ruins will tell us anything more."

Remy didn't want to be the one to bring it up, but he must. "Did you check out Todd and NuNu?"

An amused smile curved the stern mouth under the gray mustache. "Right after I left the scene. Rousted the intern from his bunk over the cab in the motorhome. Sleeps in his tighty-whities. Scrawny dude who fit the description, but the older men were still awake playing cards and vouched for him. He's off the list. No motive, good alibi. As for NuNu..." LeDoux paused to take a deep drag of coffee from a truly hideous mug. "My little granddaughter made this. Like it?"

"She shows some real artistic talent." Remy wished he'd get to the point.

"Which says you are a smooth liar. This is a mug only a grandfather could love. I'd offer you some bullpen coffee, and you'd probably claim it ain't swill. About NuNu, he wasn't at his trailer. I walked around the property. No sign of gas cans."

Grateful that NuNu possessed enough intelligence to get rid of the evidence, probably in the bayou, Remy carefully let out a breath. "So, did you track him down?"

"Sure. Out at the Barn flipping burgers and frying catfish like he does every Saturday night. All the kitchen workers swore he'd been there since six when his shift started. No time cards used out there. Old Broussard says he trusts his employees to arrive when they should and do their job."

Remy very nearly blurted out that they'd seen NuNu at his trailer around seven, which he guessed was the chief's intent. He held it in and prayed the man wouldn't question Julia too. He stood and gathered the reports. "Thanks for your diligence. Lots of people have taken sides on the issue of the Queen. I guess we'll never know who tried to burn her down."

The sheriff took another swig from the lumpy mug heavily adorned with purple unicorns and rainbows. "Mostly the Broussards against the town as usual. Might be they lose this one. If you want to protect your property, even for salvage, you better think about hiring a guard."

"I'll give that some thought."

Remy found his way out, zigzagging around close packed desks. He had plenty of time to drive out to the Hartz mansion for the meeting. He'd expected to meet the big man in a boardroom on the campus of Hartz Technology, but Jonathan had developed the common touch since moving to Chapelle and marrying local. He could two-step and bass fish with the best of the Cajuns and belonged to nearly every organization in town, even Ducks Unlimited, though he didn't hunt. They'd have their discussion at his Pecan Grove home, keeping it casual. The word beloved came to mind concerning

Jonathan Hartz.

Remy figured he'd never earn that adjective, not the way this project was going. Truly, he meant to give this mostly rural parish a development they could tout and profit from, but the populace proved to be stuck in the past like so much of the South. He tried to soothe himself on the way out of town, passing the beautifully landscaped technology plant that employed so many, and heading beyond it into the country where Hartz lived by Indian Lake.

Pink Mexican primroses, hiding the wayside debris of beer bottles and fast food wrappers, festooned the edges of the deep ditches. Beautiful land if only people wouldn't trash it. Crap, now he thought like Jane Tauzin. He arrived at the Grove a half-hour early, bad form, showed eagerness. Remy was only eager to get the meeting over and done. He took the gravel road running between the wall of the Hartz estate and a vast sugarcane field. Driving alongside the levee and hoping to distract himself with some eagle watching, Remy parked by the docks and waited, but only the usual blue herons and great white egrets appeared stalking prey in the shallows.

Two Indian mounds rose out of the haze on the far side of the lake. Known as the Twin Sisters, local lover boys had also dubbed them the Two Tits. Another place to take a girl not afraid to hike through a cane field at night and lie on a blanket under a starry sky. Julia came immediately to mind, naked and willing. No use loitering anymore, Remy turned his truck toward Pecan Grove and whatever waited there.

As soon as he'd been cleared at the gate by some serious hired muscle, Remy found Julia's Regal

Restorations truck already sat in front of the mansion. No sign of Jane's hybrid. Good, though Celine Hartz would surely be inside. He parked and mounted the brick steps of the portico with its four slender white pillars. A ring of the bell brought Hartz's Hispanic housekeeper to the door. She escorted him past a truly magnificent hanging staircase and hand-painted wallpaper murals of Louisiana swamp scenes to a cozy breakfast room at the rear of the mansion.

There they waited, four against one, lacking only Jane Tauzin. Hartz, sitting at the head of a blue distressed table Remy would call shabby chic, rose to offer his hand. Nothing forbidding about the slight man with the expensive haircut that kept his blond hair from falling into baby blue eyes framed today with barely noticeable eyeglasses. He had a cordial smile for Remy and offered coffee from a carafe, a bottle of water, and a delectable assortment of Pommier's pastries. If Remy recalled correctly, the housekeeper had married LeJeune Pommier and sometimes worked at the bakery, only one of several strange matches in the house.

Celine, the Cajun bride, sat on her husband's right and his personal assistant, a tall, severe woman with blue eyes so sharp they could probably cut paper, held the place on his left. Inexplicably, this all-business female was the billionaire's sister-in-law through an alliance with Celine's brother, the game warden of Indian Lake. Yes, people still talked about that one too. Must be something in their water. Remy didn't judge. To each her own. He wondered if the town gossips already speculated about himself and Julia. Let them say what they will.

What did bother him was Todd standing squeezed

up against a tree-trunk side table festooned with ferns and other houseplants as if he were part of the display. Considering his build, he had large, long-fingered hands, and both rested on the rear of Julia's chair as if guarding her back. Todd's usually bland face scowled Remy's way. Bearing a grudge, he guessed, about being accused of arson. Couldn't be helped.

Julia merely nodded to acknowledge his presence and sent no smile his way even though he took a chair next to her. She wore her business attire and her no-nonsense face to the meeting. Sipping her coffee from a china cup, she selected and ate a mini-éclair in two precise bites. Instead of licking her fingers as she had at the picnic, she wiped them on a cloth napkin before speaking. "We lack only Jane before we can start."

Celine Hartz with a smile as sunny as her husband's poured coffee for Remy and passed it to him. Why all the happy, Remy wondered? She indicated the sugar and cream, real stuff, and the refreshments. "Jane said she might be late and to begin without her."

Remy tested the coffee and added a bit of cream, fairly sure the beverage had been made with Starbuck's beans since Hartz missed his Seattle brew and made sure the brand became available in Chapelle. The billionaire possessed the money to create whatever he wanted, wherever he wanted it. His proposal should be interesting.

With his assistant taking notes on a HartzPad, the billionaire started immediately. "To keep things short and sweet, I'll offer you four times what you paid for the Queen, and reimburse you for the bush-hogging and the new dock if you supply me with the receipts for the work."

"A generous offer, but I have investors who want the Black Diamonds development to be built on that land. I cannot renege."

"Would they consider another site?"

Remy chuckled. Exactly how long had Hartz lived in the Ste. Jeanne d'Arc Parish? "What other site? Lots of agricultural land surrounds the town, but no one will sell, at least for a reasonable price. Remember when the Dollar Store paid big bucks for a ramshackle place to tear down and put up their building?"

Hartz nodded. "Yes, now everyone thinks their backyard is worth a million."

"We need a lot more land than that for Black Diamonds. Being on the bayou is a huge selling point." A thought occurred to Remy, one he might as well propose though he couldn't be sure Old Brossard would approve. But, trying to cooperate might gain him some points from Julia. He didn't care about refusing Hartz.

"That sugarcane field next door to you—it runs down to the levee road. Maybe Indian Lake could be a draw. Ever try to buy it?"

Hartz issued a rueful grin. "Often. The Patin family owns it and the sugar mill. Their board of directors is made up solely of relatives. Their policy is not one acre of cane land will be sold lest their heritage and livelihood be harmed. They mean it too."

Curious, Remy asked, "What did you plan to do with the field?"

"I like my privacy out here and preserving the environment. I thought I might put in an arboretum. I'll admit having a condo complex right next door does not appeal even if I could get the land."

Remy shrugged. "Probably too far out of town

anyhow." He swept a glance past Julia to see if she'd been impressed by his effort to find a new location for his project. Her usually expressive face remained as stiff as a plaster of Paris figurine. Not impressed.

Hartz fingered through a second proposal. "What if I became your partner to restore the Bayou Queen? I buy out your current investors and provide forty-nine percent of the funds to leave you in control of the project. We use my money to get matching grants giving other organizations some stake in the renovation. The more diverse the support we have, the better."

Julia spoke for the first time. "Jane is already looking into available grants. Your matching funds would make the process so much easier."

Yeah, maybe if Remy were as rich as Jonathan Hartz he could buy her love. No, no, he meant her admiration.

Hartz shoved the papers Remy's way. "Study this. Take the idea to your investors. See what they think. They can go in with us, or I can buy them out. Then their cash will still be available for Black Diamonds when an alternate place is found."

"I can ask them, but I don't think…"

The doorbell rang at the front of the house, followed by the thud of running shoes, and the appearance of Jane Tauzin flapping a set of papers. She wore a rumpled skirt and blouse, having obviously been in and out of her car so often the vehicle did not cool off between stops. Her brown bangs hung in sweaty strands glued on her forehead. "We got it—the historical designation for the Queen. And more! An injunction against its demolition." Jane rounded the table and kissed Jonathan Hartz on the forehead and both cheeks. "Thank you, thank you for making those calls. I can start writing the grants now."

His nerd-pale face colored. "Happy to do it, Jane, but don't tell your husband you kissed me, okay?"

"Ha! He'll understand. If you kissed me, it might be another story."

Remy closed his eyes for a moment, then said the words that would only anger Julia further. "We'll fight that injunction—because I doubt my investors will buy into the plan. They like things their own way."

Hartz nodded. "The Broussards. Stubborn people. Hard to deal with them. But you will present the plan?"

So, he did know the ins and outs of the parish. "Yes, but don't get your expectations up."

He addressed this statement to Julia whose blue eyes blazed with new hope. Behind her, Todd wore a self-satisfied smirk. Remy gathered the paperwork and stood to let Julia pass, but he cut between her and the intern. She couldn't leave without Todd—or without speaking to him. They left Jane behind glugging a bottle of water.

Out on the portico, he headed Jules off before she could bolt for her truck. "Give me a minute! You did see I tried to suggest another site for Black Diamonds."

"You knew it wasn't possible. Weren't you the one who told me how precious land is around here?"

She'd remembered, but she wasn't done with him. "You owe Todd an apology for accusing him and—and embarrassing him—in an attempt to keep your own kin out of jail." She shoved the intern forward and between them.

"NuNu isn't in jail. He had an alibi too." Remy tried to peer around the guy, skinny as a beanpole without the greens growing on it, but Julia evaded his try. "Okay, okay, Todd, I'm sorry I implicated you and caused Sheriff LeDoux to drag you out of bed in your tighty-whities. At least, you had something on. He would have caught me in the raw." Maybe he implied that's the way real men slept.

Though Julia's eyes peeking through Todd's akimbo arms showed a flicker of interest at his last statement, she wasn't ready to relent. "Now, you've embarrassed him again. I doubt your sincerity."

"It's the best I can do. I'll take this proposal to the old man and see what he says, but Julia, you have no idea how dangerous it is to interfere."

"You mean he'll send another arsonist to burn the Queen."

"The sheriff did say he thought I should post a guard, but I can't see the expense to protect a building that *will* be demolished sooner or later. Not what I meant though. Intimidation is the Broussard style. I don't want anything to happen to you—or Todd, I guess."

"I can take care of Ms. Rossi and myself," Todd stated, folding his arms across his thin chest.

"Please do that." Remy found he meant it. Talk about heartfelt sincerity. He gave up and turned to leave.

Julia stepped out from behind her defender. "When will you talk to your grandfather?"

"Probably tomorrow."

"Well, you be safe too."

Maybe she cared a little. "They probably won't kill me." At least, he hoped so.

Chapter Nineteen

Julia's team of preservationists scored big with the historic designation and the injunction. She should be buoyant, but felt as if she had her feet stuck in her own plaster unable to move forward without trampling Remy's dreams. She realized it wasn't simply a project to him, something to be put on the back burner until he found another site. His plans were elegant and would bring new life to the parish consistently losing population as young people moved away for better jobs, or so Celine told her. If only they might compromise, but she didn't see how. Having to stay away from him physically didn't improve her mood either.

But she had work to do both at Alleman and with her volunteers. "Todd"—she said as they drove away from Pecan Grove—"activate the phone tree. We'll need people watching the Queen twenty-four seven since Remy won't pay to protect her. They can park across the road from the property, and everyone should have a buddy and a phone in case the Broussards try to intimidate them. If Miss Lolly doesn't understand, tell her it's like perpetual prayer. Set up a schedule. I'll let the sheriff know what we're doing. Maybe patrols can drive by at night and make sure all is well."

"I'd be happy to do that." Todd had a narrow face but perfect teeth thanks to great orthodontia. Still, his smile came across as somewhat vengeful.

"He did apologize to you."

"Only because he wants to be on your good side. I can't figure out what you see in him."

Julia believed that didn't require an answer, but she enumerated one in her mind. Handsome, fit, intelligent, talented, visionary, and generous in bed. No need to tell Todd. Her mouth watered a little. She swallowed as they turned in at the white brick pillars of Alleman.

"Get to work on that schedule. I'll check on the uncles and see how the crack repair is coming along. We're almost done here. The next phase belongs to the painters and paperhangers."

"New Orleans here we come!" Todd appeared overly happy about that.

"This has been an interesting project and more exciting than most with the Queen in the mix. Back in NOLA, we'll be working on bids and estimates for new projects. Not much chance to get our hands dirty."

"Yeah, I'll miss that, but not Mr. Remington Broussard."

She'd miss Remy though. She certainly would.

****

Remy returned to his tower and reluctantly set up a meeting with his great-uncle. Not much else he could do now with the injunction in force, but he'd arrange for a bulldozer and dump trucks to clear the fire debris. Perhaps, rent storage and remove the magnificent bar that he'd use one way or another. Just a step closer to razing the Queen to the ground, and he didn't feel good about it anymore. Julia had a point. No more buildings would be created out of huge cypress timbers. Trees of great size barely existed anymore. Craftsmen doing that type of meticulous parquet—gone. Those handmade bricks, not easy to duplicate unless a person did their own. He built with steel and glass and wondered if his work would last as long.

Good, in a stroke of luck both the dozer and the dump trucks were available first thing in the morning. One more item to check off his list. At least, it was progress. Too bad he wasn't making any with Julia.

****

Miss Lolly and Miss Maxie pulled their behemoth of an old Lincoln Continental in behind the economy car holding the persons doing the second night shift protecting the Queen. They'd signed up for this time slot because it fit their regular attendance at early Mass. Julia provided them with one of those phones you had to be smart to use and patiently showed them how to call her number embedded somewhere inside the gadget. Along with a thermos of coffee and a couple of croissants stuffed with ham and cheese, they stood ready to do their duty until noon. If they had to pee, well, Remy had rented a couple of portable toilets for his men. They'd sneak in and use those since the high weeds were gone.

Miss Lolly and her constant companion got out and rapped on the window of the smaller vehicle. The ancient veterans in the backseat startled awake along with their assisted living aide asleep behind the wheel. "Is the enemy creeping up on us?"

"Not yet, but if you can't stay awake, you should take a daytime shift. This is dereliction of duty," Miss Maxie said, rather severely. "Go back to the home and get your breakfast. We brought ours along."

"We only nodded off around dawn. Tell her, Benita."

The aide, a heavy-set woman who'd spent an uncomfortable night with her belly pressed against a steering wheel for the sake of overtime pay, answered, "Don't know. I was sleepin'. Y'all ready to go now?"

"The Queen might have burned to the ground while you napped!" Miss Lolly accused.

"Woman, we witnessed the destruction of Europe. I think we'd notice."

The sound of heavy equipment trundling down the road drowned out their spat. A bulldozer led the way making a wide turn onto Remy's property. Three dump trucks followed. Remy brought up the rear flashing the little confab a what-the-hell-is-going-on-now glance.

"A bulldozer! Y'all saw it. Remy is breaking the law and starting the demolition. Because he's a Broussard, he thinks he can get away with it. Where's the phone. We must call Julia." Miss Lolly fumbled in the big black purse that held the croissants and her rosary. "Now how do I work it?"

"Gimme that. It's a burner, only got one number in it." Benita took over. "Two women here say a bulldozer is on the property. Okay. She be right over to stop whatever is up. You GIs ready for your oatmeal?"

"Eggs, we want eggs."

"We can do that." Benita returned the phone to Miss Lolly who immediately lost it in the depths of her purse. The aide wasted no time leaving.

"Should we march in there and sit down in front of the dozer, Lolly?"

"Let's see what Julia has to say."

They didn't have long to wait before Julia's truck parked in the space left by the economy car. "In there! In there! Dump trucks too." Miss Maxie pointed a wobbling finger toward the Queen.

"And portable toilets in case we need one—which I might. Overly excited. You lead the way, Julia."

She did with the two old ladies close behind vowing their willingness to throw themselves on the dozer immediately after they used the facilities. Julia marched right up to Remy and poked her chin at his face. "What's the meaning of this? We have an injunction!"

Remy waved a hand at the pile of charred rubble. "Removing what has already been demolished. Not attacking your beloved Queen."

"Oh well—we'll be watching." Julia turned on her heel and marched away with her small contingent following. "Mind you don't trip on the oak roots, ladies."

Miss Lolly threw Remy a defiant backwards glance. "He almost looks sad you didn't stay and argue with him longer."

"Maybe some other time."

****

Newly returned from their second surreptitious trip to Remy's necessaries—convenient he'd rented several—Lolly and Maxie prepared to finish their turn at guarding the Queen the next morning. Patty Broussard, the boy's own grandmother, and his Great-aunt Pammy, were due to spell them in half an hour. They'd passed the time reading and eating their snacks, trail mix full of peanuts for protein, dried fruit for fiber, and M&Ms for fun, occasionally throwing some out the window to feed the birds who flitted in the oak trees. No sign of action on the property, and Maxie had brought her bird watching binoculars to make sure no one approached from the bayou side without being spotted.

They didn't suspect the moving van until it drove across the culverts and down to the charred plywood blocking the rear entrance to the Queen. Two men got out and began tearing away the barrier. Miss Lolly's hand dived into her purse and fished out the burner phone. "Let's see, I put my finger here to get Julia's number—and then what?"

"For heaven's sake, Lolly, you push the thing that sort of looks like a phone to make the call. I'll bet Remy is removing the stuff he wants to salvage out of the building even if he's forbidden to tear it down. Give me that thing! I'll do it." In the struggle for possession, Maxie spilled the bag of trail mix into her lap. She opened her door and dumped it out before connecting with Julia.

"You'd better come quick. They're tearing the Queen apart. You should bring your uncles. These guys are pretty brawny if comes to a fight."

"What's she saying?"

"To stay in the car and out of the way. She'll be here shortly—with her uncles and the puny young man. Meanwhile, to call 9-1-1 and get the police out here. I guess we have to punch that in and hit the telephone thing again." Maxie beamed when someone on the other end said, "9-1-1, what is the nature of your emergency?" Unsure of what to say, she guessed, "Robbery?" and gave directions.

Lolly pointed at an oncoming red truck. "Remy is here. Good you called the cops, or it would be an unfair fight. He can easily take that skinny boy."

Remy ignored them and went to join his workers.

Lolly took up the binoculars and watched the three men enter the hotel through the gap in its walls. When Julia arrived with her own men in tow, Lolly hissed, "They've gone inside. Be careful."

No walking in this time, Jules drove straight to the Queen. Todd jumped out of the cab with her, and her uncles got down from the back. Miss Lolly applied the binoculars again. "They have their tool belts on and are going inside. Looks like a rumble to me."

The police arrived with their siren silenced. Officers Chauvin and Ancona got down. Ancona muttered, "Why us, why always us?"

Officer Chauvin stuck to the script. "What's the problem, ladies? Where's the daylight burglary in progress?"

"At the Queen. Remy Broussard is preparing to take things away in a van." Maxie waved her liver-spotted hand at the hotel.

"Ah, doesn't he own the place?" Ancona asked.

"Well, yes, but a judge said he can't tear it down." Lolly gave an empathic nod of her dyed-black head. "You'd better get in there. Julia Rossi and her uncles went to stop them. There might be violence."

"Amateurs, always amateurs. We'd better go down there with sirens. Might break it up." Chauvin agreed with Ancona. In they went.

"We should get to walking, Maxie. No way can we steer the Lincoln over that bumpy ground."

"Julia said we should stay put."

"Well, we sure can't see or hear anything out on the road. Let's go!"

By the time they hobbled to the hotel and stepped carefully through the hole in its rear wall, all the action appeared to be over—or maybe it had never begun. No blood on the floor, no bruised bodies, though Julia and her crew stood facing Remy and his with the two cops and a pile of tool belts in the middle.

"Miss Lolly, Miss Maxie, we were only removing the old mahogany bar for restoration. Officers, could we just call this a false alarm?"

"For all we knew, you were tearing up the parquet," Julia said with a stubborn tone to her words.

"Well, I'm not. Like I said, the bar will be repurposed somewhere. With the injunction in place, it's about all I can work on right now thanks to you."

"Yes, thanks to me, the Queen will be saved."

Lolly and Maxie clapped their fragile hands. The sound echoed in the vault of the hotel's lobby.

Julia hadn't finished. "You'd better not try to remove the roof slates. In this climate, that's a sure way to kill a building."

"That never occurred to me before you said it—but I won't be doing it unless we demolish the queen. Look, I meet with the Broussards this afternoon. I'll present all the proposals and let you know how it goes. Then maybe, we can put all this behind us and end the ridiculous surveillance."

"I beg your pardon. There is nothing ridiculous about well-meaning people trying to save an endangered landmark."

"Not at all, but do you really think these ladies could stop anything bad from happening?"

"That's why we called the cops!" Maxie exclaimed, showing her red-haired temper.

"Okay, okay. Sort out the tool belts. Ms. Rossi, take your men home. Remy, get on with your business.

Miss Lolly, Miss Maxie, can we give you a lift to your car?" Officer Chauvin offered.

"We'd love to ride in the squad car. But first let me have a private word with our leader." Lolly drew Julia aside. "Maybe you should try being less confrontational with Remy. I see yearning in his lovely dark eyes. Perhaps, you might go back to doing what you two were doing before—some say. I mean you'd be sacrificing yourself for a good cause."

Unfortunately, sound carried so well inside the empty Queen. Remy's laughter rebounded off the ceiling. "Small towns, big mouths, and bigger ears to hear what anyone has to tell. But yeah, I'd be willing to go back to the way things were before all this." He gestured to the police, the two sets of muscular men, and the frail old ladies.

Julia's cheeks bloomed with dusky rose. "Come on, guys, time to leave." She led her now very hostile uncles and a fuming Todd outside. The officers and her preservationists followed, getting into the squad car. A small parade, they moved down the rough lane to the road where the next shift of watchers waited.

"What happened?" asked Miss Patty and Miss Pammy.

Julia paused to answer them. "Nothing, really. Remy was removing the old bar for refurbishing."

"Why does everything exciting happen on their watch?" said Pammy, nodding toward the elderly women.

"We're just lucky, I guess. Thanks for the ride officers, but I wish you'd turned on the sirens." Miss Lolly inched her old bones behind the wheel of the Lincoln.

"Wasn't an emergency, ma'am."

Julia shook her head. "That's two false alarms in two days. Maybe we should stop watching the place. I believe we can trust Remy not to defy the injunction. He meets with his investors later today. Then, we can decide how to move ahead."

Miss Patty shook her immovable lacquered curls. "No secret who his investors are. I know my brother-in-law. No one can move him an inch—obese as he is."

"We'll see tomorrow."

Chapter Twenty

Remy skipped lunch in case he had to endure another Broussard Burger challenge. Though the setup in the Barn stayed the same with Old Broussard at the head of a table surrounded by his minions, no smell of fried onions or french fry grease filled the air, and no food appeared. NuNu only poured coffee from the big granitewear pot. Remy accepted his cup, but failed to offer so much as a thanks. Thanks for what? Trying to burn down the Queen and putting a bigger rift between him and Julia?

The old man missed nothing with those piggy eyes sunk in the flesh of his face. He called the meeting to order by saying, "First, NuNu got somet'ing to say to Remy."

NuNu kept his watery, bloodshot blue eyes on the floor as he balanced the coffeepot on the edge of the table. "I guess I jumped the gun trying to burn down the Queen. Just thought I'd help things along since it seems like the Italian bitch is leading you around by your dick. Never thought you two would be out there naked in the bayou." His wisecrack earned a few snickers

Some apology. "Julia saw you, and so did I because you didn't have the sense to run instead of watching. I lied to keep you out of jail, NuNu. Claimed the man who started the fire looked like her intern, but the sheriff knew better. I should have saved myself the trouble since your coworkers covered for you."

"Damn right dey did if dey wants to keep dose jobs," Old Broussard interrupted.

"Next time, don't do me any favors, NuNu. Lots of saleable salvage might have been destroyed. Another thing—if you ever speak of Ms. Rossi in those terms again, I'll come next door and use you for karate practice."

"Pussy whipped," NuNu muttered.

Remy pushed back his chair. "You want to start now?"

Old Broussard held up his pudgy hands where a wedding ring dug deep into the skin. "Enough. Bot' of you had your say. *Se donner la main.*"

Reluctantly, Remy shook his distant cousin's hand and dropped it as if it were a hot baked potato. "Don't try to help me again. Julia and her people are watching the place around the clock. Next time, there will be more witnesses."

"You go now, NuNu. We got business here don't concern you, no."

As NuNu slinked away, Remy handed the old man and Slick copies of the proposals made by Jonathan Hartz. They were the only folks around the table who counted. Their heads began to shake almost immediately. He doubted if they read a single word.

"Everything he offers is a great deal. If he buys me out, I'll give you half the profit. We build Black Diamonds later. If I go into business with him to restore the Queen, your investment will be placed in a special account kept separate to fund Black Diamonds when an alternative location is found. It's win-win."

"You t'ink we got you da land cheap so you could

blow us off and go into business wit' dat *etranger* rich man, heh?" Old Broussard's chins shook in multiple-layered anger.

Still, Remy pushed him. "I didn't ask for your help in buying the Queen. I could have managed that on my own."

Slick made his only comment. "Ha! Good one."

Ignoring the insult, Remy continued. "None of this means Black Diamonds won't be built. In fact, you could invest in the Queen too, and sell out when she's up and running for a nice profit if it's about the money lying idle. You have to realize with the property under a no demolition injunction, we might not be able to proceed with our original plans for years."

"Not about *pousse-pousse*." Old Broussard rubbed two fingers together as if he held a wad of money. "Dis is about family. Who you loyal to, Remy, who?"

"The Broussards of course." Though in his heart of hearts, the place where Julia claimed he wanted to restore the Queen, he wondered if that were true. He hadn't been raised here. His parents resented sending him to spend his summers in Chapelle with the demanding Patty, not to mention setting up his business here lured by a free bit of land and support for his project. They'd warned him.

"You tell Mr. Bi-yon-aire no deal. Den get your daddy or granddaddy to fight dat order."

Since his father fled to Mandeville years ago to avoid doing the family's legal business and escape Patty, Remy doubted he'd get involved now. His grandfather might come out of semi-retirement to fight the preservationists. He'd always been about progress, but touted Jonathan Hartz as among his best friends.

Doubtful if Hartz thought the same. In the end, Guidry Broussard owed his political success to his cruder relatives and a pushy wife. Yeah, he'd fight the injunction free of charge even if it aggravated his grandmother.

Remy picked up his papers. "I'll tell Hartz what you had to say."

"You do dat. Don't let us down, you." Old Broussard enveloped Remy's hand in his fleshy grip for a shake surprisingly strong and bone-crunching as he made his point.

Remy didn't wince or rub his fingers afterward. Show no fear was always good advice when dealing with dangerous animals. He nodded goodbye to everyone else at the table and NuNu listening at the entrance to the kitchen. His anger rose as he drove away from the Barn. He could have bought the Queen without help in a fair auction. The deals Hartz offered were excellent for everyone. Why couldn't one hog-headed old man see that?

He'd sleep on it—without Julia in his bed. She'd never be there again if he sided with his relatives against all reason.

In the morning with a clear head, Remy Broussard vowed make his decision for better or worse, richer or poorer, and whatever came next with Julia and the Queen.

Chapter Twenty-One

Remy awoke still angry, so angry he called Hartz immediately to ask for a few minutes of his time this morning. He got the PA, Adrienne Stone Landry, still called Heart of Stone by some of the locals, who made it abundantly clear that ten minutes was all the time the billionaire could spare. Her sleek body and alert, intelligent eyes reminded him of a Doberman, and she protected her boss/brother-in-law that well.

He had plenty of time to stop by the bank and remove the Broussard funds from his account. They were placed in a new account labeled Black Diamonds, Ltd. Someday, when the project moved forward, Old Broussard should thank him, though Remy wouldn't place bets on it. He proceeded to the Hartz Technology plant, had his name checked on a list, and received his visitor's badge, nothing warm and friendly about this part.

Remy parked where directed close to the grand lobby in spaces reserved for guests, after passing the water feature that once held gators which had gotten too friendly and been removed, and other Hartz amenities, like picnic areas and a basketball court all beautifully landscaped. He should have visited earlier to take a tour and soak in the magnificence of the lobby as impressive as any bank. The polished granite of the floor had an earthy brown tint edged in green stone. Chihuly glass sculptures hung from the two-story ceiling. Helpful signage said they were called swamp forms and did rather mimic the canopies of cypress trees, flocks of flying egrets, and maybe that one was an alligator. They didn't block the view of the Hartz logo, twin steel blue hearts pierced by a golden lightning bolt, embedded in the center of the second-floor balcony.

He headed for the reception desk to make his presence known, but halfway across the space, Mrs. Landry beckoned him to take one of the opposing staircases to join her above the lobby. Hartz supposedly never took the elevator behind the desk, part of his fitness regimen. Remy did the same.

All business, Mrs. Landy greeted him by saying, "This way," but he paused for a minute to peer over the railing at the glass sculptures. "They look different from up here as if we're in an airplane flying over the Basin. Jesus, I wish I'd designed this place. It's fantastic."

The PA allowed herself to release a small smile. "Thank you. I had some say in its design. Come along, only ten minutes, remember?"

Remy followed her brisk pace to the inner sanctum of Hartz Technology, no waiting, no second interrogation by another secretary. They sailed right in under Mrs. Landry's flag where again he felt the warmth of Hartz's greeting and received the offer of water or coffee despite their limited time. The Hartz domain spread out beyond the tinted windows, the vast, single story factory surrounded by endless fields of cane and the brown water snake of the bayou winding through them. After a shake of the hand, Hartz took his seat and asked, "Are you here to accept any of my proposals?"

"On behalf of the Broussards, no."

The billionaire's always optimistic face fell, making him appear older and less boyish. "That will be a blow to Celine and Julia, not to mention Jane. I'm sorry to hear this."

"It appears we won't need the entire ten minutes," Mrs. Landry said. "I'll show you out."

Remy stayed seated. He pulled the proposals from his briefcase. "Nor do I want to sell you the property. But, if you are still interested in entering into a partnership with me to restore the Queen, I'll sign the deal today."

The enthusiastic boy who still had a feel for what new games and products kids wanted reemerged. "Wonderful! While you will manage the project, I hope you'll accept some suggestions from your 49% partner and the women who care so much about this restoration, especially Julia."

"Yes, especially Julia. I won't move forward without her by my side."

Though Hartz and his PA exchanged glances over that comment, Mrs. Landry said, "The contracts are already drawn. I'll get them." She left by an inner door to her own upper-echelon lair.

"Do you mind if I share this news with Celine? She'll be excited." Hartz had his phone in hand.

"Not at all—but allow me to take the news to Julia. I'll be going directly to Alleman from here."

Hartz gave him an understanding smile. His PA returned with the contracts. "Sign in the indicated places. It's the same as the copies I gave you the other day. Off you go to tell Julia." He shooed Remy out of the office with a flick of his hand. The ever-vigilant Mrs. Landry tailed him until he left his guest badge at the desk and exited the building.

Feeling free and unencumbered by family obligations, he flew along the road to Alleman, ignoring the jolts caused by the potholes, and turned in at the pillars of the old plantation home. He found Marv in the kitchen, but no one else. "They're upstairs. Todd is getting a lesson in crack repair."

Remy homed in on the sound of Julia's voice as he reached the landing and made his way to a bedroom with a tester bed, a huge walnut armoire, and two marble-topped nightstands shoved in its center. Sam and Sal probably provided the muscle to move the furniture. They stood out of the way with their arms folded while Julia in full plasterer's garb lectured a rapt Todd. Remy entered quietly, content for the moment just to hear her voice full of enthusiasm for what she taught.

"Lime plaster is a living, breathing entity. Small cracks like these will open and close seasonally according to the humidity level and are not a major problem."

"Kind of eerie, though," Sammy commented. "I had an aunt with walls like that. Hated staying over at her place."

"But we can get rid of them by making them slightly broader with a crack widener. No sophomoric jokes, please. This is very sharp tool. We cut away plaster to make the cracks wider, then fill them in with patching material. Don't even think of using plaster of Paris," Julia warned as if Todd had actually dared to suggest that.

"No, ma'am, I wouldn't do that or joke about it."

"Plaster of Paris must be mixed with lime to be successful." She drew the edge of the crack widener along the gap to show the width needed for the repair, then handed it to Todd to give it a try.

"Julia," Remy said. "I have news!"

Todd's hand slipped, and he gouged the wall. "Look what you made me do."

Julia patted her intern's shoulder as if he were a favored pet. "Not a problem. We can fix that." Her tone cooled considerably when she faced Remy. "You had something say?"

"Yes. I signed a contract with Jonathan Hartz this morning to restore the Queen. I accepted the partnership. The Broussards are out of it. It's just him and me and whatever grants Jane can get. And you. Especially you, because no one is better than Regal Restorations."

"Ain' that the truth," Sal said. Not the person Remy wanted to hear from.

"Actually, you should get quotes from a variety of contractors for the best deal, but of course we will give you an estimate." Julia turned back to Todd.

"But I want *you*." He didn't know what he'd expected. Maybe the cluttered room prevented Jules from flinging herself at him in joy and rapture, but certainly more than this coldness. Remy admitted he wanted to be rewarded for taking this brave step forward. Obviously, Julia had no idea what it would cost him financially or otherwise to sever ties with the Broussards over the Queen. Possibly all of his parish business. He might have to move back to the New Orleans area. Not a hardship if Julia lived nearby.

"Jules?"

At last, she answered him. "I hoped this day might come, but didn't really believe it. Anyhow, I already have estimates drawn up for Jane to use in her grant writing. I'll get them to you. I'm looking forward to working with you."

Still, Julia didn't move from her spot, but Sam and Sal came over to slam him on the back and pump his hand. "Way to go, Remy." If only they weren't hairy Italian males.

"I came here directly from Hartz Technology to tell you myself."

"I appreciate that."

"Well, I'll leave you to your lessons." He backed from the room as if she might stab him with that crack widener.

He heard her uncles ragging on her as he left. "Jesus, Jules, why don't you just seal him in a wall and plaster it over. He came through for you." Nice to know someone was on his side.

His best hope—that she might deliver those estimates to him alone tonight.

Chapter Twenty-Two

With a glass of red wine in hand, Remy sat on his waterside deck idling swatting at mosquitoes on an evening so still he could hear a distant train pass on the other side of the bayou. Soon time to go inside. No use saving the rest of the bottle for Julia. She wasn't coming. He glanced toward Alleman with a few lights gleaming and at the dark bulk of the Queen where NuNu had ruined an epic evening. Yes, time to give up.

Someone buzzed for permission to enter at the gate. He raced inside to hit the button, not bothering to inquire who called. The Regal Restorations truck moved up the drive and parked in front of the house rather than on the pad. She wasn't planning on staying, but perhaps he could change her mind. With a wide, perfect smile, he opened his front door.

Todd got down from the truck and delivered a portfolio. "Ms. Rossi wanted you to have these tonight."

"Tell her thanks. I'll look over her estimates immediately so we can get started on the project. And Todd, once again, I am sorry for implicating you in the fire."

"You outright lied to save a relative."

Remy half-expected the guy to poke out his lower lip in a sulk the Cajuns called *bouderie*. "Family ties are important in the South. You wouldn't understand.

And I didn't lie. I only said you resembled the man who set the fire. Which you do."

"Yet you didn't turn him in."

"He coughed up an alibi. Let's let this go. I assume you will be working with us on the Queen."

"I hope, but I won't forget you made me look ridiculous to Julia. Goodnight."

So, Ms. Rossi had been replaced by Julia. Had she slept with him out of pity—because Remy couldn't imagine any other reason. "Goodnight, Todd."

He'd barely gathered up the wine bottle and the two glasses when the buzzer rang again. He'd be willing to bet Todd forgot something—or maybe Julia had relented. Again, he raced for the front door without bothering to ask who wanted to enter and stepped outside. Stupid, very stupid.

Slick's black SUV emerged from the night. He'd brought company with him. "The old man heard what you done and sent me to deal wit' you, Remy."

"Heard what?" Play dumb, back away, get inside.

"Blackie Tauzin's wife sent one of those press releases to the *Clarion* saying you and Hartz signed a contract to restore that old eyesore on the bayou. We got ears at the newspaper. We can't touch Blackie's wife, and Hartz and his lady are the golden geese of Chapelle, so they're off limits too. But you, Remy, you betrayed our family."

"Tell Nonc his money is safe in a separate account. He can have his investment back if he wants; Black Diamonds will be built someday."

"Don't make no never mind to me. You got to take your licks for selling out to Hartz. Otherwise the whole parish will think the Broussards have gone soft."

A pair of Slick's goons thudded from the SUV and approached Remy on either side. He thought he might stiff arm them and take Slick down with a sweep kick, enough to get inside the house. But someone had gotten between him and the door—NuNu who'd skulked over the fence from his lair of a trailer like a hyena ready to feed.

If he were Bruce Lee or Jackie Chan, he would do a double somersault and break free, but he wasn't that good. His martial arts skills were more defensive than combative. But he might be able to strike an important bargain. "Before you start in on me, promise that Julia Rossi has immunity too, and I won't fight you. I'd also appreciate if you'd leave my teeth intact. Grandma Patty paid for my braces. You don't want her on your back."

Slick shook his head. "I'll ask the old man about your lay. Me, I don't mind bashing a woman, but he has scruples. I know he doesn't want Patty in his face. Who would? Now, you ready to stop talking and take your punishment?"

Struggle would only make it worse. The Broussard's Barn gang secured his arms and legs. Slick blacked one eye, then the other, maybe broke Remy's nose. He pummeled the stomach, but had the decency not to attack the groin. The worse of it came from NuNu who'd worn steel-toed work boots for the occasion. When Remy sagged to the ground, his cousin lit into his ribs with savage kicks while revealing a litany of hatred.

"I hate your fuckin' house and your nice truck and your pretty face and your big deal education." Through swollen eyes, Remy watched the boot draw back for a kick to the mouth. Slick yanked NuNu away.

"Nuh-uh, son. As the old man would say, 'Not the tee't.' You do that, and I'll tell Patty."

"Fuck Patty."

"She's your great-aunt. Show some respect. One more kick, and we're done here."

NuNu delivered a good one. When the two ribs cracked, Remy passed out. He came to in the emergency room of a Lafayette hospital listening to Slick tell the doctor that his cousin had fallen down two flights of metal stairs at home. He was in no shape to deny it. Pumped full of some pretty good painkillers, he came around again in the bed of his black tower. Oh, Julia.

Chapter Twenty-Three

At three a.m., the phone rang next to Julia's ear. Crap! She'd barely gotten to sleep. Thoughts of Remy and working closely with him on the Queen circled and recircled in her mind, never coming to rest. She'd been too easy, jumping into bed with him early on, trying to have her pleasure and save the Queen too. Now, he expected to have her whenever he wanted because he'd delivered the project into her arms like an orphaned baby who needed nurturing. It went against her policy of not sleeping with co-workers, and enforcing that rule would be difficult if they were together every day.

Sure, she was still pissed about his throwing Todd under the streetcar, but the sheriff knew better right from the start. Only her intern's ego had been bruised and nothing else. Because she demanded it, Remy settled that with an apology, insincere and ill-accepted by Todd. They both needed to get over it. And her uncles. What was with them? All that back slapping and saying she'd been too hard on good, old Remy. They'd never approved of a single man she'd gotten involved with, and now they loved Remy. Men!

The phone continued to demand her attention. Only three types of calls came at this hour: family emergencies, building disasters, and pervs who dialed randomly hoping to say something obscene to women only half awake and not expecting it. Regardless, she needed to answer before voice mail asked for a message. She spoke the salutation she used when conducting business or shutting down pervs, a stern, "Rossi, here."

"Joo-ya, oh, Joo-ya."

She nearly told the perv to go to hell before she noticed the number belonged to Remy. The voice didn't sound like his. "Remy, is that you?"

"Un-huh."

"Well, I don't do booty calls at three a.m. or any other time."

"But you could make me feel sooo much better."

She considered the silly request from the usually smooth Remington Broussard and asked, "Are you drunk or high?"

"High on some really good painkillers. Feel like I'm floating a foot above the bed. I need you to climb on top and bring me back to earth."

"If you are taking painkillers, it wouldn't be worth my effort. You'll be too numb."

"That part works independently, don't cha know. Come be with me."

Julia huffed an exasperated sigh into her phone. "I don't rescue druggies, and I certainly don't sleep with them. If I'd known you had a problem…"

"No problem, a—an accident." He fumbled trying to find the right article. "Been to the hospital. Fell down my stairs. Please, please, pretty please, come make me feel better, Joo-ya. I'm all alone."

"How did you manage to get to the hospital and back again?" she questioned, all the while imagining that he'd been entertaining another woman when the accident occurred because she'd been cold to him that afternoon, making it partially her fault. Maybe they'd been drinking heavily which explained why he'd fallen down his own metal staircase.

"Had guests, Slick 'n NuNu 'n some of the gang. Drove me to Lafayette and brought me back again. Gone now. Safe to visit."

"You shouldn't be alone." She'd heard of people taking falls, being discharged, and dying of a blood clot. Remy isolated in his black tower, she couldn't bear the thought.

"Thass what I saaaid. Didn't I?"

"I'm on my way. Can you buzz me in and get to the door?"

"Nope. Doubt if my pals locked up though. C'mon in."

"Right away." She didn't bother with the niceties like a bra or underwear, simply pulled up her jeans and threw on a T-shirt, finger-combed her hair, and shoved the sneakers on her feet. Scooping up her keys, Julia eased out of her bedroom and quietly shut the door.

Despite her care, Marv, clad in black silk pajamas, appeared in his doorway. He didn't sleep well, he claimed. Now she believed him. "Is there a problem? Has the Queen been attacked again?"

"No. Remy took a fall down his stairs and had to go to the emergency room. He's all alone, so I'm going over to his place to make sure he's okay."

"How on earth did he get to a hospital and back?"

"Some of his relatives were there."

"Then, I'd say Remy didn't tumble down that staircase on his own. Be careful, Julia."

"Thanks for the warning. I'll be back in the morning early."

She went on her way, climbed into the truck, and edged it slowly past the darkened motorhome. Once on the road, she gunned the engine and sped toward the nearest bridge, crossing to Remy's side of the bayou. The gate stood open as well as his door, letting in the mosquitoes, wood roaches, and moths. She put an end to that, locked the two of them inside, turned on a light, and started for the stairs. A half-empty wine bottle and two glasses sat on his desk. He'd definitely had company, but while climbing the stairs, she noticed no splotches of blood on the metal treads or landings. Could he be faking simply to lure her in the middle to the night?

Remy heard her coming and emitted a pathetic, "Joo-ya?"

"Yes, I'm here." No, he wasn't faking.

She barely recognized the person propped up in the king-sized bed with the black satin quilt thrown over his legs and the zebra hide bunched at his feet. The area of his chest not bound by white bandages bore purple blotches. A sling held up one arm, but the worst of it was his face. His dark eyes merged with the black rings under them, bridged by a swollen nose. A split and puffy upper lip stretched into a painful white smile to welcome her. At least, he hadn't lost any teeth. However, his deep dimples were obscured by the facial swelling. Only a table lamp lit the room. How much worse would he appear in broad daylight?

"Joo-ya," he said again and held out his good arm, the wrist ringed in bruises.

Julia went to him and lifted the unkempt hair off his brow, touching him in a maternal gesture. "All this happened from a fall down the stairs?"

"Thass the story." He lifted the spread and patted the mattress.

"Really, with a broken arm you want me to sleep with you? You *are* high."

"Not broken. Dislocated shoulder. Few cracked ribs. But you'll be fine."

"I think you mean I'll be fine."

"What I said. Make me feel better."

"You want a reward for being clumsy?"

"Not for what I did. Mostly, I want your hot body next to mine."

"That sounds like the Remy I know, always hitting on me." She sat on the side of the bed, and he lost no time running his hand under her T-shirt and fondling her breast.

"You made it easy for a sick man. Thanks."

"Not my intention. I drove here in a hurry."

He tried the zipper of her jeans, but snagged it halfway down. Julia completed the maneuver herself, kicked off her shoes, and slid in beside him. "Only to keep you warm. You're shivering."

"It's the drugs. Honest, I'm fine below the waist. Wouldn't want the famed Broussard fertility messed up, now would we?"

"You're talking nonsense. Snuggle up and try to sleep—unless I can bring you an ice pack or something." Julia turned out the light on the night table, rolled on her side, and spooned her rump against his hip.

"Or something is what I want. Wide, wide awake."

"I might hurt you."

"No, no. I'll just lie here and enjoy it like a woman. Let you do all the work."

"If your ribs weren't already broken, I'd crack them for that remark." Remy worked one of his legs between hers and used his left arm to lever her over onto his pelvis. "I'd fight you on this, but you're already beat up—and hard. I cannot believe you're hard."

"As quick-setting concrete since you climbed into bed. Ease my pain, Joools."

"One wince, and we're done." She carefully lowered herself on his erection, going slow which only made him grin and split open his swollen lip again. "Your mouth is bleeding."

"Not much. Really don't feel it. All my blood is rushing somewhere else."

Julia leaned forward and positioned her arms carefully on either side of his bandaged ribs. She arched her back and pumped gently up and down. A good enough start though it did little for her—but this was for Remy. Too slow for him, also, as he surprised her with a matching hip thrust as she lowered. Then, they were in tandem, moving in the darkness, experiencing the build, the lift, the climax together. She felt that more than sex connection again, the rightness of their being as one.

He did go on longer than usual thanks to the drugs, but Julia had no complaints. By the time he bucked inside of her, she'd come twice and was ready to dismount. Cuddling would have been nice if he'd had any place left on his chest that didn't seem painfully sore. As his eyes, what she could see of them, closed in sleep, Julia resumed her spoon position and rested too. She'd done what he'd asked and all she could for the moment.

Chapter Twenty-Four

Always an early riser, a must in her profession where they often tried to beat the heat of the day, Julia tugged her T-shirt over her head at dawn and padded down to the kitchen. Scrambled eggs she figured would be best. Maybe some toast cut into strips and well-buttered. She started coffee, beat the eggs, and rejoiced to find a wedge of parmesan in the fridge and dried chives in spice rack to give the bland breakfast more flavor. Orange juice, probably not a good idea with his sore lip, but she poured some for herself while the coffee brewed and the eggs jelled in the pan. Finding a tray stored sideways in a nook of the kitchen, she loaded the breakfast for two and climbed to the bedroom. No Remy in the bed either awake or asleep.

He'd made his way to the bathroom. As he claimed, his legs worked, all of them. Julia tapped lightly on the door. "You okay in there?"

"Fine. No blood in my urine. That's good news."

"I made breakfast. You get to eat in bed today."

"Sounds good." He emerged stark naked and moved toward the covers. Though his legs and taut, slim buttocks showed no damage from the rear, he held himself stiffly trying not to aggravate his ribs. Working his way under the spread again, he held out his hand for the plate.

Julia hung onto it. In the light of day, he did look

worse. The handsome Remy she'd come to love—no, too soon, make that like very much—might never be the same again. Still, the man on the inside counted more, confident and vital and willing to take a chance on saving the Queen. That's what mattered. "Better take a couple of these pain pills with your food. Want me to make an ice pack?"

"Maybe later on the ice. Only one pill. They make me loopy."

"Yes, I noticed."

"Do you plan to feed me? I think I can manage with my left hand."

Julia handed over the food. He spilled some of the eggs on the spread, managed the toast strips fairly well, and held out his hand for the coffee mug as desired, drinking the brew with careful sips. Julia finished her plate and loaded the tray for the return to the kitchen.

"I really should leave, but I'll call you today and see if you need anything. Stay in bed and rest. Anything else I can do for you before I take off?"

"A sponge bath? I'd really like a sponge bath."

"Considering how well you ate breakfast, I think you can manage with one hand."

"Lots of places I can't reach. Don't go."

While she suspected he really wanted more physical contact, his request still tugged at her heart as she gazed on his poor, battered face. "Okay, I'll wash your back. Let's go over to the sink, and I'll fill it."

Julia put one of his thick, black towels on the floor and ran warm water in the basin. Retrieving his bath gel from the shower, she squeezed some on a washcloth, and gave it slight sniff, pure Remy, a clean, sharp scent with a spicy tang. He faced the mirror as she washed above and below his bandaged ribs, under his arms, across his rear and down his legs. He lifted his feet like an obedient horse, allowing her to clean between his toes. When she came up, he made a special request. "Clean behind my balls, would you? Gets musty back there."

Julia reached between his legs and did a thorough job, massaging each one in her hands. A glance in the mirror told her Remy had another part eager to be washed, stroked, coddled. Pressed against his rear, she reached around and wrapped the cloth over his member, worked it up and down, up and down, until the head reared back, and spread its semen on his belly. "That's what you really wanted, right?"

"Oh, yes."

"The pain pill kick in yet?"

"Not quite, but my mind isn't on pain anymore, thanks to you." He turned and took the cloth to clean himself. After he tossed it into the sink, he gave Julia the lightest of kisses. "I wish I could do better than that. You deserve more."

"Damn right, I do. Can I borrow one of your shirts? I can't return to Alleman looking like I won the wet T-shirt contest on spring break."

"You'd get my vote. Help yourself to anything I have."

"Get back into bed. Sleep, play games on your phone, whatever, but rest today."

She put on her rumpled jeans and sneakers, found a T-shirt advertising Broussard's Barn, and hung the one she'd worn to dry on his balcony railing. "I'll return after work, make sure you get fed, and are taking it easy."

"Don't go," he said again.

The incessant wasp-like buzzing of someone desiring entrance to the Black Box interrupted anything else he might have said to persuade her to stay. "Get that for me, would you?"

Julia trotted down the stairs and spoke into the box with a mock-serious inquiry. "Who goes there? Mr. Broussard is too ill for company today." Her formal voice did not fool the person on the other end.

"Exactly why I'm here, Julia Rossi. I received a call this morning from T-Fats that Remy had been in an accident and might need my help. Let me in at once."

"T-Fats? Who is that?" He'd mentioned Slick and NuNu, but no T-Fats.

"My disreputable brother-in-law, his nickname before he turned into Old Broussard. He might be old, but I am not. I demand entrance."

"Right away, Miss Patty. I'll leave the door unlocked." Julia charged up the stairs to warn Remy he had an anxious granny on the way. She broke the news immediately.

He leaned deep into his pillows as if trying to disappear. "They really do hate me. Quick—briefs, running shorts, any top with no sleeves in the bureau drawers. Easiest stuff to get on. I can't cope with her if I'm naked."

"Hey, you didn't dress up for me!"

"No desire to sleep with my granny. Help me get them on right now."

He might have been able to manage his underwear and shorts one-handed, but the top was more of a struggle involving the removal of his arm from the sling, an easing into the armhole, and the restoration of his arm support. The top covered his bandages, but not all of his bruises.

Meanwhile, Remy seemed to keep an ear cocked for the slam of a car door and the relentless tread of his grandmother on the way up the stairs, closer, closer, closer. His forehead beaded with sweat. He sank into a side chair, and held out his feet for his running shoes right before the champagne-blonde head and chubby body overfilled the doorway.

Patty breathed heavily from her climb like a dragon working up steam to shoot blasts of fire. Julia hadn't seen Remy's grandmother other than fully dressed and completely made up. Even chained to an oak tree, the woman had squatted on a cushion so as not to dirty her short-sleeved pantsuit, every hair in place, and full-face putty troweled on her aging skin. Though she certainly slept with a hairnet to preserve her coiffure between weekly salon visits, this morning many of her lacquered curls had escaped around her head, standing up like spiral macaroni. She'd failed to prime her face with foundation, or brighten it with blusher and appeared very pasty. One button on today's yellow pantsuit had missed its hole and gaped open over a plain white cotton bra. Inexplicably, Patty held a covered saucepan in her grip.

Crossing the bedroom, she raised the lid and shoved the pot under Remy's nose. "Cheese grits, your favorite. I was making them for Gid's breakfast, but he can scrounge for himself today. As soon as T-Fats called, I took them off the stove and came right over here, my baby, my poor, poor baby. In a minute, I'll go downstairs and fry an egg to go with them. You can break the yolk and mix it around in the grits just like you did as a boy."

Julia thought Remy's face registered more pain than she'd seen up to this second. "Maybe for lunch. I don't have much appetite. Julia made scrambled eggs for breakfast, so I've eaten. You don't have to stay," he said.

Funny, he'd had plenty of appetite for more than food not too long ago. Patty set the pot on the little table nearest Remy with a loud clunk. She might have been ready to breathe fire before, but now her eyes shot laser beams at Julia.

"I should have been called first, day or night, to take care of you. What exactly is *she* doing here?"

"I asked Jules to sit with me since she's staying nearby. You need your beauty rest as you often told me when I visited. In other words, help yourself to a bowl of cereal and don't wake me. I'm still following your orders."

"This is entirely different. I mean I understand why you didn't call your mother. I doubt Melody would drive up here in the middle of the night. She'd have to cancel all those house showings for her real estate business." Patty moved in close and pinched Remy's jaw to force his mouth open. He gasped at her ungentle touch. "Good, all still there. Remember I paid for those perfect teeth."

Remy rubbed his chin. "How could I forget."

"Well then, I'll take the breakfast dishes downstairs, wash them, and get to work. Time to go." Julia picked up the tray. "I can see you are in good hands. No need to linger."

"Just leave the plates. I'll take care of them. I am sure you are needed at your blue-collar job." Patty bustled over to take charge and seize the tray. Behind his grandmother's back, Remy made a desperate "call me" sign to Julia. If he'd been able to show the panicked whites of his eyes, he would have.

"Gran, Julia has two college degrees and owns that business."

"I'm sure she understands what I mean. Don't you, Julia?"

Yep, get away from her grandson, the one she'd tried to sell her on when they'd first met at the bakery. The one Julia thought might be gay. So wrong about that!

Julia sent Remy a final sympathetic smile. "Get well soon." She added a finger wave and headed for the steps.

Miss Patty's loud assessment followed her down the stairwell. "You don't need that Italian sexpot when your gran is here to help you. She doesn't have the decency to wear a bra, and don't think I didn't notice. All that bouncy jiggle when she walks. Don't even think about going running. What was she doing letting you dress like that? Let me help you into a nice pair of pajamas. You must stay in bed."

Poor Remy, her lover, her rival, now her business partner, and who knew what else?

Chapter Twenty-Five

She'd sneak inside, put on a bra, panties, and work clothes, or so Julia thought. Barely beyond the door of Alleman, Marv called, "In the kitchen, Jules. Do you want breakfast? How is Remy?"

Trapped. Now, she had to put in a brief appearance. She poked her head around the entry. Her uncles dined on omelets overstuffed with ham, cheese, onions, and green peppers. Todd went with all veggies. Marv drank coffee from an elegant, gold-rimmed cup and perused the morning paper. He glanced her way. "Don't worry, I told your crew you'd gone on an errand of mercy. Come, come, give us a full report." Marv patted the chair next to him.

Too aware of Patty's comment on her jiggling breasts, Julia stiffed her shoulders and crossed the kitchen very sedately. Her uncles averted their eyes from her chest. Todd couldn't seem to raise his higher than her neck. Marv simply poured a cup of coffee. More comfortable at the table, she accepted the coffee and gave them a report.

"Huh," Sal, who had plenty of experience with brawls, said. "Sounds more like he took a beating than fell down the stairs, somebody holding his arms while they hit him in the face and torso."

"Yeah, he'd be black and blue all over if he took a tumble," Sammy agreed.

"Whatever he did, he probably deserved it." Todd crunched his whole-wheat toast savagely.

"What I believe he did was save the Queen, Todd, so shame on you. He wouldn't admit it, but I think the Broussards got wind of his deal with Jonathan Hartz and weren't pleased. Anyhow, it's out of my hands now. Miss Patty showed up to take care of him." Julia busied herself spreading fig preserves on a biscuit she didn't really want.

"Ooooh, poor Remy." Marv shook a sympathetic head. "I thought I might take him a basket of muffins and a container of chicken soup, but I'm simply not brave enough. Regardless, the word is definitely out." He showed her the *Clarion's* headline. *Hartz cuts deal to save the Queen*. "No credit given to Remy."

"As I said, out of our hands. Let's finish repairing those cracks on the second floor today." Julia wiped her fingers on a napkin, rose, and showed the men only her back on the way out of the room to dress for work.

They labored all morning, paused for a lunch of chicken soup laced with hot sauce originally meant for Remy, and completed their task late in the day. Julia lay back in Alleman's deep, claw-footed tub and soaked away the sweat after washing her hair with the usual floral shampoo. No word from Remy, and she'd used work to stave off the urge to call him. His grandmother would probably hang up on her. Miss Patty appeared to be a great woman to have on your side and a terror to have against you.

At this point in the job, they'd pack their equipment in the trucks and steer both plus the motorhome to New Orleans. When the plaster dried, she'd return to supervise the painters and paperhangers.

They'd complete the project well before autumn when the heat broke and Mr. Getty planned to return for the festival season. She'd read the Hartz proposal making Remy the supervisor for the renovation of the Bayou Queen, but when they could start, no one knew with the condition he was in currently.

Around ten, more than ready for sleep after the previous night, Julia relented and made the call he'd begged for behind his grandmother's back. Remy answered instantly, sounded tired and groggy from his meds, but not hopped up like last evening.

"I gather the coast is clear."

"Yeah. Remember you pointed out my lack of bedrooms. Turned out to be an advantage. Even Patty wouldn't put me out of my bed in order to stay overnight. She just left. Said she's too old to sleep on my uncomfortable couches, but will definitely return in the morning to feed me, wash my back, give me a shave. I'm thinking of growing a beard. Just smother me with a pillow, and let me die. I wish they'd left me at the hospital." Misery, pure misery, sounded in his voice.

"Have you gotten in touch with your mother? Maybe she'd drive Patty away."

"She would. Mom can deal with people in the most steel magnolia kind of way, but I don't want her to see me until I've gone from black and blue to green and yellow. My parents warned me not to move here or get involved with Dad's side of the family."

"And that would have saved you from falling down the stairs?" Julia allowed skepticism to creep into her voice. "I'm not stupid, Remy."

"Far, far from stupid. It's me who lacks brains for

getting myself mixed up in all this. I only wanted to keep you out of it. So, my relatives taught me a lesson, and Patty is part of the punishment. I can take my licks if you are okay."

"Why wouldn't I be okay?"

"You will be. Are you coming over tonight?" He seemed both sure and quick to change the subject.

"No, I don't relish sneaking out of your place at dawn to avoid another run-in with your grandmother. I wouldn't want my sexpot reputation to get around town." She couldn't help the small surge of anger.

"It will. Nothing can prevent that. It's how Patty operates when a person falls out of favor. We might as well enjoy the notoriety."

"I won't. Look, we're cleaning up and going back to New Orleans tomorrow."

"Don't leave! We can start on plans to revive the Queen."

"You aren't up to walking a job site, and what I suggested is in the papers Todd delivered. Study them when you can read again, make notes, and get in touch when you are ready to talk. I have a business to run, and that's what I'm going to do. See you in a few months, Remy. Take care and don't fall down any more stairs on my account."

Julia disconnected, knowing she should have said the words, "I love you, Remy Broussard," but afraid to admit and commit. Hitting a man in a weakened state with those words made the outcome unpredictable. Considering the drugs he'd swallowed, no telling if he'd recall what she said or did.

When she returned, would the town have turned against her? She could handle that by immersing herself in the revival of the Queen. But, might Remy feel less passion, less need and desire for her after his grandmother's incessant onslaught? Better to retreat now, and come back fighting.

Chapter Twenty-Six

After two weeks, Remy reclaimed his door key and gate remote and shoved his grandmother out the door with his one good arm. Other than leaving him in drug-induced sleep at night, she'd left his side only to keep her weekly coffee klatch with Pammy, which did not last nearly long enough. He thanked Patty for her care and the refrigerator so stuffed with her special dishes he could barely close the door, but made it clear that he did not plan to spend one more morning in bed. Even felons come up for parole, and he intended to claim his. With the swelling around his eyes reduced, he wanted no more than to get to work on the plans for the Queen.

However, nothing that happened in Chapelle ever stayed in Chapelle. Cajun roots spread out wide as the live oaks to neighboring towns and cities. Mamas called their children working away or vice versa. News, or rather gossip, rode on the wind like the nearly invisible seeds of the Spanish moss. Though he hadn't left the Black Box in days he imagined word had gotten around about his "fall down the stairs." Certainly, Patty told her cousin, and informed LeJeune Pommier in addition to anyone else in the bakery of his accident. The most sympathetic would express their wishes for a swift recovery with a sad shake of the head. Miss Lolly and Miss Maxie had already called saying they'd pray for him. Not one of those people believed for a second he'd taken a spill.

Eventually, the tendrils reached Mandeville and uprooted his mother from her home and business. She arrived in her BMW a half hour after this grandmother's departure as Remy sat drinking Patty's strong Cajun coffee and finishing the stack of pancakes she'd prepared before her ouster. Tall, slim, and collected, she still wore her blonde hair long and over her shoulders. Trenchant blue eyes sat in a fair face pampered to resist wrinkles. She surveyed his healing complexion with cool reserve, no tears or gentle hugs from Melody Broussard. With uncomfortable awareness, he realized she resembled most of the women he'd dated. Not Julia though, she was the exception. His mother was capable of warmth, but not when you'd failed to take her advice and gotten yourself into trouble.

"What have they done to you, Remy?" she asked.

He shrugged and noted his shoulder barely ached anymore. "All this. Don't worry. I can still give you grandchildren."

"That thought never entered my mind. Besides, Amelia has bestowed the title of grandmother on me twice," Melody answered as if she found the idea distasteful to a former beauty queen. She eyed him up and down. "When did you start wearing pajamas? When you lived at home, you usually slouched around the house in those saggy, flannel bottoms."

No need to inform her he rarely wore even that to bed, a privilege of living alone. "Gran bought them for me when she found out I didn't own any full sets. Same store where she gets Granddad's clothes—obviously." Remy considered his garment, pale blue with darker pinstripes. Another pair, yellow with brown checks, lay in his bureau drawer. "I plan to get dressed shortly."

"Finish your breakfast. I'm in no rush." His mother poured a cup of coffee. "Decaf?"

"You've got to be kidding me. Granny made it. There's skim milk in the refrigerator if you want to water it down."

She did. "Do you have any yogurt? I only had toast before I set out. How can you find anything in here? It's so cluttered." Melody held up two containers, one of rice dressing, the other of shrimp etouffee. "With starchy foods. Do you want me to clean this stuff out?"

"No, put it in the freezer. Whatever else Patty does, she can cook."

"You need fresh fruits and vegetables to heal, lots of vitamin C." Melody ferreted out a cup of blueberry yogurt and peered at the expiration date. "Only a day overdue. Good enough."

The gate buzzer sounded before she could take a seat at Remy's table. He winced, but not with pain. "Probably Gran trying to regain entrance. She'll say she forgot something."

"I'll take care of this."

His mother would without a doubt. She slapped the yogurt container on the table and marched down the stairs to do battle, but returned only minutes later with a large fruit basket, heavy on the citrus. Melody breached the little white envelope without being invited. "Evidently, Celine and Jon Hartz believe in vitamin C too. They wish you a speedy recovery and a quick return to work on the Bayou Queen."

"You know, Mom, the swelling around my eyes has gone down. I am perfectly capable of reading for myself."

"Frankly, I wanted to see if this came from the Italian sexpot out to seduce you into marriage—some say."

Remy covered his bruised face with his hands, but didn't press very hard. Finally, he met his mother's eyes. "You should realize by now Granny started that rumor. She liked Julia well enough until she caught her taking care of me the night I was injured, trespassing on her right to smother me with affection. Jules runs Regal Restorations and led the charge to save the Queen. We were at odds until I made the deal with Hartz."

His mother had a real talent for arching her lips in a wry smile and raising her perfectly shaped brows to show skepticism. "You mean she hasn't seduced you?"

"More the other way around, or maybe she simply allowed me to make love to her. Jules has a mind of her own. Are you upset by that? Gran was."

Melody lapped up a spoonful of yogurt and rolled it on her tongue before answering. "Believe it or not, I am aware you sleep with women. Yes, I did check her out. That's what Google intends. From what I've read, Julia Rossi might be a good match for you. The work her firm does is displayed in all the architectural and preservation magazines. In fact, she's restored the homes of some of my friends. *Louisiana Life* showed a very fetching picture of her in plasterer's garb, trowel in hand. It was rather cute."

"Don't let Julia hear you say that. She rarely takes compliments well unless it regards her work. Doesn't matter. You won't run into her. She returned to New Orleans after her confrontation with Gran."

"Pity, but shows she has the good sense to get as

far from that woman as possible."

"I think I'm the one who ran Julia off. That night I came on as very needy and not much better the following night. What woman wants a man who begs her to stay like a love-stricken teen? Weak, I showed myself as weak." Feeling the need for energy after that confession, Remy broke an orange free of the basket's shrink wrap and peeled it by driving his thumbnail under its thick skin. The first section he freed tasted sour after eating pancakes with syrup. That suited his mood.

"She is returning to work on the Queen, right? You'll have another chance with her."

Remy shook his head. "I haven't heard from her since she left."

"Did you try calling her?'

"My phone vanished while Gran reigned. She declared I need peace and quiet. After a while, I thought calling her again would be weak, like I said. Besides, she hasn't bothered with me since she left. However, I plan to impress her with my thoughtful notes on her proposal for the Queen and my perfectly compatible kitchen addition."

"I'm sure she'll be astounded—and give you another chance if she has the sense I gave her credit for. Now, get dressed and walk up and down your driveway. Exercise will aid in erasing those bruises. No bones were broken, I take it?"

His mother did an excellent job of not revealing overwhelming concern, unlike his grandmother who had moaned constantly, "Oh, my handsome boy will never be the same again." Remy knew what his mother really asked.

"Only a few ribs. The doctor told me I'd look pretty much the same as before. My facial bones are intact, no separation of the retina. I have my sight and can get to work. Frankly, I think Slick pulled his punches." He'd let the truth slip, but could see that she'd already known.

"Exercise. I'll clean the dishes. I plan to stay exactly seven days, brought a sleeping bag along, as I remember how you live. I'll make sure you get good nutrition, and are on the road to full recovery before I leave. You won't have to lock me out." Melody Broussard made it clear she did not coddle her children.

Remy moved to find his running clothes hidden away by his grandmother, but paused to say, "Thanks for coming."

"Some people are too proud to ask for help."

"Not me. I begged Julia for it, and now I feel like an idiot."

"Don't. Men can't be macho all the time, nor should they be." She put the syrup away, stowed the butter, and ran water to hand wash the small stack of dishes.

Remembering how his grandmother thought, Remy found his running clothes beneath the yellow and brown checked pajamas he would never wear again. Maybe Goodwill could use them. He dressed and put on the athletic shoes with the most support to minimize the ache in his ribs. A few trips up and down the long drive should do the trick at this point in his convalescence.

The fledgling live oaks gave little shade, but the jackhammer heat of the afternoon wouldn't arrive until after noon. Dew still lay heavy on the grass, and the air smelled mildly of the horses in the neighboring field and their droppings. Good country air Old Broussard would call that. He couldn't breathe deep yet, but the sheer movement of walking helped improve his mood—until his second time around—he saw NuNu leaning on the fence and flicking the ash of his cigarette on Remy's property.

"You look fine in green and yellow, cousin," he gloated, showing shiny white incisors, a new dental bridge in place.

"I see Nonc finally paid for your repairs. A reward for doing his dirty work?"

"Oh, I would have done it for free. My pleasure to see you grovel on the ground instead of up on your high horse. I fell out of favor when I torched the Queen without running it by the old man first, but now I'm back."

"You won't be there for long because you are a screw-up, NuNu." What was he doing, taunting the guy before his ribs knit? Remy walked on, but NuNu inserted his booted feet on the first rung of the pole fence to hike himself over and intercept his cousin.

Remy forced himself to keep the same measured pace he'd set in the beginning. Show no fear to a Broussard. His goal: get to the door in one piece.

NuNu fell in beside him. "Would have damaged you more if Slick let me. He's my daddy, you know."

"You aren't much like him. Slick follows orders to a tee and keeps his promises, good or bad. That's why he's the right-hand man out at the Barn. He'll take over someday—but not you." Why did he keep picking on the man? Not wise.

NuNu intentionally stepped into his path, jostling his sore ribs. Remy retaliated with a sharp elbow to the man's skinny gut. He paid for that action with a twinge of pain.

Before NuNu could strike back, Melody appeared in the doorway. "Why Cousin NuNu, how nice of you to visit. I'm afraid Remy isn't up to company yet after that unfortunate fall, but perhaps later. We'll have you over for dinner another time. Wouldn't that be nice?" His mother could drown people in pure tupelo honey when she wanted. They floundered in the sweet stickiness.

NuNu appeared flummoxed by an elegant lady treating him nicely instead of crossing to the other side of the road when she saw him coming. "Uh, yes, ma'am. Guess I'll be going now." He retreated across the fence as if she'd set the dogs on him.

"Great, my mother had to save me from that scum. I wonder what Julia would think about that?" Remy dashed the sweat from his forehead.

"I'm sure she would have done the same, but perhaps in a different manner. Julia Rossi seems like a scrapper to me if she can succeed so well in a man's world. Come inside. Get some rest. Eat another orange."

Chapter Twenty-Seven

His mother left precisely when she swore she would. Remy spent most of his convalescence on his third-floor balcony taking a tan he thought might help with the bruises, living on his grandmother's cooking and his mom's stock of fresh produce. He worked on sketches of his conception of what the Queen should resemble when fully restored. As his ribs and shoulder mended, he'd gone to the drawing board to design the plans for the new kitchen, of which he was especially proud. Maybe Julia had been right. In his heart of hearts he'd wanted to save the hotel.

He'd rebuild the annex with brick and plaster compatible with the older building: slate floors, a dressed-up metal fire door leading into the hotel and a wide outer door for deliveries and easy escape in case of smoke and flames. All the appliances and the cooler were the most up to date he could find, along with excellent illumination for the staff.

Remy wrangled with the staircases, not the wide one in the lobby where couples could pass, but the two dark corridors leading from the ballroom floor. Good that the building had two to meet the fire codes, though the lighting would have to be considerably improved and the steps reinforced. Hell, they'd have to pull all new wiring anyhow along with replacing the plumbing to turn some of the rooms into baths. Guests today rarely wanted to queue up to brush their teeth and use the commode in the two tiny spaces set apart for their needs on the third floor. Maybe he could fit in a small, European-style elevator there instead. As for the fourth, in the Twenties, two large suites with full bathing facilities had been carved out of the single rooms. The last owners dwelled there in decaying splendor with a grand view. The deep, claw-footed tubs had rust stains and inground dirt now, but they should consider restoring the space to Art Deco glory instead of going full-nineteenth century throughout the building. He'd run that idea by Hartz—and Julia.

His eyes turned toward Alleman where the recently planted bamboo had yet to reach the height needed to give Mr. Getty his privacy. With the rain and heat spurring the bushes along exactly like the sugar cane, they'd reach full growth by fall. For now, Remy kept an eye on the place for Julia's return. He wished she lay beside him, tanning and preferably naked, giving her insight on his ideas.

Turning his head in another direction enabled him to keep track of NuNu's comings and goings. Not wanting to be caught off guard again, he took his walks after the old junker his cousin drove left for the Barn, or elsewhere. NuNu didn't act on orders. He fueled himself with jealousy. His anger rattled around in his brain like a loose nut in the metal bed of a truck. Remy needed to be cautious, ready for a next time.

Remy considered his sketch of the ballroom, adding the plaster pilasters Julia had mentioned and some potted palms along the walls. Four chandeliers hanging from the restored coffered ceiling lit the space and subtle recessed lighting the walls. A couple waltzed across the parquet floor, she in a hoop skirt, he in a Confederate uniform, perhaps the last dance before the place became a military hospital in 1863. The woman, dark hair piled high, resembled Julia, and the man bore some likeness to himself. He wondered if she would notice.

Movement at Alleman caught his eye. Not Marv, not Julia, but Todd crossing the lawn on long legs, like the bayou herons. What a letdown—but where Todd trod, Julia would not be far behind. Remy packed his sketching supplies and slipped the drawing into the portfolio. No, he would not call asking for an audience too easily refused. He'd simply drive to Alleman and lay his dreams at her feet now that Black Diamonds no longer stood between them. He'd apologize for calling in the night, begging her to come to him, begging her to stay. He'd—he'd better get into his truck and do that immediately before he decided against it.

At Alleman, the place bustled with activity. Paperhangers applied paste to long strips of period wallpaper. Painters moved up and down the staircase lugging cans, brushes, and rollers. If seeing Julia's wonderful finish coat covered gave him a pang, he wondered how much more it must bother her, but she was not among the workmen. Remy moved to Marv's domain in the kitchen where coffee urns lined the counter and trays of donuts filled the table. No Julia, no Marv, no sign of the uncles. Surely, she hadn't left the final touches in Todd's neophyte hands?

He continued out the back and surveyed the yard where crepe myrtles big as small trees bloomed in white, purple, and shades of pink, reliably putting on a show in the heat because the species had been brought to Louisiana from India centuries ago. Standing by the tubs of blue Lily of the Nile on the rear verandah, Remy shaded his eyes and found the person he least wanted to see next to NuNu: Todd, holding a clipboard like the man in charge.

Six weeks of New Orleans cooking had put some meat on his skinny bones and manual labor built up his muscles. A light tan coated his formerly pasty complexion like paint laid over plaster. Remy's mind flashed to his own fantasy of nude sunbathing with Julia and back again. The silly soul patch was no more and revealed a deep dimple in Todd's chin, exactly the kind of feature women loved to caress with their thumbs. Often enough, his sexual partners had traced the deep grooves that bracketed Remy's mouth, which he stretched into a smile.

The scar on his upper lip tugged a little, but Slick had spared his teeth as promised. Remy moved toward Todd and held up his fist for a bump. "Todd, my man, lookin' good. New Orleans must agree with you." What exactly was he doing here? Sophisticated Remy Broussard shook hands and did not bump fists. Lookin' good, my man? Did he actually want to curry favor with Todd to get on Julia's good side again?

Todd held onto the clipboard and did not return the bump. His light eyes, somehow less watery than before, maybe due to less computer time, squinted at Remy. He stood more confidently—like a man who'd slept with a woman way out of his league. "You have a head injury too?"

"No, no. Got the all clear from Dr. Bourgeois a few days ago. Is Julia around? I've been working on plans for the Queen and want to show them to her." Remy fingered the small bump on the bridge of his nose where the cartilage had separated. The doctor said he could have that repaired with rhinoplasty, but for the time being he possessed no desire for another swollen nose and blackened eyes. Still, rubbing it had become a habit he should break.

"No, she's not. I'm in charge of the punch list until she returns. I'm supposed to write down any detail not up to the standards of Regal Restorations." Todd hugged the clipboard to his slightly broader chest.

"What, no uncles to take over?"

"Sal and Sammy stayed in New Orleans. They don't like the interior design work, too girly."

"I see. Don't worry, I won't fight you for Mr. Getty's punch list." But he would for Julia. "Do you know where she's gone? Over to the Hartz place or maybe Jane's house?"

"Oh, no. She said she had a craving for the local beignets. It's not like her to hurt Marv's feelings after he made a special run to the donut shop for us. She's acting sort of odd today." *Same as you*, Todd's tone implied.

"What day of the week is it? Sorry, I kind of lost track of time while I recuperated." His urgent tone did nothing to reassure Todd about a probable head injury.

"Wednesday. Why does it matter?"

"No matter. I'll come back later. You take good care of that punch list now." He must get to town before bayou water and lime mixed together in a volatile combination.

****

Prior to returning to Chapelle, Julia considered her wardrobe carefully. Exactly what would an Italian sexpot wear? Tight jeans—she owned those, one pair so snug they defined the crack in her butt and were rarely worn. Other than that, she appeared to have only work clothes, more jeans, tons of tops, business suits, and a few gowns of the little black variety that could be dressed up or down for art openings or cocktails with clients. She finally settled on a brilliant red top that hugged her breasts and might show a little cleavage if tugged down far enough. Jules liked her breasts. Not overly large, they looked fine and stayed out of the way. Despite what Patty said, they jiggled very little. She'd have to wear a push-it-up-and-together bra to create the right effect.

Shoes, another problem. Work boots, sneakers, pumps with practical heels, and some stylish black ones with thinner, higher heels she wore with the dresses. A pair of the last must do. As for accessories, how about the crucifix on the silver chain her Aunt Franny gave her for confirmation, unworn and still in its box? Was it threateningly Italian enough? She needed hoop earrings, clip-ons since Julia remained the only girl in the Rossi family who'd never gotten around to piercing her ears. She had a pair somewhere from a Grease-themed movie party. They went with the very tight jeans. Found them buried under other costume jewelry like an unappreciated treasure and added them to the pile. Italian sexpot costume complete. Julia bagged it and stashed it in the motorhome's storage compartment.

As she sat outside Pommier's Bakery adding a slash of red lipstick and enhanced eye makeup with the aid of her truck's rearview mirror, Julia chomped on the gum she felt added to her character and pondered if what she was about to do might not be the wisest course. She'd lose the support of the Historic Preservation Committee, but Remy had signed the contract with Hartz. Technically, Patty's group had no say in the deal anymore, but Julia would miss some of its eccentric members. If his grandmother's hold over Remy was as strong as she thought, he might look elsewhere for restoration services. So be it. She'd get over him. She didn't need a wimp in her life.

Remy's battered face haunted her during her stay in the city. She tried twice to reach him. He did not pick up. He'd been out of his mind that night and possibly didn't remember services rendered. While he clearly didn't want to be left to his grandmother's mercies, family took care of family in both her world and his. Besides, while confident in bed, Julia wasn't too sure about her nurturing abilities.

Seldom ill, she tended to push through any pain, menstrual or other, like everyone else on the job. Sure, she'd patched up Sal and Sammy a few times, put an ice pack on a black eye or a butterfly bandage on a cut, but Remy's injuries went way beyond that. If she hadn't heard the cutting remark as she left, most likely she'd be thanking Patty for nursing him back to health today instead of plotting to make a scene all of Chapelle would hear about and remember. No one insulted Julia Rossi. She'd fired men for saying less.

Julia opened her door and took a minute to roll up her jeans, showing off more leg, and discarding the larger, baggy T-shirt she'd worn to escape Alleman. She fluffed her hair, already bigger than usual with the humidity, and not subdued into a tail or topknot, put her heels to the ground, and clipped into the bakery, shutting the door hard enough to set its bells jingling wildly. She received the attention she wanted. Patty's friends, occupying most of the tables in imitation of their leader, stared her way. Julia breezed by Patty and Pammy as if they did not exist and added extra sway to her hips. "LeJeune, two dozen beignets to go, please."

The hairy-armed baker goggled as if he didn't recognize her. "I have some coming out of the fryer in a minute, ma'am—Miss Julia?"

"*Grazie mille*," she answered in her minimal Italian. "I need to say hello to someone." Jiggling as much as possible, she moved toward Patty's table and held out her arms. "As you can see, the Italian sexpot is back in town. How is your grandson doing? Or did you smother him to death?"

Though Patty's cheeks rouged with more than high blood pressure, she managed to spit a little venom in Julia's direction. "Now you've let us see you as you really are, a low-class temptress trying to lead a man back to New Orleans by his—his man parts."

"I doubt Remy has a dick left after being in your care for six weeks."

Gasps from a riveted audience filled a momentary silence so complete the sizzle of the deep fat fryer emitted the loudest noise.

Patty took time to prepare her next volley. "You abandoned him in his time of need. Of course, I had to step in and take care of my grandson. My group has continued to guard the Queen in your absence. If the Broussards pushed Remy down the stairs, what might they do to the hotel while you went off to party in the city with that young intern of yours? I know you can't help yourself. It's that hot Italian blood."

That set Julia back so far she ignored the last smear

on her character and heritage. She'd thought the Queen safe once the contract went into effect, but Patty knew her kin better than she did. The wad of gum in her mouth seemed to grow larger, stopping her words. She removed it and stuck it under Patty's table. "Thank you for that. Your greatest strength is jealously guarding things. You all but shoved me out of Remy's house."

"It is what I do best because I know this town. I protect what I love. You are no better than my daughter-in-law forcing my son to move to Mandeville to cover her infidelity."

"Oh, I don't think he was forced so much as didn't want to practice law here with his father," Pammy said, realized her mistake, and shoved a pecan tart into her wide maw.

LeJeune Pommier rushed over to hand Julia two white bakery bags and hustle her out of his shop. She dug in her cleavage for the bills to pay him. They'd gone limp from her sweat.

"Ah, I'll get your change."

The bells sounded again. No one took their eyes off Patty's table.

"Keep the change. No worries, Patty. I don't need a wuss for a lover."

"Oh, Remy told her to leave after two weeks. He really hurt her feelings," Pammy said.

Patty turned on her cousin. "Shut up, dimwit. We don't need another whore in our family. As for you, Julia, if the tight top fits, you have to wear it. You're no better than a—"

Julia didn't answer. She opened one of her bags, selected a beignet mounded with powdered sugar from the top and crammed it into Patty's open mouth. It left

209

her adversary's red face white as plaster dust and stoppered her nasty words. Jules turned on her high heels to stride out the door—and ran straight into Remy's chest.

Patty spit out the donut with the aid of a backslap from Pammy. "You saw what she did to me, Remy!"

"You're tough. You can handle it." He hooked his arm around Julia's elbow and escorted her, clipping along on her heels, a little roughly toward the door.

"That's right, throw her out!" Patty shrieked. "Send her back to New Orleans."

He got Julia out on the sidewalk and slammed the door hard enough to make the little bells sound like the church chimes. He gripped her shoulders. "So you think I'm a wuss."

"You didn't call or answer mine."

"Because my grandmother took my phone, and I was in no shape to buy another. Let me get one thing clear, I am not a wuss." He swept her hair back from her ear and plucked the hoop from her lobe. His lips replaced it, sucking. Julia felt the small scar pressed against her skin. He worked his way down her neck, bending her back over his arm, possessed her mouth, and let her up only when breathless.

"Follow me to the Black Box. I have plans for you. Nice outfit by the way."

"Just something I threw together to annoy Patty."

"Save it for another time. We have a big audience. Let's get out of here."

Julia glanced toward the bakery window. Faces, some avid, some scandalized—Patty Broussard's among them—pressed against the glass. LeJeune Pommier craned to see from the back of the crowd.

Julia nodded. At this very minute, she'd follow Remy Broussard anywhere.

Chapter Twenty-Eight

Remy kept checking his rearview mirror to make sure Julia followed and did not veer off toward Alleman. She stuck to his bumper like an experienced tailgater all the way to his doorstep. Once inside, Julia cupped his face and ran her finger over the slight scar on his lip and the small bump on his nose. "I wouldn't have these fixed. They make you look tougher."

Probably not shaving for a week added to his image as well, because she caressed his beard before urgently unbuttoning the blue chambray shirt he'd thrown on with jeans the second he noticed Todd in the yard and knew Julia had returned to Chapelle. "I need to see that the rest of you is healed before I take advantage." Her hands ran over his ribs and across his stomach. "You've lost some weight. Nice tan, though."

"After I shoved Gran out the door, my mother showed up for a week. Mostly, I lived on what they left in the fridge and a huge fruit basket sent by Hartz. Not much else to do but lie around on the deck. If you're satisfied, I have plans…"

"So do I, and I'm not satisfied yet. It's been six long weeks for me, Remy." She backed him against his desk.

"Same for me, but I didn't have Todd to keep me company all day and all night."

Julia slapped his newly recovered cheek with a

force that showed she owned some muscle, no girly tap this. He rubbed at the sting she left behind and hoped he wouldn't have to nurse another bruise and concoct a story to explain it. Those blue eyes he'd found so attractive from their first meeting blazed with a fire incendiary enough to leave blisters.

"What is it with you and Todd? Did you honestly believe the rumors your grandmother spread? You should know me well enough to realize I don't sleep with my interns or my co-workers!" She poked his bare chest with a fingernail he had to be glad she kept short or she might have punctured his unguarded flesh.

"I guess I'm jealous that he's always with you while I've wasted six weeks alone."

"Days! He's with me days learning a trade and how to run a business. My uncles showed him Bourbon Street and the bars they like to frequent. I didn't get a decent day's work out of him after those sprees. Okay, once we went dancing. Todd sucks at it."

"I'm fairly good myself. We need to make a date to do that—among other things I'm better at than Todd. He wishes he could do you. Don't deny it." Her comments about the intern soothed, but her fingernail prodded him again—and left a crescent-shaped mark on his taut, tanned belly.

"I just said I don't sleep with co-workers. If we're ready to start restoring the Queen, you've become one of them."

Remy felt a distinct disappointment below the belt. He tried to counter it. "Technically, I'm hiring you, and we haven't signed that contract yet." Wrong move.

"Oh, so Patty did turn you against me."

"Patty has nothing to do with this. I apologize for

letting her push you out of my life, and for that pity call in the middle of the night. Both were unfair." There, he'd said the words without seeming too wussy.

Now, she stroked his burning cheek. "You were hurt and drugged. No apologies necessary. I doubt you remember the good parts."

"Jules, the good parts were all that kept me going these last six weeks."

His plans in paper and ink fled from his mind. His hands went to her rump in those too-tight jeans. He hiked her hard against his crotch, fully encouraged again. Julia laid her lips on his bare chest and licked her way around his nipples leaving smears of red lipstick behind like blood as if he'd been wounded again. Nope, feeling great.

Remy spun her around and hiked her hips onto his desk. He peeled off her jeans and panties, taking her high heels with them to the floor. The small statues that anchored his plans rolled and tumbled. Fly unzipped, he sank himself deep into this amazing woman—and learned one more thing about Julia Rossi. A good argument excited her. He found her ready. Both had six dry weeks to make up.

Julia lay back on the desk and drew his mouth to her lips. His hands, hot with desire, made prints on the cool surface of the glass as he drove into her. Her short nails scored his back beneath the unbuttoned shirt. He felt no pain, only ecstasy. He loved her wild like this. He loved her. Maybe, he should thank his grandmother, but never would.

****

Julia let herself go. After weeks of wondering if she and Remy had any future, she no longer doubted.

What form that took, she did not know, but for now it was enough to have him arching over her delivering pleasure with each deep stroke. The heat of his flesh, the roughness of his beard against her neck and across the tops of her breasts drove her to climax. He went on as if he didn't notice and rebuilt the fire between her thighs to blazing again before he finished.

"Not a wuss," he murmured as his head sank between the breasts he'd managed to free early in their throes.

Julia raked her fingers through that midnight hair of his and stroked his nape. "I think you are going to have to prove that to me over and over again."

"Any time, any place, anywhere." Remy raised her off the glass top of his desk and marveled that they hadn't fractured it.

The Degas ballerina suffered a broken leg, however. Julia set the one-limbed dancer upright on its pedestal. "I think NOMA carries these because of Degas' connection to New Orleans. I'll replace it, money well spent."

She drew up her red cotton bikini pants, dispensed with the hooker bra, and lowered the scarlet shirt over her breasts. Let Remy enjoy what jiggle she possessed. Jules padded toward first floor powder room to do some restoration of her own. Halfway there, she stopped, arrested by the drawings pinned over Remy's Black Diamonds designs. Her finger moved along the row: the restored lobby, the modern kitchen hidden behind a metal door embossed to fit in with the period style of the place, a suite straight out of the 1920's, and her vision of the completed ballroom captured on paper. "Oh, Remy, that's us dancing beneath the four chandeliers. You put in the pilasters. Don't you look wonderful in your Confederate uniform?"

"I recreated the image you described, but I doubt any Broussard danced there during the Civil War. One officer claimed that the Cajuns would eat anything and fought fiercely, but had to be chained to the trees at night to keep them from going home after being drafted. The French-speakers didn't consider it their conflict for the most part. They tended to rely on large families to work their small farms, not slaves. If anything, my ancestors hosted house dances—that eventually morphed into Broussard's Barn. That's my true heritage." Remy shook his head ruefully.

Julia moved to him. "My family didn't get to New Orleans until after the war, so many Italian and Sicilian immigrants at that time people began to hate and fear them. But we thrived, opening groceries and restaurants, carving stone, laying bricks, and spreading plaster. That's my family story. Still, girls do dream of beautiful, wide-skirted dresses and a waltz with a handsome man no matter what their origin. Thank you for creating that for me."

If Remy had discovered her wild side, now she revealed her tenderness. Julia Rossi—he'd never figure her out as he had other women and grown bored with them. Her hands went to his bare ribs again, almost tickling them before she buttoned his shirt. "Have you eaten breakfast?"

"I had a cup of coffee. There's still some left upstairs."

"That might go well with the twenty-three beignets I have in the car. You need feeding."

"In every way."

216

They despoiled the black satin bedspread with powdered sugar and more sex before Julia's phone rang. Gloriously naked except for her crucifix necklace, she took the call. "Yeah, yeah, I'm looking over Remy's plans for the Queen. They are great. Anything you can't handle without me? Okay, tell Marv I won't be back for lunch... Is it?" She checked her watch, two p.m. "Sorry, I lost track of time. Oh, that? You know how people in small towns exaggerate. I did tell Patty off publicly, Sal, but I'm sure she's exaggerating. Remy still wants us for the restoration project. No harm done, right?...That so. Okay, I'll tell him."

Remy brushed some powdered sugar off his dark patch of chest hair and raised his brows. "What has my grandmother done now?"

"Only what she promised, withdrawn the watchers from the Queen though she had some trouble removing Miss Lolly and Miss Maxie. The building has been unprotected since noon."

"That shouldn't be a problem. As far as the old man is concerned, I took my lumps like a man for betraying the family, and we're done. He made NuNu apologize for starting the fire. All should be well."

"That's what I thought, but she made me worry."

Remy tried to erase the crease in her forehead with his thumb. "If you are that concerned, I'll hire an off-duty cop to stay out there until we get our own people on the site."

"I believe that would be a good idea, but let's make a visit this afternoon just to be sure. We can create a timeline of how we want the renovations to proceed so it won't be a wasted journey."

"No time spent with you is wasted, Jules. One

217

more before we go?"

"Beignet or sex?"

"That's entirely up to you."

Chapter Twenty-Nine

They managed to arrive at the Queen by three-thirty. Except for the growth of the brush encouraged by the summer rains over the last weeks, the place looked about the same—until they walked along the far side of the building. Huge spray-painted scarlet letters shouted FUCK YOU, REMY! on the grimy, gray surface of the wall.

"Shit, NuNu works fast. He most likely went into town and heard the place was unguarded. I won't be surprised if his favorite hobby is tagging railroad cars and overpasses."

"Really, it's not a problem. First thing, we'll wash the exterior, get rid of all the crud, and see where repairs need to be made. Then, we'll give her a fresh new coat of stucco until she gleams in the sun again. I'd like to get my slate man up on the roof as soon as possible to check for leaks and do any repairs. Can't wait to get started on the interior." At the job site, Julia became all business, making her notes, toting up estimates of both costs and time to complete each stage.

"I guess all of Chapelle is talking about our display of exhibitionism," Remy persisted, craving a personal reply.

Unconcerned, Julia nodded. "Yes, Sal said Marv returned from grocery shopping all a-twitter over what he heard from the cashier and Mrs. Nguyen at the fish market. He's grilling black drum tonight. You're invited."

"The gossip doesn't bother you?"

"No, but it got to Todd. Sal told him to go for a walk and let off steam. Evidently, my intern was concerned about my honor and what Patty implied about us. Sweet guy, huh?"

"No, Marv is sweet. Todd wishes the rumors about him and you were true, and not just ugly gossip."

Julia cocked her head at Remy and let him have another blast from her hot blue eyes. "You're cute when you go all broody, but keep it buttoned down. We have work to do. I'll need to get some scaffolding up in the ballroom to inspect the coffers and make molds to replace the most badly damaged."

"How can you be so calm?"

"First, I have to own what I did, and I'm not ashamed. Half the town probably wishes they'd shoved a lemon meringue pie in Patty's face one time or another. I don't have to live here. You do."

Now or never. Remy sucked in a breath of hot, humid air about the same temperature as his fear of her rejecting his proposition. "I'd like you to move in with me, stay at the Black Box."

"While the project is underway? I'm thinking this is going to take a full year to do right. That's a long time to put up with me. Also, Sal and Sammy won't like the idea. They'll bring the motorhome over here as soon as Alleman is finished and stay on site. Todd is taking a break from grad school and wants see the restoration of the Queen through to the end for real practical experience. That means he'll be bunking with the uncles. I might be able to rent a room from Mr.

Getty for the duration."

He understood her head remained in business mode. She'd covered the tight, stretchy red top with a baggy T-shirt in the truck, switched out those killer heels for sneakers, and gotten rid of the silver crucifix that dangled over him when she took her turn on top. How to take her a few hours back in time to the intimacy they'd shared this morning? Remy pushed her tablet and calculator aside and bent for a kiss. Though she accepted his lips on hers and leaned into his body, Julia shoved him back before he went any farther. "None of that on the job."

"No one here to see us, and the job hasn't started yet. I wanted to remind you of the chemistry we share. I meant stay with me permanently here in Chapelle. We'd see how we get along, move on to a deeper commitment, maybe merge our businesses."

She laughed. Exactly the reaction he'd dreaded. "Oh, Remy, are you talking marriage way off in the distant future? I'm a city girl through and through, an Italian city girl. I don't take crap from small town gossips like your grandmother very well. I'd never fit in here long term."

"Patty wouldn't let go of the fact that Celine Hartz had a child out of wedlock with Pammy's son at the age of seventeen. He ran off and joined the Navy. No matter what Celine achieved, or how high she held her head, Patty kept the gossip going. Then, Celine married Jon. Now it's *won't you come have coffee with us, Mrs. Hartz?*"

"Does she?"

"No, but times have changed. The populace of Chapelle shrugs at illegitimate babies and cohabitation.

221

It's all too common now. No one will find our living together shocking."

Julia shook her still unfettered hair. He yearned to touch it, smooth it, possess it, and all the rest of her. "Celine's family goes way back here. She'd have outlasted the scandal. I'm an outsider. Always will be."

"Okay. I'm no stranger to New Orleans."

Her smile faded. Her eyes darkened with new knowledge. "You'd move to the city to be with me?"

"As soon as we complete our project here."

"I'll give it some thought. Marble finish for the ballroom, float finish for the lobby walls. Sound good?"

"It all sounds fine to me."

****

As hot days often did, this one relaxed into balmy as evening came on fast. Since Julia hired well-recommended local painters and paperhangers for sheer practicality and to give a pop to the hometown economy, her workers arrived at dawn and knocked off at three when the interior became stifling, returning to their homes for lukewarm showers and hearty Cajun cooking.

On the back verandah, Julia, her uncles, Todd, and Remy sipped wine while Marv prepared to grill the fish, bone in, heads on, as Mrs. Nguyen always suggested. The chef declared this a celebration of the completion of the formal dining room and set an elegant table accordingly, but he did not want to sully the setting with the aroma of the main course to be served with a green apple slaw and twice-baked potatoes replete with bacon, cheese, and chives. Their host put out a tray of tomato-basil bruschetta and bowls of toasted, spiced pecans to tide them over until the meal as he hovered by the grill waiting for the exact right temperature to be reached for the quick cooking of the fish.

"Yeah, this is the life." Sammy stretched out his hairy legs clad in Bermuda shorts and drove his hand into the nut bowl again.

"Same words you used when we went to Remy's place," Julia reminded him.

"Well, it is. No traffic noise or street crazies, just the bayou flowing by and mockingbirds singing in the live oaks. I could retire here, maybe in one of those condos Remy wants to build."

"They will be built somewhere. I promise that," Remy assured him as if the man were Old Broussard. "I'll put you on the prospectus list."

"Me, I could never leave the city, the old neighborhood," Sal said, taking a gulp of red wine regardless of the notion that fish should be served with white.

"That's what I said," Julia let slip. She stared at her glass sure she shouldn't have refilled it two and a half times. In wine, truth, the old saying went.

Todd caught on the fastest. "Regarding what?"

Do it now, she prompted herself. Perhaps, she'd been drinking for courage. "Remy asked me to stay with him while we restore the Queen."

"That place only has the one bedroom." Sal eyed Remy like a target for a nail gun.

"Aw, come on, Jules is getting up there. Time she settled down with someone—as long as it leads to marriage in the end," Sammy chipped in, having a more liberal view about sex and women in general.

"I think it's a bad idea, mixing business and uh…" Todd petered out before he said the word. "I mean we should have a signed contract in case their relationship doesn't work out."

Sal pointed a thick finger at him. "You're an apprentice. You got no opinions. You don't like what Jules does, go back to school. But yeah, we need a contract before anyone moves anywhere. Got that, Remy?"

"Absolutely. How soon can we draw one up? I mean, my intentions toward Julia are completely honorable." In the end, he went the old-fashioned route, Julia noticed.

"But he's the—" Again, Todd bit off his word, in this case, enemy. Judging from the pinched expression on his narrow face, doing so left a bitter taste in his mouth.

Julia showed mercy and laid a gentle hand on his arm as he'd posted himself on her far side since Remy occupied the other. "We're allies on this project now. All of us need to keep business separate from our personal lives."

"Fish is ready," Marv called from the yard as he laid their meal on a platter adorned with a bed of parsley and cherry tomatoes. "Bring the wine."

He led the procession into the house and down the hall to the formal dining room. Todd bolted ahead on long legs to open the double doors.

"Ta-da!" Marv announced.

With the Corinthian molding picked out in gold and the walls papered in a period pattern that simulated arches rounding the room, the place did look magnificent. Each faux arch held a family portrait massively framed, not of Mr. Getty's ancestors, but interesting faces he'd purchased in antique stores and at art auctions. Some appeared jovial, some very serious, a few looked down their long noses at Sal and Sammy in their shorts, Julia in the blue dress and sandals she'd worn when she first met Patty, Todd in his Regal Restorations khakis and knit shirt, and Remy still clad in chambray and jeans. Only Marv who served the fish onto gold-rimmed dishes with the aplomb of a fine butler seemed to pass muster. The apple slaw already occupied the salad plates and the twice-potatoes taken from the oven just prior to the grilling of the fish sat on the plates. Todd beat Remy in pulling out a chair for Julia.

"Before we begin, refill your glasses. I propose a toast in honor of this magnificent room." Marv expanded his arms wide to include the shining pine floor and the oriental rug that cushioned a mahogany table ringed by six chairs. Crystal, fine china, and sterling silver adorned its top. "You are the first to dine here, a reward for your hard work. May the Queen turn out as well."

"Here, here!" Sammy downed his wine.

"It will turn out just as well, perhaps better," Julia assured Marv.

"Enjoy," he replied.

No one attacked the meal. Sal held up an odd knife, broad with a pick at the tip. "What's this for?"

"Oh, your fish knife. Mr. Getty has an extensive collection of Victorian silver. I thought it would fun to use some of it for this occasion. Use flat of the knife to separate the skin from the fish, then flake some off on your fish fork, which is next to your dinner fork. Use the tip to pick out any bones."

"Right," Sammy said, but basically sat there

clutching the fish knife and waiting for someone else to begin. Finally, Julia took the plunge, managing fairly well. Remy proceeded as if he'd handled arcane Victorian flatware all his life. Maybe he had considering his southern aristocratic mother and his social-climbing granny. The thought made Julia a tad uncomfortable no matter what he said about his lowly origins. The rest did the best they could, and truly no one cared.

Marv ended the meal by bringing out coffee and warm bread pudding swimming in whiskey sauce. They lingered in the lovely setting, mostly talking about the progress at Alleman and plans for the Queen. Full darkness arrived and the question of where Julia planned to spend the night hung in the air like the gibbous moon outside.

Remy suggested it was time he left and looked at Julia pointedly as did all the other men. "I'll walk you to your truck," she said.

"More coffee, brandy?" Marv offered to relieve the tension. Three heads shook to reject the offer.

Julia rose, the men with her, and took Remy's arm, guided him out to the front portico and down the path to his vehicle. The others clustered beneath the hanging lantern that illuminated the porch. She moved to the far side of the truck for privacy.

"Why don't you pack and come with me tonight?" Remy crowded her against the side panel and pressed against her body.

Julia smiled in the light of the more than half full moon. "Not until we have a signed contract."

"How long will that be?"

"A few days. You'll want to look over it carefully

before putting your name on the agreement."

"I trust you."

"As Todd almost said, we shouldn't mix business with pleasure."

"We were having a moment here. Why bring him into it?"

"Because he's right. It won't be long, Remy. It won't be six weeks."

He initiated a kiss meant to change her mind. It did not. She trusted Remy, but his family not so much.

Chapter Thirty

Four fuckin' weeks, or rather four non-fuckin' weeks to get that contract signed. Remy rarely used the F-word. He considered it crude, along with screwing, porking—you name it. He had sex with some, made love to others, depending on the woman. In Julia's case, he always called it making love.

The initial contract arrived in two weeks. Todd, put in charge of arranging all of Julia's notes and checking her estimates, claimed the computer lost the file, and he'd had a terrible time restoring it. Ha, restoring! Once Remy did get hold of it, he read every work and requested some minor changes to show Julia an attention to detail and lack of haste that nearly killed him. Then, off the document went to Jonathan Hartz who made further changes before it returned to Julia for revamping. This time, the printer broke down. Remy snatched the papers and placed them personally in the hands of the efficient Mrs. Landy at Hartz Technology for duplication. Suspecting sabotage by Todd, he asked for extras.

In the meantime, Regal Restorations finished at Alleman. Mr. Getty appeared in a white linen suit and a Panama hat covering the pink, bald spot in his scalp—channeling Truman Capote—to sign off on the punch list. So pleased, he gave the company a bonus and immediately hung his abstract art abundantly on Julia's pristine hallway walls until not a bit of plaster showed. He also offered her a room to stay until she moved on to her next job, damn him.

As for Hartz, he wanted to make an occasion of the signing and put his wife and Mrs. Landry in charge of issuing invitations, ordering champagne, and hiring a caterer for the event to take place in the grand lobby of Hartz Technology. Yes, Pommier's could make a cake that sort of resembled the Queen, but it would take some time.

Time! It passed too slowly before the press photographed himself, Hartz, and Julia placing their signatures on the document. She copiously thanked the Live Oak Preservation Society and the Historic District Committee, plus naming the politicians who had spoken in favor of the project, always great for future goodwill. Taking the high road, Patty Broussard had been invited and lauded for her efforts. Remy's grandmother seethed to one side of the dais hoping to get her picture taken, which no amount of rancor for Julia would prevent. Finally, she photo-bombed the group by squeezing between Remy and Hartz and shoving Julia nearly out of the frame.

Jane Tauzin, who had hyped the event to the far borders of the state and assured the attendance of the press way beyond Chapelle, ended the formal part of the program by announcing that two of the original ballroom chandeliers had been discovered in storage, once purchased to adorn another hotel, and packed away when that establishment also failed. The owner offered to donate them, turning the pair over to Regal Restorations for duplication. A round of applause released the crowd for free eats and fairly decent champagne, mimosas or coffee if preferred.

Still, Remy waited as Julia circulated to each group of well-wishers, and he evaded his grandmother's clutches. Finally, the last shrimp had been dunked in cocktail sauce, and chicken salad sandwiches found their way onto paper plates covered by napkins to take home, along with slices of white cake, raspberry-filled, from the replica leaving only the plastic pillars behind as if it were a Civil War ruin. Remy swore to himself that he'd take Julia home tonight whether she'd packed or not.

Sammy approached and slung a heavy arm around his shoulders. "You should look happier. This is a big day, a very big day. Me and Sal are going to see the old ladies back to their place. Miss Lolly and Miss Maxie hit the booze a little too much. I'll drive their car, and Sal will follow in our truck. We'll move the RV over to the Queen right after we get them settled."

"What about Julia?"

"I put her bags in the back of your truck."

"Really?" News too good to be true.

"Honest to God." Sam crossed himself for emphasis. "You take good care of her now. She thinks she doesn't need it, but all women do. Just my opinion, for what it's worth." Sammy moved off after issuing a hearty backslap.

Sal stood by the exit supporting Lolly and Maxie on either arm. Miss Lolly proclaimed rather loudly, "Yes, we knew the mimosas contained champagne. That's why we were drinking them!"

"Besides, the orange juice is good for our old bones," Miss Maxie added.

Sal had a pretty glum face considering the landing

of a huge contract. Not as on board about letting go of his niece, Remy suspected. Where was she, anyhow?

Julia came up behind him and laid a hand on his arm. His reaction nearly knocked a huge cornerstone of the cake from the plate in her other hand. "Time to go to my place, Jules. A deal is a deal. Your uncles put your bags in my truck."

Julia moved her hand to touch that short beard he'd kept because she seemed to enjoy stroking it so much. "I love when you go all assertive on me, but who do you think asked them to do that?" Without turning, she said, "Todd, drive my truck over to the Queen or use it however you want. Take the afternoon off. Tomorrow the real work begins."

Her intern appeared like her shadow in sunshine, a minion toting a large box of leftovers. "You want this stuff in the truck too?" Surly, Remy thought.

"No, that's for you and my uncles. The motorhome will be on site shortly. You can stow it there. Enjoy some free time." She handed over the keys.

"If you say so." One unhappy man, Todd shambled away.

Outside the air-conditioned haven, heat radiated off the parking lot hot enough to melt the icing on the cake as Julia and Remy crossed to his vehicle and got inside. He turned the A/C on high, needing to cool off in more ways than one.

Happy and relaxed, Julia leaned her head against the rest and stretched out her legs. "My slate man will be on the roof tomorrow, and we'll start washing the building."

That's what she wanted to talk about, the project? "Hey, we also have the afternoon off. No talking shop."

"Fine with me, but I have to let you know every day won't be like this. When I'm on a job, I return home dusty, sweaty, and often dead tired. I want to sink into a hot tub and wash it all away before ordering takeout."

"I'll be right there with you."

"On the job?"

"Yep, and in that tub. Mine is big enough for two." He couldn't suppress the grin that spread across his face.

"Well, all right then." She said little else, just studied the countryside slipping by, pondering something judging by the crease above her eyes.

"Your thoughts?"

"This is a big step we're taking."

"A giant step."

"What if…"

"No what ifs today." He steered the truck through his gateway and parked it by the door. "You get to eat any of that cake today?"

"No, too busy socializing. How about you?"

"I stayed away from the cake table since my grandmother pushed the caterer aside to do the cutting. That way, everyone had to come to her. Think that chunk is safe to eat?"

"Yes, Celine put it aside for us before Patty took over. I believe we deserve dessert right now."

Naked, they ate it on the black satin bedspread, rolled in the crumbs, and used gobs of frosting creatively before making love in the afternoon, all afternoon. Afterward, they shared the tub, cleaning areas where no crumb had wandered, facing each other, Julia on his lap impaled upon his fierce erection. She threw back her wet curls and pumped with strong thighs. He ran his hands over her firm breasts slick with soap, under her arms, and around her back to lend an assist to her motion. Water sloshed over the edges of the tub and grew cold before they finished. Julia rested against his chest.

"Totally worth that four-week wait."

She nodded without raising her head and murmured, "Maybe all for the best, a real celebration."

"No, I'm not buying that. Jules, every time I'm with you it gets better and better."

"Won't always. You know we have to clean up this mess in the bathroom, and that bedspread really, really needs dry cleaning."

"I'll drop it off on my way to work."

"Good, because I'll be on the site by six a.m. before they open."

Remy groaned and not in a sexual way. "If that's the way it's got to be. Right now, I'm ordering Chinese takeout. Might as well get into the routine."

"I can't wait to get started."

Chapter Thirty-One

Gratifying to watch the clumps of moss, a rain of brown oak leaves, and other grunge sluice off the slates. Some of the crew watched in the attic of the Queen for water leaking through. Outside, Remy and Julia stood while the mildew and grime and the ugly graffiti washed from the walls and the fluted pillars of the portico leaving behind a rather weathered gray surface she couldn't wait to restore. Her roofer noted very few holes, some cracked slates, some blown away in storms. At least, the previous owners had kept the covering over their heads in decent condition. The man brought along a supply of material to match samples sent by Julia who'd harvested them from the site. Once the sun dried the tiles, his guys would be up on top repairing the worst of damage.

Striding around in her hardhat, jeans, and Regal Restorations shirt, Julia called to Todd to follow her on an inspection of the exterior walls, marking spots needing repair. In some cases, just minor cracks, while in other places the bare bones of bricks showed through. They made notes and marked the areas requiring their attention. That done, she went inside and bounded up the staircase to the ballroom and her true love—that coffered ceiling. The scaffolding her uncles set to reach up to the sixteen-foot vault stood sturdy and ready to bear her weight. She scrambled agilely to the top and waved to Remy far below.

"Attach your lifeline," he ordered.

"Will do, but I've never fallen on any of my jobs."

"I can think of a dozen platitudes right now. Always a first time. Better safe than sorry."

"I'll be right here with her," Todd said. "Don't you have other business to attend to—or are you only for decoration?"

"Todd! Stop sniping and get to work cleaning the walls so we can do an assessment in here." Julia's voice echoed in the vastness of the ballroom.

"Sorry if my work is less glamorous, Todd. I have extra portable toilets arriving this morning to accommodate more workers." He cocked his head back to address Julia. "One of them is marked Ladies especially for you."

Julia's laughter bounced off the walls. "That's sweet, but believe it or not, I've peed in the same hole as men plenty of times. Yes, you are messy pigs who can't hit the mark, but I can live with it."

"Won't have to this time. I'll be back later with lunch." Without a glance at Todd, Remy left to attend to his own duties, far more complicated than traveling outhouses.

Julia went about her business, shining her flashlight on each coffer, choosing the ones in best condition, clearing the cobwebs and dust with a soft brush, getting them ready to make the molds for replacements. She mapped out the repairs needed for each one on a grid, climbing down to help Todd move the platform and lock it into place again as she progressed. He sent up tools in a bucket if she needed extras and retrieved any that fell to the covered parquet floor, a mistake she rarely made.

Sweaty and grimy, she clambered down the scaffolding at noon when Remy appeared holding up a large Subway bag. "Roast beef for me, chicken for you, and cheese with extra veggies for Todd," he listed.

"Did you get something for my uncles?"

"Sure, twelve-inch meatballs, what else? Also, chips, drinks, and a packet of apples for Todd."

"Good job. Let's go outside and sit in the shade where it's less stifling."

"Yeah, opening those old windows didn't help much. I want to get the electrical contractor here as soon as possible to pull new wiring, maybe hook up some fans soon."

They left the building and made themselves comfortable—or as comfortable as one could be in ninety-degree heat and eighty percent humidity—under one of the oaks after washing up at the tap. Remy tossed Todd his sandwich, apples, and a bottle of water. The younger man unwrapped his meal.

"What do you say, Todd?" Julia prompted, much as a mother would have a child.

"Thanks. You're a great gofer, Rem." Her intern showed no shame for the remark.

Julia stood up to give herself a superior position to the seated Todd. "I've had enough of this! Remy is acting as both architect and general contractor on this job. He's my boss, and I'm yours. You'll treat both of us with respect."

"I've always had respect for you, Julia. It's him…"

"No. You've reached a point where you are somewhat useful to Regal Restorations, and we'd like to keep you on, but anymore of this attitude, and you're gone."

"Yes, ma'am." Todd buried his burning face in the sub.

Julia noticed Remy's smile at the use of the local idiom. Todd was catching on in more ways than one. Remy let her handle to the situation, and she appreciated that. She appreciated him more at the end of the day when he encouraged her to soak in his luxury bath. He took a quick shower before slipping in behind her, rubbing her sore shoulders and massaging her scalp as she washed her hair. If his erection did pop up suggestively between her legs, Remy didn't press the matter. At one point, she drifted off to sleep lounging against his chest and woke to find herself swathed in one of his thick black towels and covered by the zebra hide while he reheated leftover Chinese food in the microwave. She did make it up to him later in the evening.

It occurred to her that of the two of them, Remy was the romantic, the dreamer with his Black Diamonds project on hold while she had saved the Queen and lived to restore her. As soon as she could, she'd have to give some attention to more than his sexual needs.

****

Except for the snide comments from Todd—and Julia had handled that well, preventing him from knocking the guy's head against the rough bark of the oak to pound some respect into him—Remy considered the first day of the restoration project a success. He and the HVAC contractor traced the old air-conditioning ducts from the 1920s to see if they could be used for the new units to be sited next to the reconstructed kitchen and masked from the guests by shrubs. Perhaps, they might hide new ducts in the ballroom behind the plaster pilasters Julia wanted.

Running new wiring in a building as old and solid as the Queen, never easy, but after a consult with the electrician, they figured on coming down from the attic for the fourth and third floors. That the coffered ceiling in the ballroom hung from an old iron framework and hooks made the task of wiring for the chandeliers a relative breeze. Gratifying work.

But on the second day, little things began to go wrong. It seemed to Remy that he spent more time putting out small fires like pinhole leaks in the water line and having the power restored after a midnight storm rather than making forward progress. Irksome to arrive at work and find Julia's Ladies toilet tipped over by high winds, or maybe not since all the others still stood stalwartly in a row. Whether a childish prank or true vandalism didn't matter. The men on the job shoved it upright again, and Todd hosed it out for the use of his boss. Every minor problem meant a delay, and delays cost money, running up the cost of the project.

Yes, he suspected Todd of trying to drive him crazy. A security light burned bright on the property now, and the uncles camped there in the motorhome, but both of them slept like corpses and snored like freight trains after a day of work and a couple of beers. Easy for Todd to sneak out and do the damage. Yet, Remy hesitated to discuss his suspicions with Julia. She'd defend Todd, and they'd have their first real argument since he'd agreed to partner with Hartz. At home, all went smoothly. He wanted it to stay that way.

In the past, he'd never given his sexual partners a

thought from the time they left his bed until they got together again. As long as their drama didn't touch him—he'd learned well to avoid those types from his college girlfriend—the affair ran on until both grew bored or found someone else. Not so with Julia. He doubted she'd ever prove boring. She might prefer another. Once, he'd vowed to figure her out, but it appeared she'd been the one to unravel Remy Broussard.

For so long, he'd walked the line between his cruder small-town relatives and the more sophisticated life of his parents near New Orleans. When he'd reached the age of rebellion and insisted on knowing why he had to spend his summer in boring old Chapelle, his mother sat him down and revealed that Patty swore that if Melody tried to cut off access, she'd sue for custody of her son's children. Unfit parents, she'd claim, involved in adultery and wife-swapping.

"Why would she say that? Was it true?" Remy asked his mother, so afraid it might be.

"No, but the Broussards can always come up with witnesses to anything when necessary. Your grandmother tried to break our marriage. When that didn't work and we moved away from her sphere of influence, she simply tried another tactic. We weren't trying to steal you away from your father's family, only save ourselves. So, we struck up a deal of summers in Chapelle. You did enjoy them when you were small: fishing with your grandfather, wienie roasts, and street fairs. Amelia loved the endless trips to the mall and all the stuff they bought her. She wiggled her way out by asking them to send her to music camp and horseback riding camp and trips to Europe as she got older. That made them hold on even tighter to you."

Remy's reluctance to stay with them got him a vehicle, that cherry red Mustang, to drive to the larger pleasures of Lafayette and their rental of a summer house in Cypremort Point with boating and Ski-doos, fishing and shrimp boils, plus lots of babes in bikinis. He'd gotten out of working as a busboy at the Barn to learn the family business. NuNu, a kid at the time, took the offered place clearing tables and scraping garbage off the plates in the kitchen. Yes, Remy guessed he'd been spoiled—but not by his parents who expected hard work academically.

The biggest bribe to stay in the area was the sliver of land his house sat on and hope of building his premier project. As he put together dinner for the woman in his bed, he knew he'd throw it all over and follow Julia to New Orleans if she asked.

Chapter Thirty-Two

Two frickin' flats discovered on his truck's rear tires when he walked out to the road to keep an appointment with Hartz updating the man on progress and the need for additional funds Remy hated to beg. Not something he wanted to put in an email or ask over the phone. A call that he'd be late was not well received well by Mrs. Landry. "You have until three o'clock. Then, Mr. Hartz flies out to China. He'll be gone two weeks."

Without his partner's approval of the budgetary adjustments, part of their contractual agreement, the burden fell on Remy's bank account to pay the bills. The local crew he'd hired to knock out walls on the third and fourth floors to accommodate modern bathrooms would expect payment on the thirtieth of the month, not two weeks later. He'd need them for other parts of the project and couldn't afford to delay their wages, or they'd move to other jobs that paid on time. No wonder he'd noticed a couple of silver hairs in the dark forest of his hair this morning.

Who had gone to pick up plate lunches today at Nguyen Fresh Fish?—Todd. He'd taken a lot of time for such a simple errand. Long line on Fridays, he explained, and Mrs. Nguyen had gotten Julia's order wrong, grilled shrimp on her large salad, not fried. An argument ensued as to who had messed up. Todd agreed to take the fried shrimp salad if she'd make a grilled one for Julia. Eventually, he'd appeared with bags of Styrofoam boxes bearing teriyaki swai with sides of fried rice and oriental vegetables plus extra egg rolls for the uncles and Remy.

Todd eyed the piece of swai on the end of Remy's plastic fork. "I don't know about that fish. I asked if the stuff was imported, and the lady just kept yelling at me, "Good Vietnamese food. You eat.""

"I'll take my chances," Remy replied.

With stalwart digestion, the uncles were too far into eating the dish to back out and simply nodded

Directly after, he went to get his truck and found the two slashed tires. He contacted Mrs. Landry, called a garage that did road service, stormed back to the hotel, and up to the ballroom where Todd worked a repair with the very sharp crack widener. He glared at the apprentice's bony backside. Julia cradled one of the coffers from overhead as gently as a newborn baby. She lowered it into a crib of packing material supported by a sturdy crate. Remy waited for her to finish before blurting, "Someone slashed my tires, and I have an appointment with Hartz in fifteen minutes. His time isn't easy to come by."

Julia fished in her pocket for her keys. "Not a problem. Take my truck."

"There is a problem, a big problem with sabotage on this job."

Todd didn't turn, but his back stiffened like a porcupine about to throw quills, Remy noted.

"I'm sending Todd to New Orleans with the coffers I picked out for replication. He'll stay there working with my master artisans on doing the replacements. I'm

trusting him with an important task. He'll learn a lot."
Again, Julia handled the situation with complete calm
that made Remy feel like the hothead, though judging
how she'd handled his grandmother, she did have the
capacity for huge explosions.

"Okay, we'll see how it goes." He accepted her
keys and kept his appointment with Hartz, removing the
temptation to dip into the Black Diamonds fund as well
as his own.

For a while, the project ran smoothly. The trash
heap on one side of the property grew large with broken
timbers, crumbled plaster, and corroded fixtures
awaiting the dump trucks to haul it all to a landfill. The
summer's rains held off, and Julia joined her uncles in
doing external repairs. She deserved some fun, Remy
thought. Hell, so did he. The Fourth of July had come
and gone while he recuperated on his balcony watching
distant fireworks soaring into the sky and bursting into
stars and streamers of light. He'd turned down an
invitation for a cookout at his grandparent's place and
grilled a solitary steak for himself. Time he showed
Jules one of his favorite places.

On the weekend with the uncles off to hit some of
the local bars offering music for entertainment, Remy
packed his second picnic for Jules with the romantic
foods of seduction: red grapes and ripe strawberries,
soft, mild brie to spread on fresh French bread, some
thin slices of hard salami in tribute to her Italian
heritage, chocolate truffles, and of course, wine, pretty
much the same menu that worked the first time he'd
been with Julia. He hoped she remembered.

Turning onto a cane field road and parking out of
sight in a bend, he helped Julia down, hands around her

waist, for the sheer pleasure of doing it. She no longer refused his assistance. Progress. He gave her the basket and loaded himself with the wine in insulated coolers, blankets, and the necessary bug repellent. Turning on a flashlight, he cautioned, "Watch out for fire ant mounds and snakes. The gators won't be a problem. They stay on the lakeside."

"This is one of your favorite things, hiking through cane fields at night?"

"Wait until you see what's at the other end."

As expected, Julia didn't chicken out. Two dark hillocks, too steep-sided to plow, rose up before them, the Two Tits, the space between referred to as the cleavage, fairly disrespectful of their antiquity. The name on the maps said the Twin Sisters.

"Ancient Indian mounds," Remy announced without giving away their nickname or their status as a make-out spot. He headed for a path up one side worn by many pairs of lovers. Before they reached the apex, both heard the giggles and groans of another couple. "Shit," Remy said as they topped the mound.

A much younger pair engaged in some preliminary dry humping on a beach blanket amid a couple of six-packs half gone and boxes of Popeye's fried chicken. The boy looked up, but kept his hands on both of his companion's breasts under her T-shirt. "Get lost. We were here first. Aren't you kind of old to be out here anyhow?"

"I'll give you a hundred bucks to go elsewhere."

"Why, you winded from the climb, old man?"

Remy shone his light on the freckled cheeks and red hair of the boy, the blushing face and blonde hair of the girl. He studied them for a moment. He drew on the worst threat available to control small town kids. "Miss, I know your mama. You want me to call her to come pick you up?" In fact, he'd brought her mother up here years ago, but she'd gotten pregnant at the local college by another guy, married, and gone on the mommy track, stuck in Chapelle forever.

"Jayden! Take the money. Don't let him call her."

Remy put the spotlight on the boy's face again. "You work for the newspaper. I figure you're over eighteen, and she's what, maybe fifteen? I can call the cops if you want to make headlines for statutory rape."

"I'm sixteen," the girl insisted

"You know it's not like that, dude. She's willing," her boyfriend claimed.

The girl pushed Jayden aside and sat up. "I was, but now I only want to get out of here. Take the money, Jay. We can spend the night in the boat until the warden opens the levee road gates in the morning."

"Yeah, that will be comfortable, and we might get fined. No one is supposed to be on the lake at night disturbing or poaching Mr. Hartz's precious birds, Mindy."

Mindy twisted a lock of her hair around a finger and delivered a coy look worthy of her mom. "I'll make it worthwhile. Mama thinks I'll be at Savannah's all night."

Remy handed her the hundred. The girl rose, tucked the bill into her hip pocket, and rolled up the towel.

"Please pack out your garbage," Julia said from her place in the shadows.

While Mindy gathered beer cans, full and empty, in addition to the chicken boxes, Jayden sulked. "Say, aren't you the Italian sexpot the whole town is talking about? You want to be a headline too?"

"The difference is I'm way over twenty-one and can go on a picnic at night without lying to my mother on my whereabouts." Nope, Julia Rossi did not back down.

"Move your boat while you're at it," Remy added. "Use the oars. You won't get caught if the warden is on patrol." He'd done that more than once.

The advice went unappreciated, but faced with two people completely unfazed by his threat, Jayden grabbed the full six-pack from his girlfriend and followed her down the far side of the hill. "See if I ever give you free publicity again," he promised before stumbling after Mindy.

"The less I see of the press, the better I like it," Remy said only loud enough for Jules to hear. No sense in arguing with belligerent children. He shook out a thick blanket and anchored it with citronella candles, lighting each one to keep off the mosquitoes. Far too hot for sleeping bags. "You ready to eat?" No use proceeding until the kids were long gone. He freed a wine bottle from its pack and applied a corkscrew.

"Sure." Julia stood contemplating Indian Lake. "I take it you've brought lots of women here. I'm one among many."

"No, I brought girls here when I was as young and randy and as bored in Chapelle as Jayden. You're the first and only woman I've brought to this spot. I came here in the daylight, too, with my sketchpad and a pair of binoculars to get away from my grandparents. Did some bird watching." He handed her chilled white wine in a glass.

"You don't seem the type." Julia took a sip and regarded the view: moonlight and the shadows of cypress trees on the water, white egrets perched in the rookery, the ripple of an alligator on the hunt.

"I was. Haven't been up here in a long, long time." He unpacked the basket and laid out the fruit, bread, and cheese while Julia did a three-sixty exploration of the top of the mound.

She paused with her back to the lake and peered over the rows of cane, their bent leaves silvery in the moonlight and swaying in a light breeze good for keeping down the mosquitoes. "I wonder why these mounds were built."

"No one really knows. For ceremonies or burials, I'd guess. Some say people could gather here if the lake flooded. The kids like to think virgin sacrifices took place, but most likely maidens lost their virginity here in more recent years. Anyhow, the landowner didn't want the mounds excavated, folks say."

"Who does own the land—Hartz or the Patin family?

"Not Hartz. He has title to the lake only. Not sure if the Patins lease it for farming or own it. Why does it matter? Come here and sit down." Remy patted the place beside him and dangled a juicy strawberry as bait.

"That would have more allure if it were covered in chocolate," Julia said, but gave into the coaxing. She sucked the berry from the stem and licked his fingertips.

"I promise there is chocolate to come, paired nicely with the red zinfandel."

Julia broke off the heel of the French bread and spread it with the ripened brie. "Ah, there is going to be dessert that isn't me this time." She did remember.

"Yes, both kinds." Yet, she didn't seem entirely with him as if her mind wandered through the cane fields.

They fed each other grapes and bits of salami, made a mess of the truffles melted a little in the heat, but enjoyed tasting chocolate in each other's mouths. The zinfandel did its work, and finally Julia peeled off that tight red top she'd worn the day of the scene with his grandmother and unhooked her bra. Remy immediately rubbed chocolate on her nipples and laved them clean. He discarded his shirt, craving flesh-to-flesh contact. They fell kissing on the blanket, each massaging the other's back. The pressure built, urging him to get entirely naked and Jules with him. Remy reached for the snap of her cutoffs.

Sirens screamed so loudly across the lake a cloud of egrets took flight circling in the night sky like shooting stars. Wails came from all directions. Julia sat up. "Sounds like a big fire. More than one firehouse is responding."

Remy attempted to bring her back in his embrace. "Nothing we can do about it."

But Julia stood up following the direction of the engines heading south. "Look at that light on the horizon."

"Probably just the streetlamps in Chapelle."

"No, bigger, brighter. Remy, I think the Queen might be burning. We have to go." She scrambled into her bra and top, tossed him his shirt.

Remy dashed everything into the basket and heard a wineglass break in the rush. Blowing out the candles and throwing them on top of the remains of the picnic, he rolled the blanket faster than Mindy had her beach towel. Rough going down the hill and over the ruts of the dirt road in haste, with only the flashlight and the moon for guidance. If there were snakes, they slithered out of the way. The deep marks of their sneakers roused the fire ants in the smashed mounds, but Julia and Remy were gone before they swarmed.

They raced the truck through the sleepy end of Chapelle, then more carefully past the bars with men lounging on the sidewalk outside, some staggering into the street trying to get to the other side. Remy moved them swiftly to the roadblock without killing anyone. The vehicles of the volunteers lined the street on both sides. A man Remy recognized as one of the Queen's previous protectors removed the barricade and let them in, shouting, "Not the hotel, the scrap pile, Miss Julia."

"Thank God," said Jules.

Four fire trucks fought the blaze, though two of them trained their hoses to dampen the wall of the hotel and the woods bordering the property.

"Thought you'd be here quicker since you live across the way," Chief Blaise addressed Remy.

"We went out for dinner. How did this get started?"

"No storms or dry lightning tonight. Same as last time. You could smell the accelerant."

"Gasoline?"

"Yes, it's cheap and hard to trace. Hell, no one around here thinks anything of a man filling a few cans to fuel his ATV or his boat. Go one parish over and not a soul knows who you are, just another guy planning to go off road or fishing. The fact that it hasn't rained lately helped things along too. Are you going to ask the sheriff to check out the apprentice again?"

"He's in New Orleans." Julia inserted herself into the conversation.

"He might have driven…"

"Remy, enough! Todd is staying with Sam's family and doesn't have a car. How about your cousin for a suspect?"

"Old Broussard told him to lay off. He rules that branch of the family. But the sheriff can call on him. NuNu will be at the barn making burgers all weekend."

"Yeah, like he was the last time." Julia let the sarcasm drip from her words.

"I'll set up a meeting with Nonc on Tuesday. The Barn is closed on Sunday. The old man considers it a sacred day. He does go to church and spends the afternoon resting. No one disturbs him. I'll see if I can prevent this stuff from happening again. I paid the price for the Queen. He should honor that."

"The beating, you mean. I want to go with you, Remy."

"To protect me? Ha! Not a good idea. You'll only put yourself in jeopardy."

"I want to talk to him personally."

"No, just no."

Telling Julia no put the damper on the rest of evening as sure as the fire hoses doused the flames and soaked the embers. They stayed until the firemen stowed their equipment and prepared to leave after receiving sincere thanks for their quick action. Sal and Sammy returned in the meantime, shamed-faced at being slightly shit-faced in a bar when the crime occurred.

"One of us should stay here every night. We'll take

turns going out for a little R & R from now on," Sammy offered.

Not a big fan of the firefighting efforts, Sal shook his head. "We're gonna have to redo all the patches on that side of the building. The plaster wasn't cured enough stand up to that blast of water. Get lucky on the weather, then this crap happens."

"All jobs have setbacks. We'll get to it again on Monday," Julia consoled her uncles. "Time for us all to get some sleep."

She really meant sleep, Remy figured, and nothing else.

Chapter Thirty-Three

Used to early rising, Julia slipped from bed before Remy woke. Tempted as she was to stay under the newly cleaned black satin spread and arouse him by running her fingers through his thick hair and smoothing his short beard, she let him sleep. Business before pleasure, a phrase that reminded her of Todd unjustly exiled in New Orleans, not that he wouldn't learn a bunch from her plaster artisans. Maybe he'd hook up with one of Sammy's daughters, a couple of whom—unbeknownst to their father while he stayed on the job sites—appeared to have inherited her uncle's sex drive.

Julia sliced the remains of last night's loaf to dip in an egg-cinnamon-vanilla mixture and prepared the rest of the berries, some of them crushed in the bottom of the picnic basket, for a fancy breakfast of French toast. She tossed the wineglass broken across the stem and prepared a pot of strong coffee. Taking an unearthed chocolate truffle and a cup of brew out to the kitchen level balcony, she placed a call to Jane Tauzin.

"Sorry to disturb you so early on a Sunday," Julia said, though from the sounds of roughhousing in the background, all the Tauzins were wide awake.

"I have two young boys in the house all revved up about going to an air show out of town this afternoon, though heaven knows we'll be able to fry eggs on the tarmac. They've been up since six. Merlin likes to do something special with them when he's onshore for the weekend. But I'm glad you called. I was going to save the news until Monday figuring you and Remy have more romantic Sundays than us. Once you have kids…"

"Jane, what's the news," Jules said.

"A grant came through for the restoration of the chandeliers and the replacement of the other two. I'm not sure what we'll do about the legendary centerpiece that hung in the lobby."

"Yes, when we were still speaking, Patty mentioned it often. Likely, it's been broken up to make smaller pieces. My thoughts are we replicate a large version of the ones in the ballroom—but we don't need to worry about that immediately. I wanted to ask if you know who owns the land where the Indian mounds sit."

"Not offhand. The we-won't-sell-an-acre-of-cane-land Patins probably. They farm most of that area."

"Could you check Monday morning at the clerk of courts office and get a copy of the plat to make sure?"

"Hey, you saved the Queen. I'll be at their door when the office opens. Should be pretty easy. Everyone is familiar with that area. Can I ask why you need the information?"

"I'll tell you when we have the answer. Have a great day at the air show."

"Ha! I'll be sitting in the shade with a cold drink while the boys, all three of them, crawl through stifling static displays. Enjoy your day too. Bye."

"Who were you talking to so early?" Dressed in the hideous yellow and brown checked pajama bottoms, Remy stood in the doorway and still looked tempting with his chest bared and that patch of dark hair between

253

his tanned pecs. He cast a glance at NuNu's shabby trailer before he stepped outside barefoot. "I'm glad we put up those bamboo blinds on either side of the top balcony.

"Yes, no sense giving NuNu or Mr. Getty a thrill. Jane had some great news she couldn't keep to herself. She found a grant to restore and replicate the ballroom chandeliers." Julia offered him a disarming smile along with her little white lie.

"That is something, a drop in the bucket against the cost of this project, but every bit helps. Is there coffee?" Remy looked like he needed it after tossing in his sleep all night, maybe reliving his beating or the first conflagration, Julia couldn't be sure.

"Freshly brewed. We might consider the fire last night another savings. No need to pay for dump trucks or the tippage fee at the landfill."

"I guess we could look at it that way instead of considering it another attempt to sabotage the project. Got any ideas for breakfast? Should I make a beignet run?"

"No, I have french toast with crushed strawberries ready to go. From what you've told me, your mother would approve of the use of fruit instead of syrup."

"She would. She'd approve of you too. We should go down to Mandeville one Sunday and have dinner with my parents."

That suggestion—not high on Julia's list of what to do on the weekend. "Did they hear about the scene I created at the bakery?"

"Yes. When I called to tell them you'd moved in with me, my mom said, 'Good, I wish I'd smashed something in Patty's face years ago.' Mom has her sources in Chapelle. You'd get along."

"Probably," Julia said with some caution. "Let me get the french toast started."

While she heated the griddle, Remy trekked to the end of the lane to get the Sunday paper, which he threw on the table in disgust upon return. "Not worth the walk. Look at that headline, *Fire at the Bayou Queen*. I didn't see anyone from the press out there. Someone wrote it up from the crime report. At least, we know it wasn't Jayden."

Julia sifted a little powdered sugar over the slices of toast and topped them with the strawberries. She set the dish in front of him with a flourish. "See, I can cook, but rarely have the time."

"You run a business. I understand. From that headline, you'd think the building caught fire. Just trying to get more sales." His dark eyes scanned to the end of the article. "Naturally, whoever wrote this mentions the previous arson and our conflict over the building."

"That's what journalists do. A burning trash pile isn't big news. They need to fill the space."

Julia poured more coffee and studied Remy over the rim of her cup as she sipped. He'd complained this project made his hair turn gray. She did notice a few strands of silver that hadn't been there before taking up with her. He needed some relaxation. He needed his own dreams to come true, not only hers. "Why don't we take the boat out on the bayou today and forget about all this for an afternoon?" she suggested.

"Good idea. I know a place upstream where we can dock, step ashore, and have Sunday dinner. One day, people will do that at the Queen."

"Yes, they will," she said with certitude. One day, Black Diamonds would be built too.

They passed a perfect day making love in the afternoon after they returned from boating and bayou-side dining. Julia wanted to prove to Remy she didn't miss Todd all that much, though in a way she did. Not many were as enthusiastic about plasterwork as her intern. But she made such a wonderful job of convincing Remy, neither wanted to get out of bed to cook anything for supper. However, Sundays in Chapelle meant the restaurants served the church crowd at noon and shut at two, unless you wanted Chinese buffet. She and Remy settled on firing up the grill to make burgers with a side of baked beans from a can jazzed up with mustard, ketchup, onions, and brown sugar. Wine and watching the sunset rounded out their day

They returned refreshed to the job on Monday, a bit later than usual, as they'd again found it hard to leave their bed. The damage done to the exterior plaster patches on the fire-side of the wall was already repaired.

"We worked Sunday. Our fault someone snuck in here and made trouble again," Sal said.

"Yeah, we'll move inside now and take up the crack repair where Todd left off. When the weather improves this fall, we can bring in the big crew to do the exterior."

Julia gave both unbusinesslike hugs. "That's why I love you guys. You are the best."

A chattering that did not belong to quarreling squirrels in the oak trees made her turn. Miss Lolly and Miss Maxie were tottering up the rough path to the hotel. "Quick, go grab their arms before their ankles snap like matchsticks. Whatever are they doing here?"

Sal and Sammy hurried to provide a gentlemanly arm for the old ladies and steered them to Julia. Miss Lolly offered their explanation. "We saw in the Sunday paper about the fire, but not a single picture to show us how bad it really was."

"We came here right after early Mass. Prayed for you and the hotel, of course." Miss Maxie added. "Where's the damage?"

"Only a pile of ash where the trash pile sat. No harm done. Would you like my uncles to show you to your car?' Julia hinted.

"Oh my, I suppose we're in the way. We should be wearing those." Lolly tapped Sal's hardhat.

"Not really. We're just getting started for the day." Julia noticed the disappointment on the faces of the old women. "Sam, would you get the ladies some hardhats, and I'll give them a brief tour to show what progress we've made."

Sammy crowned both with bright yellow hardhats, lowering them carefully onto their fragile skulls and thin hair. "There you go."

Miss Lolly fished in her purse for the phone she'd gotten from Julia. "Do you think it takes pictures?"

"Probably, most do."

"Would you?" Lolly handed the phone to Sal and latched onto Julia's arm. Maxie got on her other side. Both rolled back smiles so wide, they exposed the tops of their dentures. Sal showed them the results, and they twittered like the sparrows in the trees with excitement. "Now for our tour."

His phone also in hand, Remy appeared around a

corner. "We're giving tours now? A little early for that. Maybe we should set up a lemonade stand and sell hot link sandwiches out by the road too."

"That would make a wonderful fundraiser for the Queen," Maxie said. "We'll talk to some of our groups about it."

Remy held up his hands in surrender. "Only joking. Not much to see yet, but we are moving along. If the accidents stop happening."

"Did you set up that appointment with the Broussards?" Julia should have known better.

"I did for ten tomorrow at the Barn. Once we've had it out, these incidents should stop."

"Trouble with the Broussards? You must take me along to speak with Arnoult. I understand him," Miss Lolly claimed.

"Who's Arnoult?"

"Why, your great-uncle, Remy. Of course, he's been known as T-Fats most of his life, and now they call him Old Broussard, though he's much younger than Maxie and I. I taught him in third grade. The other children teased him unmercifully about his weight."

"I think it's a genetic condition that comes down in that line of the family." Miss Maxie ogled Remy's slim torso. "You should be glad you take after the Remingtons in all but the hair, eyes, and skin tone."

"You see, despite my best efforts to prevent it, Arnoult was bullied and at recess often hid behind my skirts. Poor boy. But sometimes, those who are bullied become bullies. He inherited the Barn and all the power that goes with it." Miss Lolly sighed as if she'd failed her student personally. "However, I do believe he is fond of me. I can help you get on his good side."

"The Barn is a rough place. I really don't think…"

"You don't believe I danced out there in my youthful days, Remy Broussard. Well, we did, didn't we, Maxie?"

"Yes, we cut quite a rug."

"I am sure you were a sight, but…"

The area bustled now with the arrival of the carpenters framing the new walls on the third and fourth floors to make space for bathrooms. Right behind them marched Jane Tauzin flapping some papers in her hand.

"Remy, would you give these ladies a little tour since I need to speak with Jane? They've been our most stalwart supporters," Julia asked.

"I should be upstairs…"

"Oh, we'd love to go upstairs." The elderly twosome headed in the direction of the front entry. Remy took two long strides and caught up. With no choice left, he offered them his arms.

"You are so lucky to have a high metabolism the way your granny tried to stuff you with pastries as a child, and such a handsome and charming child you were too," Miss Maxie observed."

"Still is charming and handsome." Miss Lolly pinched Remy's cheek as they pushed forward like turtles toward a head of lettuce. They crept around the bend, out of sight and hopefully out of hearing as Jane dashed up to Jules.

"You won't believe this! The Broussards own that piece of land. The Patins only farm it." Despite her enthusiasm for her discovery, Jane paused. "Why does it matter?"

Julia took the plat and the rest of the

documentation. "I'll tell you after we meet with Remy's family tomorrow."

"You're going out to the Barn with him? Isn't that dangerous considering what they did to him?" Jane's nature-green eyes widened.

"I'm not supposed to be there, but I will be—along with Miss Lolly. She thinks she can make a difference. With these papers, I know I can."

Jane's cheeks reddened with excitement, or perhaps the early morning heat. "Please take me with you. If I can get someone to watch the boys, I'll bring my husband. No one messes with him, and he's in tight with the Broussards, or was once."

"We're getting quite a crowd already."

"The more witnesses the better. They can't kill us all."

"Jane, too much drama. No one is going to die tomorrow."

"Right. We'll come in our own car. You bring Miss Lolly. What time?"

Julia gave in to the inevitable. "Ten." She took the papers to shove into the glove compartment of a Regal Restorations truck before Remy returned. He'd thank her for her interference later.

Chapter Thirty-Four

Julia waved Remy off the next day with a cheery, "Good luck." Giving him a ten-minute head start that seemed like an hour, she finally dashed to her truck and drove helter-skelter to the prim white cottage engulfed in purple crepe myrtles that Miss Lolly shared with Miss Maxie. Feeling a little guilty about asking the elderly woman to wait on the curb to save time, she started to get down to help her aboard, but Lolly already had the door open.

The retired teacher did accept a hand extended across the front seat to haul her into the cab. "Not too decrepit to seat myself." Lolly settled herself and crisply snapped the seatbelt.

As Julia expected, Remy had already gone inside by the time they arrived at the Barn. Welcome or not, she helped Miss Lolly down. They proceeded to the old general merchandise, more a convenience store now, that fronted the Barn. A burly man running the cash register stepped out from behind the counter when they headed directly to the corridor leading to the interior. "Can I help you ladies find something?"

Pretty sure the guy wasn't there only to sell potato chips, Julia answered with a smile, "I'm bringing some papers forgotten by Mr. Remington Broussard to the meeting." She figured nearly everyone there answered to the same last name.

"The old lady too?" Such suspicion.

"Well, I couldn't leave her in the truck on a hot day like this. The elderly dehydrate so rapidly."

"Humph," uttered Miss Lolly, miffed at having her role in the adventure mitigated. She peered hard at the young man. "I do believe I taught your mama in grade school. How is she doing these days?"

"Ah, good I guess, but…"

"You should never have to guess about your mama's status. Give her a call right now, and we'll proceed to the meeting."

"Only Remy was expected."

Julia waved the papers in his face. "He needs these asap!"

Before the man could react, a long, dark shadow fell over their group as the door opened again. Merlin Tauzin stood for a moment letting his eyes adjust to the dim interior, prepared to fight a hidden enemy. His big, black-stubbled chin hardened. His blue eyes burned cold. "Let them in, Len. I'll vouch for their behavior."

Eyeing Jane tucked against her husband's side, Len answered, "It's a private meeting. Some women are born to cause trouble."

"Not this time. Move along, ladies." Merlin Tauzin walked behind covering their backs in case Len might go for the pearl-handled pistol known to be kept under the counter. Unfortunately, they had to move at Miss Lolly's pace. The corridor connecting the store to the Barn seemed to telescope in length as they crept slowly toward the rough voices sounding in the cavernous space ahead.

"I tell you, me, I got nuttin' to do with dat new fire. You took your beating like a man for selling out da family. I give you immunity for your woman and dat old hotel. You callin' me a liar, Remy?" A solid fist pounded on a tabletop and set coffee cups clattering as their group entered. Old Broussard sat enthroned in his oversized chair and surrounded by his usual retinue.

Slick Broussard was first to his feet. Ignoring the women, he said, "Blackie, what are you doing way out here?"

Merlin, responding to his old nickname, answered, "Escorting my wife to this meeting. I understand she and these other ladies have something to add."

"Your wife always got something to add."

"*Mais*, yeah. If she didn't push for dat ordinance stopping trash burning in the parish, you coulda torched dat trash pile yourself and saved lots of money on dump trucks and tippage. Someone done you a favor, boy," Old Broussard said to Remy.

"Accidental brush fires are down fifty percent, the fire chief says. That saves the taxpayer money—and the air is cleaner," Jane answered, not willing to be ignored. "I wish I could have gotten the council to ban burning off the cane stubble in the fall too."

Blackie Tauzin clamped a firm hand on her shoulder. "Not going to happen with all the influence the cane farmers have. Take your victories where you can, babe. Now, let the other women have their say."

"You should put a hand over her mouth," Slick suggested with an angry glance at Jane.

"Oh, she'd just bite me."

Slick reconsidered Jane, not the flashiest woman he'd ever seen, and everyone knew he loved flashy. "I do like me a woman with spirit."

"You'd have to fight me for her." Having no idea

what role Miss Lolly planned to play, Merlin redirected the conversation to Julia. "I believe Ms. Rossi has some important information you need to hear."

"Ah, yes, I see you started with coffee and haven't gotten to this part yet," Julia said.

Miss Lolly moved glacially but steadily toward Old Broussard who pushed his bulk up by the thick arms of his special chair to honor her presence. "Slick, get my favorite teacher a chair. Pour her some coffee." After a moment, he sank into his seat like a heap of lava hardening into place.

The large pot sat on the table, no NuNu in sight to pour. Slick obeyed and moved the sugar and milk closer if she desired any.

All tucked in, Lolly said, "Why, thank you, Arnault. You were one of my favorite students too. Let's hear what Julia has to say."

Jules went to stand beside Remy, almost touching elbows with him. "It's come to our attention that you own the land where the Indian mounds sit and lease it for sugar cane farming to the Patin family."

Old Broussard heaved the fat of his shoulders. "Yeah, so, been knowing dem for years. Da Broussards bought dat field during da Depression when lotsa land went up for sale." He turned a hostile, piggy gaze on Jane. "Dis gonna be some kind of trouble with da Chitimacha tribe wanting their sacred land back? Dat why you here?"

Jane, leaning comfortably against her husband since they hadn't been offered a place at the table, shook her head. "Not that I know of—but I believe those mounds precede their occupation in the area."

"Good, I didn't never let nobody dig in dose hills

'cause maybe we have some Injun blood in the family way back from when da Cajuns first come here."

"We plan to honor that in the new Black Diamonds development," Julia rushed to say. "Remy is the artist, but I took the liberty of sketching in the layout of the site. I am aware he wanted his buildings to reflect in the bayou, or in this case the lake. Instead of one long mass of buildings, we've split them in two to be built on either side of the mounds with a tower on each end. On the roadside, the planned gardens, pool, clubhouse— and a small museum at the base of the mounds to explain *your* heritage to visitors." Grateful he hadn't dressed up for this meeting, she grabbed a carpenter's pencil from Remy's hip pocket and added a new square to the plat. "There, the museum. If we can get permission from Jonathan Hartz, a dock and boat launch might be added to give access to the lake. I can envision the clientele of this project fishing and bird watching. Both hobbies have his approval." She paused to take in some air.

Jane chipped in by saying, "Once the crop is in, we could do an environmental impact study and get some salvage archaeologists from the university to search the base of the mounds for artifacts. They could also use ground penetrating radar to look inside without disturbing them."

"Probably hold up the project for years," Slick complained.

Miss Lolly jumped right over his protest. "Isn't that exciting, Arnault?—how they can use technology to search without destroying." She squeezed the obese arm of her former student.

"Gimme a looksee." Old Broussard seized the plat

and shared it reverently with his teacher. "I like dis, me. Why you don't come right out and show me dese plans, Remy? *On doit pas se plainer avec le ventre plein.*"

"That's translates as don't complain on a full stomach. I have some Cajun in my background just as you have Native American. My grandfather spoke nothing but French. You are supposed to use the term Native American now, Arnault, not Injun," Miss Lolly directed, ever the instructor.

Remy, his face dark, said, "Neither project can go ahead while we are concerned with safety. I don't see NuNu lurking around today. Where was he on Saturday night?"

"Not here. We caught him doing crystal meth. You know how the old man feels about that shit. Give him two weeks' notice, but he came in next day and said he got a regular job better than flippin' burgers, and we could just fuck off," Slick said. "Sorry for the language, Miss Lolly."

"Where?"

"Don't know."

"I told him las' time you come here to let t'ings be, but dat boy, he *tetu.*" Old Broussard knocked a pudgy fist against his head.

"Hardheaded," Miss Lolly said. "But you are not, Arnault. I failed to teach you good English, but oh, how you shone in mathematics. No wonder you've made such a big success of the Barn, better than in your grandfather's day when I sometimes shook a leg out here. You should grasp this new opportunity."

"Your investment money is still in the bank. I told Slick to pass that along to you. Not a cent is going into the Queen."

"He tole me, Remy." Old Broussard stroked his bristly multiple chins.

"I also recall your keen interest in history. That explains why you kept those mounds safe from destruction. Perhaps you'd like to contribute to the restoration of the Queen. I am sure Remy would place your name on one of the rooms." Miss Lolly maundered on as if this idea just occurred to her.

Julia held her breath. Truly, she didn't want her beautiful ballroom to be named for the graceless Arnault Broussard. Remy came up with an immediate and better idea.

"We have a magnificent mahogany bar we're having refurbished off-site, and we're rebuilding a modern kitchen. How does Broussard's Bar and Eatery sound to you?"

"Too many Broussards around here. How about T-Fat's Bar and Restaurant? Me, I could kick in for fixin' up dat bar."

"Oh, but Arnault, you shouldn't call yourself that. It is degrading," Miss Lolly said.

"Miss Lolly, you about da only one who remembers my given name is Arnault. And look, me, I'm fat." Old Broussard flapped his flesh-heavy arms. "It ain't no insult now. I'm as famous around here as Fats Domino. Dat name never did him no harm."

Remy proposed the compromise. "T-Fats' Bar and Arnault's Eatery."

"*Bon.* Shake on it now, but gimme some papers soon. I got to tell the Patins dere's another sugar cane field gone. They ain't gonna like it, but too bad." He summoned Remy forward and engulfed his hand.

"It's a deal, Nonc."

"All you, sit down. Have some coffee before you go. Slick, you talk to your boy again when you find him. Say Old Broussard wants the Queen left alone— and dis lady here with da big plans." He gestured to Julia to sit on his left. "See if we got any cookies in da kitchen too."

No cookies, but Slick returned with a pecan pie— one of the few desserts the Barn offered besides ice cream and bread pudding. With a fist full of forks, a knife, and a stack of plates crowded onto a tray, he muttered about his no-good son NuNu as he set the places. Old Broussard sent him back for a container of vanilla ice cream to top the pie all around. Julia ate her portion with gusto. She'd work it off today and with a clear mind—the Queen saved, and Black Diamonds being built. Both problems solved.

Chapter Thirty-Five

Back in the parking lot, Miss Lolly allowed Merlin to lift her into the cab of Julia's truck. He spun her around once before seating her. "Great job in there," he said in that basso voice of his.

"I knew I could be of assistance. Inside that grossly overweight body is a good man with a fine brain, a man who can see reason."

Remy had the broken ribs to doubt that, but he kept quiet as Tauzin put his hands around Jane's waist, gave her a spin, and lofted her into his immense truck painted a custom electric blue that matched his eyes. He drove a double cab to accommodate his boys, but it was still a mean machine.

Jane leaned out the window. "Always gives me a thrill when he does that. Julia, wonderful work. I can't wait to tell Celine and Jon. So glad I came along."

"You did the research. I can't thank you and Miss Lolly enough." Julia waved as their vehicle ground up the oyster shells on the lot and left.

Remy held the door of the Regal Restorations truck open for Jules. "Want me to twirl you around and lift you into the driver's seat?"

"Don't you dare."

"Oh, my dear, you should never turn down the opportunity to let a man be a man, especially tall, dark handsome men," Miss Lolly commented, having gotten her own thrill from Merlin. That explained her lack of protest.

Regardless, Julia seated herself. "I'll see you back at the Queen."

"It's half past eleven. Meet me at the Black Box for an early lunch." From the light in Julia's blue eyes, he could tell she thought that was a euphemism for celebratory sex. Not what he had in mind.

"After that pie, I don't have much of an appetite—for food. But I'll be right behind you."

Remy noticed she ran a yellow light to keep that promise. He didn't bother to help her down from the truck, but held the door into the Box for her. She laid the sheaf of papers with the property's details and the crude sketch she'd drawn on his desk, anchored it with the new ballerina she'd brought back from New Orleans, and sailed into his arms.

"We need to talk," he said.

Jules took a step back. The light in her eyes faded. Her expression became one that Remy imagined he wore when women broke up with him, but he'd never cared for any of them like he did for Julia.

"Aren't you pleased with today's results? Both our projects are moving forward."

"Jules, you took my dream and changed it without consulting me. You must have come up with this idea when we were standing on top of the mound before the trash fire—yet not one word. I stood there like a fool today letting you do all the talking because I had no idea what was going on. I went to the Barn to make certain you and Queen were safe, not to let you outshine me in every way. As Miss Lolly said, sometimes you have to let a man be a man."

"It wasn't my intention to take over the meeting. I had to wait until Jane verified who owned the property. If the Patins held it, no sense moving forward with the idea. Only another disappointment for you."

Remy placed his hands on her shoulders and looked into her eyes. "When did Jane bring the papers to you? I suspect it was yesterday when you foisted the old ladies off on me for a tour."

She stared down at the toes of her work boots. "I didn't know if Jane had good or bad news and didn't want you to hear."

"What about last night? You couldn't have told me then, brought me in on your plans, let me do some proper sketches to show the old man?"

Julia raised her eyes. "You don't like my layout. I'm no architect. That's your job. Now that we have the land, you can build Black Diamonds any way you want out by the lake."

"I think you are a little too used to being the boss."

He didn't expect the hard shove to his chest that backed him up against the desk. "I wanted to restore your dream, surprise you with the gift of Black Diamonds, the project you gave up for me. Being the boss had nothing to do with it. I thought we worked well in tandem at the Queen, so well that Black Diamonds could be our project too, not only yours. Sorry for my stupid mistake. I'll keep my hands off!"

Remy thought she'd finished, sure if she had a beignet handy, she would grind it into his face right now. How wrong he was. Blue lightning struck from her eyes.

"You didn't tell me you took that beating to protect me, not simply to square things with the Broussards. I

271

had to overhear it when I walked into the room today. Do you know how hard it was to move forward, to speak calmly after that? It's fine for you to sacrifice for me, but I'm not allowed to give anything back?"

"Jules, you still aren't safe. Weren't you listening? The old man and Slick have lost control of NuNu. They won't bother you, but he might."

"Then, I'll have to look out for myself and guard the Queen too." Jules checked her watch. "You're the boss on this project, and I'm still on the clock. I need to get back to work as soon as I pack my stuff." She turned and mounted his metal staircase, the one he'd never fallen down. She made the steps ring as she rounded the second floor and headed for the third. He rushed after her, setting up his own clamor in the stairwell.

Remy took the stairs two at a time and still didn't arrive in time to prevent her from flinging her clothes into bags and sweeping her cosmetics from her side of the sink. Rage packing.

"I knew this wouldn't work." The words Remy most dreaded hearing from her lips.

"You aren't giving us a real chance. We hit our first bump in the road. Are you going to let that send us both into a ditch?"

"I have to rethink this."

"Where? How?"

"Going to stay in the motorhome for a while. The uncles will look out for me if I need looking after at all, and we'll watch over the Queen day and night."

At least, she wasn't returning to New Orleans where Todd waited ready to console her, he'd bet his life. Maybe the guy wasn't trying to harm the project, but he sure as hell had fallen in love with Jules. Remy understood how that could happen all too well. He needed to fix this. He eyed the bed and held out his arms.

"Not now, Remy." Julia hefted her bags and started down the staircase. He didn't dare offer to help.

Chapter Thirty-Six

Remy gave Jules an hour to simmer down—always wise, he figured. Then while making a sandwich and coffee he didn't really want, he fretted that she'd think he lacked passion because he hadn't followed her immediately to duke it out. Yeah, he'd been to Italy and witnessed some really public shouting matches between lovers both in person and over cell phones. Remy, the ever cool one, didn't think he had that in him, not on a job site and not at home. Were they really compatible? He had to hope opposites attracted.

Back at the Queen, he searched the site for Jules, but found only her uncles working on crack repairs in the lobby walls. An impressive scaffold like some kind of complicated jungle gym reaching much higher than the one in the ballroom filled the center of the vast space. He approached Sal setting up a patch for a wider area. "Have you seen Julia?"

"You better believe we have. She threw her stuff in the motorhome and put clean sheets on the overhead bunk. What did you do to piss her off?"

He couldn't truthfully answer nothing—but a complicated issue like this wasn't meant to be shared. When Remy failed to answer, Sam said, "Yeah, Julies is pretty even tempered most of the time, but when she blows up, it's big." He cupped his lips and shouted, "Fire in the hole!"

"You do realize I can hear every word you say up here. This dome is like an echo chamber." Julia rolled to the side of platform where she'd been lying on her back taking pictures of the fruit and flowers plaster medallion in the ceiling and peered over the edge.

Remy moved toward the scaffold. "Do you have your lifeline attached?"

"I will when I stand up to start the cleaning." She shoved herself upright. A whiskbroom in her hand fell free.

Remy jumped back. If it had hit him, not much damage would have been done, not as much as say one of her pointed metal finishing trowels plummeting toward the floor. He couldn't help but remember how she'd handled the crowbar and hammer when he came across her trespassing, how magnificently unafraid she was. That time, he'd held a shotgun. This seemed like a similar standoff. She had the height to her advantage.

"You need to put up some nets if you keep dropping things," Remy shouted.

"Not like Jules to be so clumsy," Sal remarked.

"Sorry. I usually have Todd to pick things up. Put it in the bucket. I'll hoist it." Julia's voice reverberated in the dome.

She sure knew how to push his buttons. If this was a test, Remy planned to pass with high grades. "I'll bring it to you."

If it wasn't, for certain she couldn't run out on him again. While he didn't fear heights, Remy preferred the solidity of a bucket truck when he did inspections that many feet off the ground. Regardless, he placed a foot on the built-in ladder and scaled it to the top.

"Oh-ho, look at him go," Sammy shouted,

thoroughly enjoying the spectacle.

Jules sat cross-legged waiting. Remy ducked under the guardrail. He cocked his hardhat back and squatted in front of her. "Your whiskbroom." He offered it to her as if holding a dozen American Beauty roses bouquet.

She accepted it like it was—only a whiskbroom. "Thanks. You can leave now. If you stay here, better get your lifeline on."

"You are my lifeline, my partner in this and all projects to come." He put the warmth of hot lime into his words.

Far below, one of the uncles said, "Aww, ain't that sweet?"

Julia remained unimpressed. "Very romantic. Todd's line is hooked on right over there. Use it."

"You brought Todd up here?"

"In the ballroom. I wanted to show him some things—and don't even let your mind go there. What is your problem with the guy?'

"I told you. It's all the time you spend with him—and the absolute fact that he is in love with you. I know that feeling well." He would have said, "I love you too" if the uncles hadn't been eavesdropping.

"I'd describe it more as admiration, hero worship if I were a man. I sent Todd away to keep the peace. Regardless, I'll be seeing him tomorrow. Some of the casts for the ballroom ceiling are finished. I need to take a look and bring a few back to see how they fit."

"I'll go with you. I want to see your operation."

"If this is really about Todd…"

"No, it isn't." Maybe it was a little bit, but he didn't have to admit that. "What time do you want to leave?"

"Five a.m. I can get there and back the same day even if I'm ambushed for lunch or dinner by my mom."

"I'll be ready to go. Your truck or mine?"

"Mine. I'll pick you up."

"Won't you consider coming back to the Box tonight?"

"Like I said, I need to think. See you tomorrow, five sharp."

"I'll be ready." He cast Todd's lifeline aside and climbed down. As he passed the highly amused uncles, he muttered. "She's tough."

"You better believe it. That's our Jules," Sal said, knowing his niece heard.

Sammy whispered in his ear, "But so worth the effort."

Remy nodded and went about his business for the day, checking the framing of the doorways and bathrooms on the upper floors. He found a couple of doorframes so poorly done he summoned the foreman. "This is crappy work. The lintel isn't even level. Rip this mess out."

"Sorry. New apprentice. I'll make him do them again and stand over him while he does."

Apprentices, the bane of Remy's existence right now. He'd like to take the hide off this Todd substitute, but wisely left it to the foreman. "I'll be back to inspect again before I leave for the day."

He took himself off to supervise the laying of the slab for the new kitchen and hoped that would take his mind off of Julia for a few hours. He knew he wouldn't sleep well tonight, not without her within his arm's reach, her warmth burning off the chill of their argument. Five a.m., he'd be ready to go.

Chapter Thirty-Seven

Jules knew she'd been spoiled by Remy. For one thing, even with the new bump in his nose, he didn't snore nearly as hard as her uncles. The tepid shower in the motorhome hardly compared to the luxurious bath and shower in the Black Box, both big enough to fit two. As usual, Sal and Sam went out for something fried for dinner and insisted she go along as pie and ice cream in the morning did not make a meal, and she hadn't touched the box of donuts during break. Oh, for Remy whipping up an omelet or ordering takeout because she was too tired to cook. And for the king-sized bed with Remy in it, a solid presence against her back, one she could turn to any time she wanted.

No, she would not make this easy on him. The gates at the Black Box stood wide open like welcoming arms waiting to receive her at five a.m. Nicely dressed for the excursion, Remy had gone with pressed khakis and blue chambray open at the collar, so tempting, so inviting with that deep-dimpled smile on his face. Really, they didn't need to leave before sunup. They could...no!"

Remy climbed aboard, briefly noting her all-business work jeans and Regal Restorations shirt, but saying nothing except, "I made coffee for the trip. It's for both of us." He held up a stainless-steel thermos.

"Thoughtful of you."

"I know a hole-in-the-wall place on the way with the best biscuits. They'll stuff them with whatever you want: a fried egg, ham, bacon, sausage, cheese, all of the above."

"I think that's called McDonald's."

"No, better than that. They'll do steak too, even fried catfish. Mind if I turn on the radio?"

"Whatever you want." She'd decided on crabby as the best way to keep him at bay. Julia let the classical music flow over her, replacing conversation, then the usual depressing news of the day as the sun rose hot enough to fry the aforementioned egg on the concrete highway as they passed thorough small towns and over swampy ground. Remy poured coffee for her and put it in the cup holder, probably hoping to get her in a better mood. At the rundown diner, he took her order, went inside and waited since she'd made it clear she didn't want to get down and waste time. Truly, she feared facing him in a cracked vinyl booth and feeling the tug of his attraction. They might end up in a motel along the way.

Julia ran the air-conditioning and drank the coffee as she waited for breakfast to be delivered directly into her hands. An only child, her father called her headstrong, her mother stubborn, and her many cousins, bossy. She guessed she was and probably couldn't cure herself enough to be anyone's wife. No reason to tell him right now. He stepped into the cab, bringing with him the aroma of bacon and the steam of hot biscuits. She accepted one with no egg, suspecting she'd be wearing the dribbles on her shirt if she did, and set out on the road to New Orleans again.

"I could drive while you eat," Remy suggested.

"No, I'm fine." Let him see how willful she was. Let him be the one to call things off between them because hard as she tried, she couldn't end it.

Julia selected an off-ramp well before they reached the heart of New Orleans. She took Remy to an area of warehouses, row upon row, and parked beside one with Regal Restorations scrolling out along its exterior in blue paint. Other than that, her base of operations appeared crude and unadorned. She led Remy inside where her crew of thirty plaster artisans already worked hard on their individual repair projects using instruments as fine as dental picks and tiny brushes. All was as Julia demanded it be: molds mounted on the walls out of the way, the saws and drill presses gleaming and ready for use, the area for the making of metal templates already busy with workers cutting, filing, and sanding the blades needed to form exact reproductions. Only a few raised their eyes and voices to greet her.

An impressively feathered plaster eagle, taller than she, perched in one corner keeping a keen and beady eye on the operations. "Our mascot, Egg Head, we salvaged him from a building we were unable to save."

Along one wall a master artisan berated a small clutch of apprentices examining a batch of newly cast crown moldings in the egg and dart pattern consisting of a series of ovals and points. Jules recognized Todd, gangling and blond, standing among the dark and stocky descendants of Italian immigrants as if he'd been hatched in the wrong nest.

"Do you see the flaws here? You must constantly run a blade across the top until it dries. Otherwise, the plaster swells out of the mold. Never turn your back on it. We'll try this again, mix, pour, set, unmold." Row upon row of plaster moldings curing in casts spread out across the floor.

Julia heard a low whistle behind her. "Impressive," Remy said.

"Thank you, but take a look at the men working at the tables. What color is their hair if they still have any left?"

"Gray."

"Yes, it takes ten years to master ornamental plaster. I've known some of these men since I was child. They'd let me cast plaster rosettes and paint them. Mostly, their children aren't going into the trade. We need people with heart, stamina, and a good grasp of mathematics to do what we do here. They're dying out. That's why I require guys like Todd."

"I hate to admit architects are a dime a dozen in New Orleans, my primary reason for being in Chapelle."

"Well, it is more glamorous than plasterwork. You are the designers. We are the restorers."

"How much room do you have here?"

"Eighteen-thousand square feet, all of it in use."

Remy pointed to a complex mold. "I recognize that, the Corinthian molding from Alleman."

"Yeah, incredibly difficult, all that detail."

"You don't use silicone for the molds?'

"No, urethane rubber. It's far cheaper and can reproduce the finest detail."

Remy continued to ask intelligent questions and did not mask the admiration in his voice. "Where are all the others, the roofers, the floor refinishers?"

"Files on my computer. They are sub-contractors

we call in for big projects, but plaster is my true love."

"You really don't need a spare architect, do you?" Did she detect regret in that last statement?

"Depends on the architect," she answered at once. "Seen enough?"

"Maybe too much."

"Almost time for the lunch break. Someone informed my mother I'd be in town. We're expected at her house for pasta salad."

The clock struck noon, and the artisans carefully laid aside their tools, headed for a break room, and opened old-fashioned lunchboxes releasing the odors of salami and garlic. Some moved toward the food trucks parked along the road this time of day, Todd among them.

"Hey, Ms. Rossi," he said carefully in front of his co-workers bound to take offense if he seemed too familiar with the boss. "Can I get you something from one of the trucks?"

"Don't you have moldings to watch over?" Remy asked.

"We're taking turns during the break."

"Thanks, Todd, but my mother expects us."

"Nice lady, your mom. She fed me a few times. It's always good. I wish I didn't have to stay here."

"Are you getting a good taste of all we do?"

"Yes, ma'am. But I'm not nearly good enough to do most of the work. I don't like babysitting the molds." He looked at Julia with pleading gray eyes.

"Being a cornice hen is an important job. Stay with it. I'll be back to get a couple of the new coffers for the Queen's ceiling to try out."

"I'd like to see how they fit in person."

"Maybe that can be arranged." Julia waited for a protest of some sort from Remy, but none came. "Off we go to Little Palermo."

"Looks like the French Quarter to me," Remy remarked as they left the highway for the Vieux Carre and delved into a side street near St. Mary's Church and the Old Ursuline Convent.

"With so many Italians settling here after the Civil War they started calling this section the Sicilian Quarter. A lot of the old families have pulled out for the suburbs, but not mine. We own most of the block."

Jules failed to find a space in front of the brick row homes and turned down a narrow alley. She parked near a locked rear gate and let them into a long, skinny yard where staked tomato plants, bushy eggplants, and zucchini vines yellowed, long past the end of their season under the onslaught of the August sun. They made their way up a brick walk and mounted three tall cement steps to the backdoor. Jules banged on it with a fist, then tried the knob.

Unlocked. They entered an old-fashioned kitchen painted a cheery yellow and hosting a linoleum-topped table with three chairs guarded by a print of the Holy Family along one wall and an array of outdated appliances along the other. Judging by the wear on the surface of the table, and the ring left by a cup near the sugar bowl, Mrs. Rossi took her coffee and most of her meals there, but the woman was nowhere in sight.

"In here, my darlin' daughter," she called from another room.

"Mama, how many times have I told you to keep your backdoor locked? This neighborhood isn't as safe as it was when I was little."

"What are they going to steal? Eggplants from the garden? Great-aunt Gertie's antimacassars?" Mrs. Rossi entered, shorter and plumper than her daughter, dark auburn hair streaked with gray, a smile of welcome on her face, but a wee bit of a bite to her words. "So, this is the young man who seduced my daughter."

She eyed him head to toe much as Julia had once done. Jules watched Remy go off-kilter for a few seconds. Then, he unleashed his enticing smile. "I believe *she* might have seduced *me*. I can certainly see where she gets her Irish blue eyes and dazzling smile."

"As my granny would say, this one kissed the Blarney Stone. She also warned me to stay away from the Italian boys. I think Cajun lads might fall into the same category."

"You married an Italian boy, Mom."

"Exactly. I didn't take her advice. Maybe you shouldn't take mine. Well, the table is set for lunch. Go right in and seat yourselves."

Julia led the way to a dining room dominated by a Victorian breakfront full of knickknacks from a pottery rooster pitcher to fancy floral-painted teacups too nice to be used, and a large mahogany table. A starter plate of garden fresh tomatoes and mozzarella slices sat at each place on Irish linen placemats edged in lace. Cruets of vinegar and olive oil were placed handily nearby along with a sliced loaf of Italian bread on a marble slab, and a bowl of pasta salad studded with ham that appeared large enough to feed half of Julia's work crew. Mrs. Rossi had iced tea poured, but offered lemonade or wine. Remy accepted a glass of the latter. "I'm not the one driving,"

"My Marco would never let me drive." Mrs. Rossi

passed the pasta bowl. "Sometimes I miss his bossy ways—but then I still have Julia always telling me what to do." Clearly, she knew her daughter well.

Remy sidestepped the trap of agreeing with her. "This is a delicious meal," he said instead.

"A fine lunch for summer. We have lemon icebox pie for dessert. You'll have to come back in winter for my Irish stew and soda bread."

"I'd like that if Julia keeps me around."

Jules didn't fall into that pit either. "Who knows what the future holds?"

"I can recommend a fortuneteller by Jackson Square who might know. She said my daughter would meet a tall, dark, handsome stranger, and she so has."

"I'm fairly certain she tells every woman something like that." Julia steered the conversation to another topic. "You know I could renovate this place for you, new kitchen, open up these small rooms to make it more spacious like my place."

"I lived here with your father for thirty-five years. You won't touch a thing."

"Stubborn."

"Like my daughter. She wouldn't be this way if we'd had more children, some brothers to keep her in line, but it wasn't to be. Bad complications after her birth. My hysterectomy—"

"Mama, please, not the hysterectomy story at lunch."

"Well you see, my daughter is my only hope for grandchildren and not getting any younger. Would you like to have a family, Mr. Broussard?"

"Oh, six at least. My family is big on reproduction." Remy winked at Jules across the table.

"Please call me Remy."

"Mom, his house has only one bedroom. He didn't plan any space for children."

"He an architect, now, isn't he? Certainly, he could build another place if he wanted."

Jules declined to answer the obvious. Yes, he could if he wanted a family, but Remy had shown no sign that he did, six indeed! She started telling her mom of their progress on the Queen and held onto the topic until the icebox pie was consumed and coffee served.

Julia breathed a sigh of relief when they prepared to leave burdened down by containers of pasta salad including some for the uncles and a small one for Todd. "Such a nice young man but far too skinny."

Jules didn't want to get her started on Todd. "We need to go. I have to pick up the ceiling coffers. Coming, Remy?"

"As soon as I thank your mother for the wonderful hospitality. Mrs. Rossi, it has been a pleasure."

"It's Katie to you." Her mother fluttered.

As she headed for the door, Julia wished she hadn't heard her mom's last remark to Remy. "I do like Todd, but Jules has ten years on him. I think you have the edge."

"Are you coming or not?" With Remy trailing, Julia paused at the gate, loaded him with the stack of plastic containers, and let them out. In the alley, she tested him again. "I want Todd…"

"If he's what you want, then I guess we're…" Grim described his face.

Done. Over. *C'est finis* as the French would say. Julia rushed to finish her sentence. "I want Todd to return as my assistant at the Queen if the two of you won't bicker."

Relief washed over his handsome features. "I can keep up my end of the bargain if he keeps his."

"Good. We'll take him back with us." She handed him the truck keys and scooped up the containers.

"What, me take the wheel under the influence of one glass of rather sweet wine?"

"I think you are sober enough for both of us. See, I'm sharing."

"And I'm sharing this." He bent for a kiss that would have been way better and lasted much longer if the pasta containers weren't in the way. Remy opened the passenger door for her and waited until she stowed the leftovers in the back before taking the chance that she'd kick him when he twirled her around and lifted her into the seat. Julia did not protest.

Miss Lolly knew a thing or two for a maiden lady. Sometimes you had to let a man be a man.

Chapter Thirty-Eight

Only off the site one damn day and the framing of the upstairs rooms had gone to hell again. Remy couldn't blame Todd for any of it. No, the apprentice squeezed behind the front seat among the pasta containers for the long ride back to Chapelle as happy as man newly released from prison. They had to go by Sammy's house to collect Todd's belongings, which meant meeting Sam's wife and several of his daughters, one of whom seemed really, really sad the apprentice was leaving. Pressed to stay for coffee and Italian cream cake, they did, and that meant stopping for dinner at an IHOP on the way back and arriving at the Queen around eight to drop Todd at the motorhome.

As the uncles accepted the pasta salad and additional slices of cream cake, Todd unfolded his long, cramped legs and hauled his stuff to the RV. After Julia took him aside at the Regal Restorations building, he'd remained mostly silent on the trip, probably sleeping when he wasn't raiding the leftovers with a plastic fork. Now, uncertainty hung in the air like the ninety-eight percent humidity left behind by the afternoon thunderstorm.

In Todd's absence, Remy asked in a low tone the uncles wouldn't hear, "Are you coming back with me?"

Julia's lips quirked. "Did you think I'd sleep with Todd in the over-cab bunk?"

"I never know what you're going to do next."

"That's good for you. Keeps you on your toes. Yes, I'll be coming home with you."

He didn't miss that she'd used the word home, one he had avoided. No sex last night, though Remy suspected they both wanted it, but at the moment, they negotiated a rocky stretch of road in their relationship, one that had to be traveled cautiously. To have her snuggled deceptively soft and tame as a kitten against his backside would do for now, not for too long. To see Julia sipping coffee at his table in the morning and sharing a plate of eggs and toast with her seemed a privilege since she'd stormed out on him two days ago. No more taking Jules for granted, he promised himself.

The two them were early on the work site. Remy inspected the kitchen annex, good solid framing, the smooth concrete floor pierced by the conduits for plumbing the sinks, dishwasher, icemaker, prep area. Once the concrete floor cured, they'd move to wiring and insulation, set in place the metal lath to hold the keys of the plaster walls, raise the brick exterior and stucco it over to blend seamlessly with the Queen under its own slate roof. Still a way to go, but coming along.

Afterward, he'd gone to the upper floors and found more shoddy carpentry work. This time Remy didn't chew out the foreman. He called his sub-contractor and reamed his ass, handed the phone to the foreman who had the same done to him by his boss.

"Yes, sir. Yes, the guy will be gone by the end of the day." The foreman mopped his face with a bandana hanging loose around his bull neck, ready to soak up the sweat of the day. "Better to fire a person late in the shift. Not as much upheaval then. He can just walk out like nothing happened and save his dignity. Meanwhile, I'll have him fix this mess he made. Claimed he'd been to trade school, and gave a decent demonstration, but it sure doesn't show now."

"Next time, check the references." Remy left him to it. Micromanaging seldom went down well with construction crews who often considered architects to be suits or sissies. He had an appointment with the electrician, delayed because of the trip to New Orleans. He looked in on the ballroom where Todd and Julia plus the uncles were setting up the rolling scaffold again, but didn't linger. Remy returned at the lunch break where he convinced Julia if they ate leftover pasta salad, they'd have time for afternoon delight as a dessert. Despite a bad start, the day improved hourly.

As the time came to knock off in the heat of the afternoon, Remy sought the foreman again. "Is he gone?"

"Yeah, I gave him the heave-ho a half hour ago."

"Did you make sure he left the property?"

"He was walking toward the road last time I checked."

"Pissed off?"

"Not happy for sure, but I don't think he'll make trouble."

Remy had to accept that. With Sam and Sal and even Todd living at the site, not likely the man would come back in the night to take revenge on the project. As usual, Jules was among the last to leave the building. He waited for her by the kitchen annex while her men split off for the trailer. With no one else around, Remy pressed a quick kiss onto lips tasting of the salt sweat of the day and ran his fingers through the mass of her damp dark hair, flattened from being under the hardhat dangling from her fingers. "Shower together?" he asked.

"You bet. You'd think I'd be too dehydrated to pee, but I've been up on the scaffold for hours. We're running new channel iron to stabilize the existing coffers and reinforcing the ties before we start hanging the new units. I didn't want to climb down in the middle of all that. Let me use my personal Port-O-Let before we leave. No need to get it for me, but I admit I enjoy having it all to myself."

Remy had learned well enough not to comment she always used her private john at the end of each work day before they left the site and once the other workers had gone. Still smiling his way, Julia opened the door stenciled with Ladies and stepped inside the dim interior. She slammed it shut with such force, the structure rattled. The unit rocked as elbows rammed against the molded plastic walls and feet kicked at the entry trying to escape. A snake inside, Remy thought at first, gauging the distance to his shotgun mounted in the truck against the number of steps to the portable outhouse. He ran toward Julia's struggle. Get her out first. Murder a snake later.

When still feet away, the slide lock popped, and Julia stumbled forward, her body moving, struggling, but her neck in the grasp of the fired carpenter who held a knife to her throat. He stepped down and kneed her in the back. "Stay still if you want to live a few seconds longer, bitch."

Not a snake, a snake in the grass, NuNu had changed his appearance enough to fool Remy from a distance, but not up close. He'd seen the narrow-shouldered, hunched form, head bowed before the foreman tearing into him, but no dirty blond ponytail hung down that back. Sideburns of dark brown showed below the rim of the hardhat, and a sparse dark mustache crawled along his upper lip. The guy wore shades indoors, a sign of drug use, Remy believed, which explained the erratic carpentry. Now the shades were off, the pale blue eyes dilated, wild, and crazy. Sweat from the time NuNu spent hiding in the plastic sauna of the toilet leached the dye from his lip hair and sideburns and sent it streaking down his pale face in dirty rivulets.

"Stay still, Remy. I got your woman, and she's gonna pay for your mistakes." NuNu jerked Julia's head higher with the arm under her jaw and exposed more of the graceful, tanned column of her neck. "Y'all think you're so smart with your college degrees. I been here weeks messing with the framing, wasting your time and money, and you never caught on. Hoped the trash fire would spread to the hotel, but it never did. If Slick hadn't held me back when we give you that beating, I'd a kicked your pretty white teeth up into your brain and left you dead. But, the family turned its back on me, not you."

For doing crystal, not his other transgressions, a fact Remy left unsaid. NuNu probably had himself hopped up on the drug right now, making him paranoid and violent. Remy made an offer he hoped the man could not refuse. "Julia has no part in this. Come on, cousin. I'll take you on unarmed." Out of the corner of his eye he saw the reinforcements stumble from the motorhome, Sal with a pistol, Sam holding the two-by-four he used as footrest, and Todd, a cell phone pressed to his ear. So did NuNu.

"Drop that shit, all y'all." He pricked Julia's neck to make his point. The droplet ran down her neck and left a small purple stain on her blue Regal Restorations shirt. They did as he told them, but Remy moved a foot forward before NuNu's eyes swiveled back to his. "Stay put! She has to pay for coming here and stirring up the people against the old man's project. With her gone, this one is dead in the water—like Julia's gonna be."

"Not so. I went out to the barn after the trash fire to make peace. Nonc is buying into the Queen, paying for the bar and restaurant. We're going to build Black Diamonds on some property he owns around the Indian mounds. Our quarrel is over. Now, let Julia go."

"It's not over for me. All my life you treated me like dog shit you had to wipe off your boots. Always had a fancy car and the prettiest girls like this one, but I got her now." NuNu pricked Julia again for the sheer pleasure it seemed to give him. She didn't flinch. In fact, her hand inched toward the tool belt she'd been in too much of a hurry to shed before entering the Ladies Port-O-Let.

Remy had to keep NuNu talking and be ready when Julia made her move. "You were a little kid I hardly noticed, and I wanted to be the coolest guy in town at seventeen. I didn't hang out with children. It wasn't personal."

"I had to listen to my own daddy saying he wished he had a son like you, so sharp, so cool. He didn't run your Mustang off the road. I did. But, it didn't do me no good. Just wasted a nice ride. You got luck, Remy, and I got none."

"What? You couldn't have been more than twelve or thirteen." Keep him talking. Keep him talking.

"You think it takes any skill to drive an automatic? Daddy let me drive his car around on the cane roads from the time I could reach the pedals. One night, I took it out by myself, tracked you down, and scared you into that ditch. Not a scratch on my daddy's car. Now that takes skill."

"It does. You can cook and do carpentry work too. Those are good skills to have."

"Ha! You went off to get a fine education, and I went to jail trying to be cool like you, boosting hot cars to get the girls. Made some great money with a chop shop and showed the ladies at good time until I got busted. Seventeen, and they tried me as an adult. I didn't lose my front teeth in a barroom brawl like I told the old man. I lost 'em in prison. Skinny guys like me, they make you their bitch."

As if she'd heard enough of that word, Julia palmed the crack cutter from its holder and drove the blade—so sharp it could cut through plaster—into NuNu's thigh. His knife hand jerked across her throat. She fell at his feet as his lock on her neck released.

Remy charged forward, shouting, "Julia!", unable to aid her because NuNu raised the hunting knife, heavy and sharp enough to skin a six-point buck, with the intent to drive it into her chest. He did the flying kick he'd wanted to use when this criminal helped beat him unconscious. Jeans were not designed for motion like the *karate gi*, nor were boots for great purchase on the ground. Remy hit NuNu's elbow, not his knife hand, maybe for the best. The knife dropped into the dirt on Julia's far side. His opponent scrambled to make a grab for the weapon with his left hand and got a clumsy grip on the handle. Remy landed another kick under NuNu's jaw that should have stunned him or possibly snapped his neck, which wouldn't have been a shame, but the man seemed to feel no pain. NuNu shook his head, still looming over Julia in a fighter's crouch like a hungry wolf guarding his prey.

A bullet whizzed past the two of them and buried itself in the front of the outhouse. Todd yammered on his phone, an odd distraction, while Sammy advanced with his two-by-four trying to find an opening. Remy wanted to give him one, but with NuNu backed against the Port-O-Let and still too close to Julia, he didn't dare give him any room to move. If necessary, he'd block any attack on her with his own body—if she still lived. Remy's eyes flickered toward her oozing neck, not spurting, and that was good, but he noticed something else, her hand moving again toward her tool belt where one of her sharply pointed steel finishing trowels hung. He took the hint and whipped it out of its holder. Did Julia smile?

Sensation returning to his elbow, NuNu flipped the knife to his right hand and smirked. "You gonna take on a hunting knife with a trowel? I guess you ain't that smart after all." He feinted at Remy over Julia's still form, found himself blocked by the triangular piece of steel, and cursed. "She-it."

Remy prayed the trowel could stand up to the heavy tempered blade, at least long enough for Sal to get a good bead on NuNu. Their arms were locked in the struggle when Julia rolled backward and grabbed the leg of the man who had tried to murder her. He pitched against the Port-O-Let. Two-handed, Remy drove the point of the trowel deep into NuNu's chest. Surprise registered in the wild blue eyes before they went blank. His last word, "Bitch."

Julia pulled herself from under the fallen body and rested on her elbows. "*Now*, I'm tired of people calling me a bitch."

"I'll remember that always." Remy knelt beside her, taking her into his embrace. "Promise you won't die in my arms."

"The cut didn't go deep. I thought I'd better play dead."

"That's our Jules," Sal said, as proud of his niece as if she'd just completed another plaster masterpiece. "Want me to put a bullet into that little shit's head just to make sure?"

"No, I think we are done with NuNu for good this time. Leave something for the undertakers."

Todd came running with the first aid kit. "Let me put pressure on your wound until the ambulance arrives. Should be here any minute along with the cops."

"It's nothing, I tell you. Just help me up."

"Stay down!" all three men shouted and kept her there with Todd holding a gauze pad against her neck, Remy grasping her hand, and the uncles looking as if they'd tackle her if she moved. The medics arrived, put Julia a gurney, and rushed her to the local clinic. The doctor used fourteen stiches to close the gash, assured her the scar would fade, and sent her back to the Black Box with a bottle of painkillers she promptly threw away.

"You are one tough woman, Julia Rossi," Remy said. "Is there anything I can do for you?"

"Yes, run a deep, hot bubble bath and join me there."

Chapter Thirty-Nine

Despite the suffocating summer heat, Remy dressed in a lightweight pale gray suit and knotted a blue tie the same shade as a Regal Restorations shirt around his neck. Most of the Broussards attending NuNu's funeral would be far more casually dressed, but he intended to show his respect for the family if not the person lying in the casket. Not likely they'd attack him at Moity's low-end funeral home selected for the burial rather than ponying up for classy Duchamp's, even if Blackie Tauzin's brother-in-law who owned the place offered them a good discount.

Julia walked him to the door of the Black Box. "I'd be willing to go with you." She wore a necklace of dark stitches around her throat.

"No, it's a family matter."

"Okay." She backed off. Both were learning their boundaries. "I realize I'm not a family member—yet." That and a farewell kiss filled him with optimism and hope for their future.

The coroner found the trowel embedded in NuNu's chest and enough drugs in his system to explain the reason for his rage. Easy to ascertain the cause of death as a severed artery. After a week, Malcolm Moity drove his circa 1960s hearse to the morgue and picked up the body for embalming. The sheriff interviewed all the witnesses, declared the incident self-defense, and declined to press any charges. A few said the Broussards could get away with murder—most that NuNu had been in trouble since the day he came into the world and went out the same way. The talk would die down eventually, and be raked up from time to time as the occasion demanded.

The truck barely cooled off by the time he parked in Moity's gravel lot by the railroad track. Remy stopped in the restroom before entering the parlor assigned to Nolan Broussard. Not wanting his family to think it was flop sweat, he wiped the perspiration from his face and made sure his hands were dry before walking on the worn runner toward NuNu's coffin. Chilly as the grave inside the mortuary.

Dozens of dark, nearly black Broussard eyes turned his way when he entered and tracked him to the front of the room. Not a chair stood empty, but not a tear in any of those eyes. Flower arrangements sat on either end of the casket, nowhere else in the room. He stood behind two of NuNu's pals. One dropped a roach of marijuana, still in its clip, by the pale hands crossed at the waist. The other placed a six-pack of beer at the shiny shoes of the corpse who, judging by the way it hung on the thin body, wore a suit that probably belonged to someone else. The cosmetologist had washed away the dye job and returned the hair to dirty blond. The two druggies slinked past the family in the first row and left the hall.

When Remy's turn came, he bowed his head and committed NuNu to hell in his mind, but crossed himself as he'd been taught since childhood. He guessed he'd have to confess that someday, being unable to forgive. He turned to face Old Broussard sitting in his chair brought from the Barn and the long row of people beside him consisting of Slick, a few of his brothers, and a couple of his older sons—the pallbearer brigade. All of them wore their black Barn attire while the old man had donned his Sunday best.

Nonc took his offered hand without uttering a word and jerked his head toward Slick sitting beside him. The old man held up an arm that brought Mal Moity running on his stubby legs, his pot-belly shaking like newly unmolded aspic beneath his white shirt and black suit. "Get dat crap out da coffin. It's disrespectful." Mal reached into the casket and removed the beer and roach, carrying off the offerings.

Shoulders back, jaw firm, Remy stood before Slick. "I regret I had to kill your son. He tried to murder Julia." To say he was truly sorry would have been a lie, though he would rather have sent NuNu to prison than the grave. Remy held out his hand to NuNu's father. They shook. The tension leaked from the frigid, floral-scented air of the funeral home.

"Come talk wit' me." Slick rose and led the way outside, offered Remy a cigarette, got a refusal, and lit one for himself. "Not so sure he was my son. His mama was one of our whores. Leila she called herself. We caught her shooting up and were ready to toss her out when she claimed to be carrying my child. I was sixteen. Scared the crap out of me. No telling who the father really was, but yeah, it could have been mine. I never could resist a big-haired, bosomy blonde. So we kept her on. Had to detox both of them when the kid was born. He didn't look nuttin' like me. Put the baby in day care and in the hands of my mama at night. I guess Leila thought the family would set her up somewhere nice. When that didn't happen, she took off with one of her johns, left the baby behind."

"You never did a blood test?"

Slick took a deep drag on his cigarette. "No point after she abandoned the kid. Ma had a heavy hand with children, and he cried all the time. Never was right in the head. After a while, the day cares wouldn't take him neither. Too much trouble. He got passed around the family, didn't last too long in any home. Good thing we have a lot of relatives. Anyhow, we tried to raise him, and he ends up in jail before he finishes high school. The old man and me thought working at the Barn after he got out might settle him. It didn't. So, he'll be buried under a headstone calling him Nolan Broussard and his dates. That's all. Beloved by nobody and regretted by none."

What a terrible epitaph for anyone. Remy felt a twinge of pity for the child. He might have been nicer to the kid if he hadn't been a typical self-involved teen. As for the man NuNu became, no sympathy there. He could have stayed clean, followed orders, and remained safely under the dark wings of the Broussard family for the rest of his life, but wasn't capable of that.

"Just wanted you to know the whole story, Remy. No one is coming after you about this. Hell, you're one of our success stories. NuNu was a screw-up."

Remy had said those same words to the dead man's face. Awful the rest of the family felt the same. He found himself offering the manly hug favored by his family, as he had no words of consolation. "If you ever want to retire to Black Diamonds, say the word."

Slick shook his head. "Broussards don't retire. Someone got to run the Barn and all the other stuff. I'm next in line, and my daddy's ticker ain't so good. I imagine I'll be taking over sooner rather than later. I appreciate you came, and we settled this."

"Me too."

Slick ground out his cigarette in an urn filled with wilted impatiens and returned to the viewing. Remy decided against going to the hour-long funeral Mass, the cemetery, the reception at Slick's house afterwards. He got in his truck and returned to the Black Box to change his clothes. Julia, of course, had gone to work.

Chapter Forty

Remy found Julia and her crew patching cracks in the ballroom. Todd worked nearest the large entry doors. "She's been waiting for you," he said in a surly voice. Obviously, the apprentice still had a big chip on his shoulder, probably one made out of plaster. Todd frowned as Jules put aside her work and rushed to take Remy's hands.

"How did it go with the Broussards? You look good on the outside. No internal damage, I hope."

"No, I'm square with Slick and the rest of the family. No more troubles for us or the Queen."

"Great! We finished running the new channel iron, but I wanted to wait until you were here to place the replica coffers and see how they fit."

"A big moment."

"You bet it is. Just watch." She moved to the far side of the scaffold positioned under two gaps in the ornate ceiling and climbed to the top with confidence.

"Lifeline," both Remy and Todd prompted.

She laughed and shook her head, but clipped the line around her waist, and fastened the other end to the guard rail. "Todd, send up the first coffer."

Her apprentice raised the precious object slowly, carefully, into Julia's hands. She maneuvered it onto one of the ties. "See that! Fits as tight as a lady's white kid glove. We'll point the joints later. Todd, give me the next."

Julia received the second coffer into her capable hands. She walked to the far end of the platform toward the next gap. Todd mimicked her motion, stalking along the base of the scaffold as if Julia might require his help at any moment. Remy took up a position at the end to get a better view. As Julia reached up to tie the coffer to the framework, the platform shifted under her weight. The lifeline zinged along the railing as she dropped through a gap with the scaffolding beneath her buckling in the middle. She dangled fifteen feet above the ballroom floor still holding the coffer to her chest.

"Don't move!" Todd shouted—and she laughed.

"Where did you think I'd go?"

The apprentice bumped Remy aside. "Release the lifeline. I'll catch you!"

"No way. You don't have the muscle." Remy pushed Todd. "I'll do it."

"No, me!"

Sal and Sam moved between them. "This is Jules' life you're arguing about. We'll all catch her." The scaffold emitted an ominous screech of metal. "Unless you want us to get a ladder or call the fire department?"

"I just want to get down before the whole thing goes."

"Drop the coffer first," Remy suggested.

"Nope, we're coming together." She wrapped one arm tightly around the plaster square. "Get ready. On the count of three—one, two, three." Jules released the lifeline and plummeted into four sets of strong arms woven together to make a basket. They lifted her to her feet. Sal relieved her of the weighty coffer and placed it out of harm's way.

"Jules!" Remy wanted to hold her, make sure every bone her body was okay, but Julia didn't spare the time for so much as a quiver. She went to examine the scaffold.

"I don't get it. This is top-notch equipment. We put it together ourselves. It shouldn't have failed."

"Yeah, both Sal and me were up there yesterday finishing the channel framework. No problem, and we weigh lots more than Jules."

"Maybe the Broussards aren't done sabotaging this project." Todd's light eyes looked nearly as wild as NuNu's before his death. Red spots burned on his pale cheeks.

"Certainly wasn't NuNu. I saw him in his coffin. About every Broussard in the parish is at the funeral home. Lots of them sat a wake last night. My family may be many things, but when they say we're good, we are. They keep their word." Remy dearly wanted to point a finger at Todd, but he'd given a promise to Jules too.

Julia did the pointing. "I asked Todd to check the bolts early this morning since I knew I'd be up there hanging the coffers. We can't go ahead with the project until we know what caused the accident. Todd said we were ready to go. Were we?" Remy had never seen her blue eyes go so hard, not even when he'd angered her.

Todd's head drooped. "I-I wanted to be your hero, save you like Remy did the other day. So, I loosened a few of the bolts. I knew where the scaffolding would fail and planned to be there to catch you. Remy got in my way."

"First of all, Remy didn't save me from NuNu. We worked together to defeat that scum. Sal and Sam were ready to pounce if he took Remy down. You did your part by calling the police and the ambulance. Today, all of these arms were held out to save me. This isn't about being a hero, Todd; it's about teamwork. That's what gets a project done. I'm going to let you go. You should still have time to enroll for the fall semester and finish your master's in historic preservation. I think you will excel at it, and you learned a lot this summer. Take that knowledge with you and leave."

"But, Julia, I realize what I did was stupid. I wanted you to see me as more than an apprentice. Remington Broussard and his family aren't good enough for you."

Remy answered him. "I'm aware of that. But, as Julia said, it's about forming a team you can trust. You failed at that. Only one more thing I want to know—were you responsible for any of the other sabotage around here?"

Evidently, Todd decided to get it all off his narrow chest. "I walked to the Queen one night when Sal told me to cool off and caught NuNu in the act of tagging the building. He dropped the can of spray paint and ran, but I finished the job by adding Remy after the Fuck You and ditched the evidence. I held up the paperwork with the agreement between you and Hartz and jammed the copier, thinking maybe Julia would reconsider working with you if she had more time to go over the details."

"Todd, I am so disappointed in you." Jules shook her head. "Get your things out of the motorhome. Sal or Sam will take you to the bus station. We'll pay your way home. And one last word of advice, never fall in love with your boss."

Chapter Forty-One

After Todd's departure, the Bayou Queen project moved ahead as well as any other Remy had supervised, which is to say they found new problems that had to be fixed, some sub-contractors fell behind and held up others from completing their work, fixtures didn't arrive on time, etc. Still, with Julia's amazing efficiency and contacts, he thought May instead of June for the opening.

In the Black Box, their experiment in living together went about the same. He and Julia had some small squabbles and jockeyed for drawer and closet space when she moved more of her things from New Orleans. They survived a formal Christmas Eve dinner in Mandeville with his family, then crossed the causeway and celebrated Christmas Day with hers. All of this stress was offset by amazing sex and the feeling of moving forward toward a completion that wasn't purely physical.

Remy pondered when to make his next move and spent some time researching Italian wedding customs. Number One on the internet list: gain the permission of the bride's father to seek her hand in marriage. That meant approaching Sal and Sammy with his honorable intentions one evening when Julia went to New Orleans to check on some other projects in the works for Regal Restorations. On a Saturday early in February when the first hints of spring color showed in a spurt of wildflowers along ditches and a pleasant warmth filled the air, he invited them over for a cookout on the deck. Once the uncles downed a few beers and mellowed some, Remy turned with the grill fork in his hand, the thick-cut steaks sizzling behind him, to say his carefully rehearsed words.

"I love and admire your niece, Julia, and would like to ask for permission to seek her hand in marriage."

Sal squeezed his beer can so hard suds surged from the top. Sammy slapped the bare, hairy knee exposed by his Bermuda shorts. Remy held the grill fork in a defensive position, tines out—until both men burst out laughing until tears ran down their broad faces.

Once they caught their breath, Sal said, "Have you asked Jules yet?"

"No. I read up on your customs and thought I should speak to you first."

That set off another round of chortles. Sammy wiped his eyes on the hem of his purple and gold T-shirt. "Our customs, that's hilarious. This ain't the Old Country. I sure hope your proposal is more romantic. If you want, I could coach you. I'm good with the ladies."

Sal slurped some beer to clear his throat. "Better not tell Jules you asked us first, or she'll move back into the motorhome again. We'll have to hear over and over how her personal life is none of our business."

"A little clarification needed. Do I have your consent?"

"Oh, hell yes. We seen this coming months ago. You're kinda slow off the mark. If fighting NuNu for her life—which was pretty damn impressive—didn't do it, nothing will. You shoulda asked her right after that, but Jules has a mind all her own. You not only got our permission. We wish you all the luck in the world. Pay attention to those steaks now. I like mine medium rare, not charred clear through. Wine, we should have wine to toast your upcoming nuptials," Sal suggested.

"I have some upstairs. So, you think she'll say yes."

No gaffaws this time. "Can't tell with Jules," Sammy admitted.

"I've been concerned about her last words to Todd—about not falling love with your boss. Technically, I'm her boss right now."

"Yeah, I almost felt sorry for that poor jerk. Todd had a real talent for plasterwork and threw it all away for a dame, even if Jules is the best. He cried on the way to the bus station. Anyhow, I wouldn't wait, my friend. While you're finishing this project another Todd with lots more sense could come along and make an offer." Sal chugged the last of his dented can of beer and flattened it under his heel, not a gesture that gave Remy confidence.

Sammy—possibly the more sensitive of the two—stepped up with a plasterer's hawk load of encouragement. "But her mama loves you. That helps. She's staying over with her tonight. I know Katie will be filling her ears with your praises. You made an impression at Christmas."

"Yeah, complimented her mom's cooking and didn't get drunk. Brought her that little present, the framed sketch of Julia you did, and helped with the dishes when you should have been sitting among the men watching sports and swilling wine. You're a little wussy sometimes for my taste, but I ain't marrying you."

"Come on, Sal, give the guy a break. He held off a hunting knife with a trowel—a god-damned trowel—and killed the guy with it. Remy can cover my back in a bar fight any night."

"I'd like to think I'm a twenty-first century kind of man, not a Neanderthal. Let me get that wine." Remy flipped the steaks and turned the fork over to the other men who started debating which had the most Neanderthal blood.

Killing a man didn't make him a hero, made him a little sick inside in fact, but he'd do it again to save Julia. Life without her seemed more and more impossible, but her answer to his proposal came with no guarantee. She hadn't been in any rush to move into the Black Box. Could be she wanted out when the project came to an end.

Remy ran up the flight of stairs, retrieved the bottle of robust red, glasses, and one other item. By the time he returned, they'd decided Sammy had more caveman blood because who ever heard of a bald Neanderthal like Sal?

"Take a look at this while I plate the steaks." Remy turned over his design for an engagement ring for their approval. "I think I was supposed to show you the ring first, but it's taking a little longer than I figured."

Sal and Sammy studied the sketch. "Hey, that's an egg and dart pattern on the band with a rosette center."

"Julia said that was her favorite type of cornice, the one she chose for the Queen's rooms too. I plan to put a two-carat diamond in the rosette. A jeweler in New Orleans is working on it right now."

"Nice," said Sal.

"Thoughtful," said Sammy. "When do you plan to give it to her? Valentine's Day? It's coming up fast."

"Too obvious. Maybe the next weekend in a special spot."

Sal raised his glass. "Here's to your *nozze*."

"My nose?" Remy fingered the small bump in his bridge that he'd had no time to fix.

"Italian for wedding." The uncles tossed back their wine and smashed Remy's glasses on the deck. "May you and Jules have as many happy years together as the number of these shards."

"Lots and lots of shards there. Thank you, I guess. Don't get up. I'll fetch a broom. Enjoy your steaks." Marrying into the Rossi family—obviously going to provide a world of new experiences.

Chapter Forty-Two

The weekend after Valentine's Day, Julia found herself hiking through a cane field again with Remy. This time, they parked boldly on the road and trudged along with no cover from the tall stalks, all of them harvested for the last time. The deep furrows that once drained the crop rows lay flattened and now sprouted only the wooden stakes outlining the ground for the Black Diamonds development rather than the production of stubble cane. Heavy rain the night before left large puddles behind in the landscape. At least the lane, compacted by years of heavy, high-wheeled tractors, harvesters, and carts sat high and dry.

Remy, unusually quiet on their trek to the mounds, muttered about getting some fill for the low places, but the toads and frogs croaked merrily calling for mates to come out and play.

Julia started a conversation. "Jane has completed her environmental assessment and says as long as you have an adequate and self-contained sewer plant for the development all should be well. In fact, this side of the lake might become healthier without the sprays and pesticides from cane farming running off into the water."

"Yes, I read the report. Glad to hear it."

"Great that the Cypress Lake Casino and the Chitimacha Nation are funding the small museum out here. They want it done right. Mostly, the university found lots of potsherds around the base of the mounds. They think all that broken pottery washed down from the top where sacrifices may have been made to the sun god. Nothing inside the mounds, but the radar showed how they were layered up with basketfuls of earth over a period of time. The positioning might have something to do with the solstice too. The gamekeeper out here— he's the formidable Mrs. Landry's husband—says if you stand on the east bank and face the mounds on the right day in winter, the rays of the rising sun will hit the gap between them. The cleavage, the kids call it. Interesting, huh?"

"Yeah, I read that report too." Remy walked on lighting the way with his flashlight as dark closed in on them, early this time of year.

He'd been like this since her return from New Orleans, terse and distracted. This evening, Remy, the ever-cool, seemed nervous, off-balance somehow. Julia thought they'd been doing so well together. Christmas Eve came off all right in the end. She'd met his mother and dad, his sister and brother-in-law, plus the two charming, mischievous blond grandchildren. The kids took some of the edge off the formality of the affair by getting early into the presents piled beneath an interior designer's dream of a Christmas tree, flocked and covered every square inch by huge ornaments in silver and gold. The boy spilled his milk on the pristine linen tablecloth set with a holly-sprigged pattern designed especially for the season and the girl refused to eat the braised Brussels sprouts prepared by a personal chef in the kitchen whose assistant brought dinner out course by course. The minor chaos made her feel more at home like a Rossi Christmas with children underfoot and the occasional dish getting broken as she and her mother always celebrated with Sal and Sammy's big families, taking turns at each of the houses.

She'd expected Melody Broussard to be upset by the disruptions. So beautiful and reserved, she looked the type. Instead, she said of the children in their booster seats, "How are they going to learn good manners unless they observe them? If they see us eating the sprouts, eventually they will try them." Their grandmother personally mopped up the spilled milk and brought more from the kitchen. She placed half a Brussel sprout on each of their plates and ignored whether they ate them or not. When the little girl did, but made a face, Melody placed a green mint by her plate to take away the taste. Her brother followed that lead, claimed he liked his, and received two mints for not making a face. A clever family, this branch of the Broussards.

Accompanied by coffee, hot chocolate, and heavily iced ginger cookies for dessert, they opened presents by the tree and beside a gas log glowing in the fireplace. Julia could see as she looked around the room where Remy got his taste for clean, modern designs and reflections in the water as the house sat by the lake and possessed its own large deck and dock visible from floor to ceiling living room windows.

She'd molded pairs of highly detailed plaster of Paris angels for the two women and gilded them herself. For the kids, figurines of sea creatures easy to color with the water-based paints she provided, a hit with the little girl, not so much for the boy, Julia admitted. The men, always a problem to buy for, got excellent bottles of Italian wines and that included Remy. His assortment contained Mondoro Asti Spumante, a sparkling wine that paired well with chocolate, just in case they had something big to celebrate.

Their gifts were the kind she might have expected in this family: silk scarves, expensive perfumes, and tasteful jewelry for all the women including her. Jules had little use for the first two and couldn't imagine where she'd display the classic diamond tennis bracelet from Remy on her wrist other than at the Rossi Christmas party the next day to awe her female cousins. She knew she'd see disappointment in her mother's face that it hadn't been an engagement ring. Maybe she felt a little of that letdown herself when New Year's Eve passed and then Valentine's Day, celebrated with red roses and a nice dinner out, but no commitment from Remy.

What saved the evening for her was one last rectangular box that had some weight to it. "This is especially for Julia," Melody said coyly as she handed over the package wrapped in gold and ornamented with a white dove of peace nestled in the bow. Carefully setting the bow aside, Jules stripped the paper and withdrew a carton of Café du Monde's beignet mix.

"In case Remy's grandmother visits, you might want to have something to stuff in her mouth," Melody explained. All the adults filled the room with chuckles, but the children wanted to make donuts right away. Julia left their household the next morning feeling like an accepted member of the family. Perhaps not.

As she trudged through the former cane field lugging another picnic basket Remy had packed, it occurred to her that men truly believed breaking up in a very public place prevented a woman from making a scene. Remy told her once about the college girlfriend who'd punched him in the balls at an expensive restaurant over her disappointment about not getting a ring. Well, Julia Rossi could do better than that. They might be in the middle of nowhere where none would hear her scream or rant or see her drop kick Remy off the lake side of the mound after she took the truck keys and left him for the gators or the gamekeeper to find.

Her part of the restoration of the Bayou Queen neared completion as soon as Remy signed off on it. The exterior of the hotel, plastered and painted, shone white again. The lobby had its swirling float coat and the upper bedrooms their flat plaster walls and ceilings and cornice embellishments. She'd brought in an entire crew to finish the work and assigned her best masters to the coffered ceiling, gilding it in place and repointing each section. The marble finish made the walls glow. Her pilasters hid the A/C ducts rising behind them, and she'd applied the gold accents personally. This week, her parquet men worked on polishing the floor they'd meticulously restored and sealed against damage. Once the electrician hung the chandeliers, the ballroom would be ready to host dancing—and wedding receptions again. She'd thought maybe hers would be held there. Yet, not a hint from Remy about their status when he'd been all hot for marriage and a business merger when she first moved into the Black Box.

Hadn't she and Remy worked so well together on this restoration as the time drew nigh to turn the grounds over to the landscaper and the interior to the decorator? Hadn't she given him all of herself just as passionately? Now, he planned to dump her out here and take all the credit for the revival of the Bayou Queen.

They reached the bottom of the mound, its grassy covering dew-heavy and slippery from the rain. Remy offered her a hand. Julia batted it away. "I'm fine. I can climb a hill without your help." Under her current head of steam, she could probably defeat Mount Everest.

At the apex, Remy laid out a waterproof tarp and topped it with a blanket while Julia restlessly prowled the mound. As he lit the citronella candles, both practical and lovely, to keep off the mosquitoes that hatched with the rain, she stared over the muddy field, the one she'd secured for him and gotten no thanks for her effort. Most likely why he wanted to humiliate her—nice work on the Queen, but we're finished. Thanks for all the sex. I want to do Black Diamonds on my own.

"How about sitting down, Jules? Nothing to see out there yet, but the stars over the lake are shimmering with all the water in the air."

"I'd rather stand." She braced her legs and folded her arms under her breasts.

"All right then." Remy dropped to his knees and took an object from the picnic basket she'd toted across the field. He popped open the small box. "Julia Rossi, would you do me the honor of being my bride, my partner in life and many projects to come?"

His hands shook a little, but nowhere near as much as her knees. Julia sank to the blanket, leaned across his open hands, and offered the kiss of a lifetime, one that sealed the deal and signed the biggest contract she'd ever undertake. "Yes! Certainly, yes!"

By the light of the flickering candles, he rewarded her answer with that deep-dimpled smile she'd been missing all week since the arrival of a package sent by special messenger from New Orleans, its contents not shared with her. "It's nothing," he'd said and turned away. Now he placed that object on her finger and shone the flashlight on the ring. "I forgot it would be too dark out here for you to see the details."

"Oh, Remy! The egg and dart pattern with the diamond set in a rosette, its perfect, perfect for me."

"I was afraid you wouldn't accept it, not until you'd completed our contract, after what you said to Todd about not falling in love with your boss."

"I think I was cautioning myself as well. What if you waited to break up with me until after we finished the Queen? All week I thought you were laying the groundwork to tell me our relationship wasn't working out for you."

"I took a big chance here—because you never said you loved me—and technically I am your boss."

"You have all my love. I can't believe you didn't know that."

"Even a man likes to be told."

"Well into this project I stopped thinking of you as my boss, but rather as my partner."

"For life." Remy opened the bottle of Asti Spumante and let it foam into the flutes. He handed her the bubbling wine. "To us—but don't break the glass. I'm running low on them."

"Why would I do that? Sure, last time we came here, one got broken when we packed in haste, but…"

"I've been reading up on Italian customs. I think we should skip the glass smashing, but I am good with confetti and doves and an endless reception—at the Queen."

"I think you might know more about those than I do, but there is one snag. My family will expect me to get married at St. Mary's in New Orleans, a long way from here."

"Get married in the morning, say ten. One-hour Catholic Mass, transfer everyone by bus and limo to Chapelle where most of my family will be waiting and already into the cocktails and antipasto. Dinner at two, dancing all night, start the honeymoon in one of the Art Deco suites." Remy removed a gold box of Godiva chocolates from the hamper and offered her the selection. "Pairs well with chocolate."

Julia selected a delicate white shell filled with chocolate ganache, popped it into her mouth, followed that with a sip of the wine. "It certainly does. You've given this wedding way more thought than I have."

"Don't girls plan their weddings at an early age?"

"Not me. I spent my time learning to plaster. What else did you have in mind?"

"Right now? Getting naked with you on this blanket. I'll show you the wedding prospectus I've drawn up later. You can make any changes you want. It's only a starting point. Speaking of starting points, last time, we only got halfway before NuNu lit the trash fire."

"You'd just finished licking chocolate off my nipples."

"I do recall." Remy drew off her top, let her breasts spill free, broke open a cream, and recreated that scene.

Just before Julia gave herself over to the rhythm of love making with her ring as bright against the tanned skin of Remy's back as the stars were in the night sky, she thought he had no idea how complicated weddings of any kind could be, more difficult than restoring a magnificent hotel, but so worth the effort.

Chapter Forty-Three

Julia sat at Remy's glass-topped desk and studied the document headed *Prospectus: Rossi-Broussard Wedding.* "First of all, you have the date wrong. It should be next June, not this June."

He looked over her shoulder. "No, that's correct."

"Remy, how long did your sister's wedding take to complete?"

"About a year, though I don't see why. Jonathan Hartz and Celine pulled theirs together in eight weeks complete with golden canopies in the trees and salmon flown in from Seattle. It's a local legend. Granny attended and knows all the details. I want ours to be the talk of the town too. I mean we have nearly four months to put it together if we go for late June."

Julia turned and shot him a glance meant to convey unbelievable. "Who was their miraculous wedding planner?"

"His PA, Mrs. Landry, I believe."

"Well, we don't have her or infinite wealth. I'm not asking my mother or the uncles for a cent. Mom very stubbornly lives on my dad's social security and won't take money from me. Sam has four daughters to marry off and Sal two. We'll pay for this ourselves, remembering we aren't billionaires." She returned to studying the prospectus.

"Agreed. Though I bet we could get the loan of

Mrs. Landry since you are tight with Celine."

"Maybe, but St. Mary's will be booked solid by now, and St. Mary's it must be."

"Put down Ste. Jeanne's here in town as an alternate."

Julia tossed her hair. Remy buried his face in it, inhaling the magnolia scent, lifted its mass, and kissed her nape.

"Stop that! You're ruining my concentration. Ste. Jeanne's probably has a full schedule of June weddings too. We'll check, but I am not hopeful. Why June anyhow? Seems fairly unoriginal for you."

"According to my research, Italians aren't supposed to marry during Advent, Lent, in May because of the veneration of the Virgin, or in August because it's unlucky. That takes up half the year."

"I don't think those rules hold anymore. Let's put a question mark by the date and move on from there. Reception at the Bayou Queen Hotel is a given." She swiveled in the chair to give him a waist-level hug.

Remy kissed the top of her head. "No, it's not. I'm already getting inquiries for events, but I told them we aren't taking reservations yet—not until we pick our date." His hands traveled down her back and strayed to her backside, taking her in close against his pelvis.

Knowing where that might lead, Julia turned her chair back to the desk. "Keep that up, and we'll never get done. Time's a-wasting. Why don't you go call Ste. Jeanne's and see if they have any June openings even though my family will have a fit if we use your church and not mine. Do that out on the deck, please. Let me concentrate."

He went reluctantly. Jules drew a line through

Hand-written Invitations done by a Calligrapher and wrote in Engraved, acceptable and much faster. Under Folklore he'd written groom keeps iron in his pocket, bride does not wear gold until after the ceremony. Bride tears veil to ward off evil spirits. She crossed out the last. "Not going to tear my veil." Truthfully, she'd be reluctant not to wear her engagement ring, but could put it on later. He'd already crossed out break a glass at the end of the ceremony. She checked okay next to tie a white ribbon to the church door.

Remy returned with a scowl on his face. "Yeah, Ste. Jeanne's is booked solid. I tried St. Mary's too. Same story, but we are on a list if cancellations occur."

"Ah, my dear, dear Remy, people who spend a year planning a wedding do not cancel. Their Save the Date cards have already gone out by now."

"It's happened," he insisted. "Granny and her friends showed up for a wedding here in Chapelle and found a note on the door saying the couple had cancelled."

"Maybe they simply didn't want her at their wedding, but there is no way we can keep her from ours." Julia buried her face in her hands.

Remy rubbed her shoulders. "Don't tense up over it. We put her, Pammy, and my grandfather in a limo with a bottle of champagne and transport them wherever we end up having the ceremony. They should be mellow by the time they arrive. It's under Transportation."

"Great, Miss Lolly and Miss Maxie can ride with them too. We can't leave them out. On to the Bridal Party. 'Italian wedding parties are small, just a maid of honor and a best man.'" Oh, that might work in the real

Palermo, but not in Little Palermo. At the very least, I have to have all six of my female cousins—and your sister as matron of honor, which will cut down on the squabbling over who gets to hold my bouquet. So, seven attendants, and your niece and nephew as flower girl and ring bearer. How about your groomsmen?"

The way he rubbed the bump on his nose, she could tell he hadn't given this any thought. "Ah, I guess my brother-in-law and, hey, how about Sal and Sammy and Marv?"

Julia noted the names and wrote Need Three More. "Procession—bride and groom walk to the church together and down the aisle as a couple symbolizing the marital journey. I like that one—because no one gives away Julia Rossi. She gives herself."

"Your wedding band will match the engagement ring. It's already made. Here's the sketch for mine."

Julia snatched it away. "Let me take care of that." He noted the edge in her voice.

"Ready for a break?" Remy eyed the staircase to the bedroom.

"We finish this first. I'm fine with the confetti throwing, but releasing doves. Doesn't New Orleans have enough pigeons?"

"They are trained to return to their dovecote. I made sure of that. Just be sure not to throw birdseed, or they'll linger and poop everywhere. The dove rental guy told me that. He only needs our time, place, and date, and how many birds to bring. His phone number is at the end."

"On to the reception at the Queen. Cocktail hour, with large antipasto trays on tables. Dinner, starting with a cup of Italian wedding soup followed by lots of courses (discuss with chef at the Queen). *Mille-foglia* for wedding cake. Nope on the last."

"Don't know what it is?" Remy said a little smugly. "I had some when I was in Italy."

"I know what it is, but layers of filo pastry filled with vanilla and chocolate cream and strawberries is going to be very messy. We'll do an American cake. Yes, we can have *wanda* on the side, even if strips of fried dough covered in powdered sugar aren't very healthy. It's only one day."

"Our day."

"Right. Flowers: green garlands studded with red carnations and baby's breath on the staircase, small arrangements of the same for the tables, the colors of Italy. Did Marv help you with this? I can't see you asking for baby's breath."

"No, I called Beau's Blooms. He thinks you should choose your own bouquet."

"How right he is, but I like the garlands. Band: must be able to play a tarantella as well as Cajun music and regular songs. That's going to be a challenge."

"We're going to have lots of challenges, like the guest list. I figure on three-hundred."

"Remy! That's excessive."

"Listen." He enumerated on his fingers. "At least one-hundred Broussards. The Remington side of my family is small, only a divorced uncle and his two grown children. My grandparents are gone. Your immediate family isn't large, but your mother will want her friends and you'll insist on inviting your artisans, especially after all the work they did on the Queen. Then, you owe the Live Oak Preservation ladies and the Historic District Committee, plus Jane and Celine, their spouses and families. It's mounting up."

"I see your point, but my people will want to give speeches and do toasts. We'll be there all night." Julia rubbed her temples.

"Only a short way to our suite in the hotel. We bus your guests from New Orleans and back again unless they want to book a room overnight. No worries about too much drinking, and we give them departure times, one earlier, one later. I estimate two sixty-person buses should do the trick, three limos for the wedding party, my close Broussard relatives, your mom and aunts, and the Remington side of the family. Again, phone numbers for the bus and limo company at the end just waiting for date and time."

Julia grew suspicious. "You've put in all those numbers because you expect me to do all the work."

"Well, I'll be tied up with Black Diamonds by then, and you did say once that after the Queen project ended you wanted to take some time off."

"I thought a trip to the Bahamas, not planning a wedding!"

Remy spun her chair around and gripped her shoulders. "You are the most competent and efficient person I know. You can do this. And we'll get you some helpers."

If he'd told her she was beautiful, sweet, and kind, Julia might have given him a black eye that exceeded Slick's punch, but he'd learned her weakness. Above all, the she prided herself on getting a job done well and on schedule.

"I can put my aunts, female cousins, and mom on making confetti bags, church flowers, and addressing envelopes once the date is set. From what I've heard,

Jane's wedding was pretty eccentric, but Celine and Mrs. Landry can help me on this end. We'll have the entire staff of the Queen eager to prove themselves at a big event. It can be done!"

"With Julia Rossi style."

"Don't lay it on too thick, or I'll consider backing out."

She read Remy's eyes reflecting uncertainty for perhaps five seconds before his confidence returned. "Turn to the last page," he said.

"Honeymoon—Sicily."

"I'll be planning that. Anywhere you want to go and for how long."

"You'd delay the Black Diamonds project for a month?"

"For you, anything."

Not too certain she'd do likewise for him, but touched just the same, Julia rose up and mouthed, "Two weeks in Italy" against his lips. They opened for her, took her in, and began the foreplay as Remy backed her toward the staircase. At the first step, he scooped her up and began the ascent.

"Hey, I'm too heavy to carry all the way to the third floor! Don't you dare hurt your back before the wedding!"

"We can take a break on the living room sofa. Mostly, I believe we need lots and lots of practice for the honeymoon starting today."

Chapter Forty-Four

Julia learned that weddings possessed much in common with construction projects: delays, changes in plans, unexpected difficulties, and surprises both good and bad. Among the good, a cancellation at St. Mary's. Too bad for Maria Remini that she'd caught her fiancé in bed with her maid of honor shortly after Remy placed their own wedding on the waiting list. By her special day the last weekend in June, Julia had solved her list of problems with an amazing crew of women: her mom, aunts, and cousins, Jane, Celine, and Adrienne Landry.

She left her mother's home on Remy's arm with the wedding party to walk the few blocks to St. Mary's full of confidence that all would go according to plan—hopefully. They set out fifteen minutes before the ten a.m. ceremony once the arrival of the bus from Chapelle bearing some of the Broussards had been confirmed by phone. The morning heat remained bearable, and she clipped along on satin pumps sensible enough to survive the cracked sidewalks and a night of dancing. Her ankle-length gown with a fitted lace bodice and many diaphanous layers of skirts swung about her hips and did not drag on the ground or in the gutters they crossed. No gold around her neck, but a lace choker covered the slowly fading scar. She carried red roses accented with silver sprigs of olive leaves bound with white ribbons and her old Irish granny's crystal rosary. Remy, tuxedo-handsome, had a square-headed iron nail she'd found on the grounds of the Queen in his pocket.

Because this was New Orleans, they somehow acquired a second line of well-wishers and a three-piece brass band—trumpet, trombone, and tuba—all the way to the church door sporting the white ribbons that proclaimed a wedding. Plain as a piece of pound cake on the outside, the doors to St. Mary's opened onto golden vaults, crystal chandeliers, and a many-columned altar. Rossis and Broussards jammed the pews. Julia, as she processed down the aisle by Remy's side noted and ignored that his grandmother had obviously been crying for some time before their arrival. Everyone else wore smiles, including herself. Her best burst forth when she placed Remy's ring on his finger, his own design, a wide band in egg and dart, cast in platinum, and sporting a small black diamond in the center of each of the ovals, her own addition.

They sat for the lengthy communion and stayed to pose before the altar for formal photographs with their somewhat unorthodox attendants. Oh, not the women garbed in emerald green that honored her Italian and Irish heritage and looked good on both the many brunettes and the single blonde, but the assorted groomsmen, the last three drafted by their wives. Remy refused to have any Broussards, or to call old college friends he'd lost contact with long ago. So, the towering Merlin Tauzin stood next to Amelia's tall, blond husband, then her two squat uncles, the lithe Marvin Holcomb next to Adrienne Landry's gamekeeper husband, and last of all, billionaire Jonathan Hartz wearing his custom tux. If she'd had to rate the most uncomfortable, the prizes would go to Sal in third, Sammy in second, and Merlin in first place, though he'd been stroked into complying by Jane's many suggestive compliments about how men in formal wear turned her on. They'd gotten a sitter for their boys and a room for the night at the Queen.

Julia and Remy emerged from the church into a hurricane of confetti and a flurry of dove wings as the brass band stuck up a Dixieland tune in hopes of getting tips in their open trumpet case. Remy slipped them a folded bill, and his bride suspected their appearance hadn't been an accident. With everyone loaded into a bus or limo, they began the long journey to Chapelle fueled by champagne. It soothed Marv, hired as the Queen's general manager, when he feared the Broussards remaining behind in Chapelle would devour all the antipasto before the rest of the guests arrived. "A second round of trays is being held back in the kitchen," Julia told him.

The next snag occurred when they debarked at the Bayou Queen. Remy's gran emerged with the front of her pink crepe de Chine suit drenched down the front. His parents followed with amused smiles on their faces. Julia's mother and aunts, who had ridden with them as well as Lolly and Maxie, came out squawking they wouldn't share a wedding table with Patty. Miss Lolly supplied the skinny on the why. "Patty suggested the wedding was planned in such a rush because you must be pregnant. All three of the Rossi women doused her with their champagne."

His attack of nerves over, Marv stepped up. "I'll make certain the place cards are changed. Don't fret."

He put on a concerned face. "I see you've had a little accident, Miss Patty. Let me take you to a room, and we'll fix that with a hairdryer. Plenty of time before dinner is served."

"Oh, Marvin, you are queer but dear."

"A queen of the bayou for the Bayou Queen," Marv quipped

Patty failed to smile. "Truly, Remy has married into a violent family. I fear for his life." Holcomb led her away before any of the Rossis brained her with an antipasto tray.

Remy shook his head. "I'm more likely to be killed by the Broussards."

"My fault," Julia acknowledged. "I thought the women could get to know each other. Maybe they did a little too well."

"Forget about Granny, and let's enjoy. I have iron in my pocket to ward off evil."

"Somehow, I keep thinking that iron was meant to encourage the wedding night, but that's my own take."

"Which I wish we could begin now, but..." Remy led his bride to a throne-like chair worthy of Henry the Eighth sitting at the side of the vast, gleaming mahogany bar with its polished brass rail where Old Broussard held court. A sign on dark wood with gold block lettering hung above the mirror proclaimed it to be T-Fat's Bar.

"Step right up. Da best selection of liquor in da parish and free tonight only," the old man declared in a voice like a Bourbon Street barker. Guests lined up three-deep to take advantage of the offer after shaking his hand. "Here dey come, da bride and groom. Julia, welcome to my family."

He pointed to his pudgy cheek, shaved clean for the occasion, and Julia dropped a kiss on it. "Thank you for making the bar and kitchen possible, Arnault."

"You family now. Call me Nonc like Remy does. I tell you me, you got a smart wife here, Remy."

Remy agreed. "All that and more."

"Have a drink on me, and go pass a good time, eh."

They settled on champagne as the most readily available and already poured at one end of the bar where red-coated bartenders worked frantically to keep up with demand. "Did we make a mistake having both an open bar and putting a bottle of wine on each table?" Julia questioned.

"To quote Nonc, you can ever have too much food or too much booze, no. I have the limos waiting to transport any locals too drunk to drive and the buses will take all of yours safely back to New Orleans. Slick and his boys are standing by to escort any drunk who doesn't want to leave outside. I think we've got this nailed." Remy fingered the iron in his pocket.

A shriek pierced the jolly, well-lubricated atmosphere, and Louisa, Sammy's second eldest daughter, split screaming from the group of bridesmaids like a streaking green skyrocket. "You came! You came!" She wound her arms around Todd Whitcomb.

"Todd," Remy said to his new wife as if he'd been betrayed. "You invited Todd." He stared at Julia's former apprentice nicely dressed in a suit and tie as if the man were a brain-eating zombie come for a good meal. "What if he came to cause trouble?"

Keeping secrets from each other they ought to have shared had separated them once before, and Julia realized she must act quickly. "Not intentionally.

Louisa asked if she could have a plus one, and I told her to give the name to Marv. We kept what Todd did among the four of us so she had no way of knowing he wouldn't be welcome. After all, the graffiti and holding up the contract really did no long-term damage."

"Jules, you could have been killed when the scaffolding collapsed."

"Not likely. I did have my lifeline and all your strong arms to catch me. I never go up alone in case I run into trouble. Why ruin Todd's life by pressing charges? He has a real passion for plaster."

"You're making excuses for him. He has a real passion for you." Remy's arm muscles hardened under Julia's hand.

Todd found them in the crowd. Hesitant and jumpy at all the attention his date's voice caused, he moved forward with Louisa clamped to his arm. As he approached, Remy took the nail from his pocket and put the pointed end between two fingers. "If we need help, I'm certain some of the Broussards are packing, especially Slick. I don't see any signs of a weapon on Todd, but small things can do big damage." He moved in front of Julia. Clearly, he'd fight for her again right here, right now.

Todd extended his hand, the universal sign of being unarmed.

"Put that nail away!" Julia whispered and stepped out from behind Remy's sheltering body. She took Todd's offered hand. "Good to see you again. Have you finished your studies?"

"Yes, got my master's in May. The place looks great. You did the float work walls using brooms. I wish I could have been more a part of it. I'm looking for another apprenticeship in plastering. I don't suppose…"

"No, it's best you find another company, but I'll give you a reference."

"Thank you for overlooking my foolishness last summer. I've never met a woman like—"

Louisa tugged on his arm. "You've made your manners with the bride and groom. Now, come sit with me. The soup is being served. Dancing after the meal. An Italian band out of New Orleans for the first half, then a switch to Cajun for the second part of the night."

"I'm not sure I can do either. But, Jules, Mrs. Broussard, will you save one dance for me?"

"Only one." Remy pocketed the nail. "Good luck charm," he explained, but the tone of his voice said otherwise. "Go and enjoy Louisa's company and the dinner. We have a chef from New Orleans."

Indeed, waiters swarmed from the kitchen designated in gold lettering as Arnault's Eatery with trays of small soup cups. Louisa staked her claim on Todd's arm again and pointed him in the right direction.

"We should take our seats too."

They got through the soup course, the pasta and shrimp alfredo, baked redfish in salsa, herbed lamb chops, and zucchini parmigiana, right down to the sorbet to cleanse the palate for the *dolce* of sugared almonds, *wanda*, little boxes of nougats that could be taken home if desired, and of course, the wedding cake, white and gilded like the hotel itself and topped with sugar doves.

Marv skillfully orchestrated the many toasts and speeches interspersed throughout the courses, consulting his list and tapping each contributor when their turn came. Many simply wished the bride and groom *evviva gli sposi,* long live the newlyweds, or similar sentiments in Italian or Cajun French. Uncle Sal's eyes filled with tears as he described Julia's childhood and her talent with plaster from an early age and wished them happiness and many children. Sammy's speech was similar, but ended without encouraging numerous offspring.

"Will it ever end?" Remy whispered to Julia as he responded to yet another toast with a raised glass that he barely sipped.

She replied, "You wanted an Italian wedding, you got it."

Marv announced, "Let the music begin."

At last, the couple mounted the grand staircase with its garlands of red, green, and white. As Remy led Julia through the central double doors of the room on which she'd lavished such care, she glanced up and saw the gold and while plaque on the wall above the entrance, Julia's Ballroom.

"Oh, Remy. I think I'm going to cry, and I so rarely do."

"Please, don't. That's not my Jules."

She held back the tears with a blinding smile.

They entered to a drum roll from the band set up along one wall and moved to the head table before the arched windows. Every facet of the four chandeliers sparkled, casting their glitter on the parquet floor. Golden brocade settees lined the walls interspersed with bandy-legged Louis the Fourteenth tables and chairs for four. Palms in alabaster jardinières added color and the spice of red carnations filled the air. Best of all, Julia's perfectly plastered walls shone like marble. If she had dreamed of a wedding as a girl, this would be it.

Their first dance as man and wife might have been to some corny old Dean Martin song because she'd left the choice up to the bandleader, but Remy twirled her out and brought her back again into his arms in what she suspected to be a Cajun dance move. All she wanted to do was rest her head on his shoulder and close her eyes as Remy guided her around the hall.

Julia swore she could hear the swish of hoop skirts as they circled, interrupted with a hint of jazz music now and then. If she opened her eyes she imagined soldiers wearing the uniforms of three wars might be lining the walls enjoying the music. But no, her relatives stood there with money and checks to stuff in the *borsa*, the satin purse her Aunt Rosa made and insisted she wear, for a dance with the bride. Remy's family, determined to uphold Cajun customs when their music started, handed out straight pins to attach bills to her veil for the same honor.

Strange that she was the one who felt such affinity to this place when Julia knew Remy would always be the romantic, the visionary in their relationship. She'd supply the practicality, plastering over any small cracks, repairing the cornices chipped over the years, helping to build an edifice of marriage that would stand as long and be solid as the Bayou Queen.

A word about the author...

Once a librarian, now a writer of romance, Lynn Shurr grew up in Pennsylvania Dutch country. She attended a state college and earned a very impractical B.A. in English Literature. Her first job out of school really was working as a cashier in a burger joint. Moving from one humble job to another, she traveled to North Carolina, then Germany, then California, where she buckled down and studied for an M.A. in Librarianship.

New degree in hand, she found her first reference job in the Heart of Cajun Country, Lafayette, Louisiana. For her, the old saying "Once you've tasted bayou water, you will always stay here" came true. She raised three children not far from the Bayou Teche and lives there still with her astronomer husband.

When not writing, Lynn likes to paint, cheer for the New Orleans Saints and LSU Tigers, and take long road trips nearly anywhere. Her love of the bayou country, its history and customs, often shows in the background of her books.

You may contact Lynn at www.lynnshurr.com, lynn.shurr@yahoo.com, or visit her blog—lynnshurr.blogspot.com.